PENGUIN STUDENT EDITIONS

CAL

Bernard Mac Laverty was born in Belfast in 1942. After leaving school he worked for ten years as a medical laboratory technician before studying English at Queen's University, Belfast. In 1967 he married Madeleine, with whom he has had four children. After he graduated from Queen's University he moved to Scotland with his family and taught for a number of years in Edinburgh and Glasgow. He gave up teaching in 1981 to write full time. He has written three novels, *Lamb*, *Cal* (both made into successful films) and *Grace Notes*. He has published four collections of short stories, *Secrets*, *A Time to Dance*, *The Great Profondo* and *Walking the Dog*. Bernard Mac Laverty's work has won numerous awards and has been consistently well reviewed. The *New Statesman* described *Lamb* as having 'the gently quickening pace of the best thrillers and the remorselessness of tragedy', and the *Spectator* said of *Cal*: 'Mr Mac Laverty describes the sad, straitened, passionate lives of his characters with tremendously moving skill'.

Ronald Carter is Professor of Modern English Language in the School of English Studies, University of Nottingham. He has published widely in the field of language and literature studies and applied linguistics and English teaching. He is the co-author with John McRae of *The Penguin Guide to English Literature* (1996) and *The Routledge History of Literature in English: Britain and Ireland* (1997).

Valerie Durow recently completed a doctoral thesis on the modern British novel. She is currently administering post-graduate courses and research programmes in the School of English Studies, University of Nottingham.

John McRae is Special Professor of Language in Literature Studies in the School of English Studies at the University of Nottingham. He is the author or editor of more than forty books, including, with Ronald Carter, *The Penguin Guide to English Literature*. He has lectured in over forty countries worldwide.

Penguin Student Editions

Series editors: Ronald Carter and John McRae

Other titles in this series:

Bernard Mac Laverty

Cal

Edited by Ronald Carter and Valerie Durow

PENGUIN BOOKS

PENGUIN BOOKS

Published by the Penguin Group
Penguin Books Ltd, 80 Strand, London WC2R 0RL, England
Penguin Putnam Inc., 375 Hudson Street, New York, New York 10014, USA
Penguin Books Australia Ltd, 250 Camberwell Road, Camberwell, Victoria 3124, Australia
Penguin Books Canada Ltd, 10 Alcorn Avenue, Toronto, Ontario, Canada M4V 3B2
Penguin Books India (P) Ltd, 11 Community Centre, Panchsheel Park, New Delhi – 110 017, India
Penguin Books (NZ) Ltd, Cnr Rosedale and Airborne Roads, Albany, Auckland, New Zealand
Penguin Books (South Africa) (Pty) Ltd, 24 Sturdee Avenue, Rosebank 2196, South Africa

Penguin Books Ltd, Registered Offices: 80 Strand, London WC2R 0RL, England

www.penguin.com

First published by Jonathan Cape 1983
Published in Penguin Books 1984
Published in Penguin Student Editions 2000
14

Copyright © Bernard Mac Laverty, 1983
Introduction and Notes copyright © Ronald Carter and Valerie Durow, 2000
All rights reserved

The moral right of the author and editors has been asserted

Set in 9.75/12.5 pt PostScript Monotype Plantin
Typeset by Rowland Phototypesetting Ltd, Bury St Edmunds, Suffolk
Printed in England by Clays Ltd, St Ives plc

ISBN-13: 978–0–140–81789–8
ISBN-10: 0–140–81789–1

Contents

Introduction

People were dying every day, men and women were being crippled and turned into vegetables in the name of Ireland. An Ireland which never was and never could be. It was the people of Ulster who were heroic, caught between the jaws of two opposing ideals trying to grind each other out of existence. (*Cal*, 82.08)

He was in love with the one woman in the world who was forbidden him. (91.21)

The blood-dimmed tide is loosed, and everywhere
The ceremony of innocence is drowned . . .
(W. B. Yeats, *The Second Coming*)

Cal is a novel of contrasts and contradictions.

In just the first few pages of the novel, a range of contrasts is established. We see how Cal is nauseated by the violence, noise and 'humane' killing of the abattoir, and how he seeks relaxation in the peace and quiet of the library where Marcella works. We are shown how he and his father, Shamie, live on a predominantly Protestant estate, and yet both of them are Catholics. We witness Cal's frustrated attempts to discover his own identity as an Irish Catholic by trying to learn Gaelic, and the underlying hostility to him of his neighbourhood with its loyalty to the queen, flag and language of England. We see, too, the contrast between Cal being 'in' and wanting 'out' ('I'm far enough in to want out', 19.28): his uncertain involvement in the 'Cause' of the political minority, of which he is a part, and his growing distaste for the violence it begets. And we observe how, although Cal goes to church and holds dear the memory of his mother, a deeply religious woman, his own commitment to the church and to religious belief is tenuous.

Numerous contradictions are established, too, from the very beginning of the novel. Cal is alone, unemployed and isolated, and yet he wants to work and needs to find love. He wants to feel part of a community but not part of that section of the community which needs him. He dreams more than he acts; yet his acts cause him increasing nightmares. Cal's dreams and reveries transport him into a different world, but the physical reality and violence of contemporary Ireland is never far away. He receives notes through his letter box with the words:

GET OUT YOU FENYAN SCUM OR WE'LL BURN YOU OUT. THIS IS YOUR 2ND WARNING, THERE WILL BE NO OTHER. (23.20)

The outcome of one of his recurring dreams is of a beautiful and distressed young girl who 'need[s] his help' but who jumps through a glass window to lie 'skewered on some railings, screaming unceasingly' (31.09). There is also the contrast between the urban and the rural, between the peace of the rural scenes in the novel and the clamour of the city where Cal lives and works. But there is a contradiction here too. The violence and noise of the city and of a divided Ireland are in reality never very far away, and constantly invade the tranquillity of the farm where Cal finds temporary refuge.

And above all there is the central paradox between his growing attraction and fondness for Marcella and his realization that she is the widow of the man he was involved in killing.

It is also something of a contradiction that the more Cal faces up to and understands the consequences of the violent acts in which he has participated, the more he discovers within himself what he wants and needs, and begins to understand the meaning of love, tenderness and sacrifice. The more he confronts the inhumane, the more humane he himself becomes. The more he accepts the consequences of experience, the more he proves himself worthy of redemption. Gradually, Cal begins to see in the dark which surrounds him.

His sin clawed at him, demanding attention. He fought it for as long as he could but there was little to distract him except the cold. In the pitch darkness his eyes, with nothing to do, naturally turned inside himself. Tired of pacing, he lay down on the floor with his knees to his chest for warmth. He lay inert on broken glass, his eyes open to the night, and saw again the terrible thing that he had done. (82.14)

Paradoxically, it is by working on the farm of Mrs Morton, whose son he has helped to murder and whose husband he has helped to maim, that he begins to cleanse his thoughts and feelings.

. . . although he ended up each day physically filthy, work had a cleansing effect on him. It was as if idleness had allowed dirt to accumulate on his soul, to clog his mind, and work moved him through it untouched. (53.28)

Paradoxically, too, it is on Mrs Morton's farm, as a Catholic boy on a Protestant farm, that he grows closer to Marcella, a Catholic within a Protestant family and married to Robert Morton, the officer in the Police Reserve who is murdered by Crilly with Cal's help. It is against the dark and cold background of pain and suffering that Cal finds the warmth and tenderness of feeling which his relationship with Marcella generates.

In contrast to the increasing warmth of feeling between Cal and Marcella, however, there are none the less constant reminders that any future hope is conditioned by the actions of the past and the violence of the present. At the end of the fourth chapter, a peaceful and idyllic walk with Marcella and Lucy is brought to an abrupt end when Cal comes across a cow blown apart by a landmine – evidence of the continuing religious and spiritual war.

It was half a cow – udders, hindquarters with muscles red-raw and still jigging. He froze, frightened of stepping on another mine. He looked around him and saw something red, high on a tree in the hedge. He narrowed his eyes and recognized one of the Preacher's red tin plaques.

'The Kingdom of God is within You.' (120.20)

Cal is a novel which tells of a divided society. It tells of people divided in religion, divided in their allegiance to different values and where even the strongest are divided within their own minds and spirits. It is a society in which love and tolerance and sensitivity are almost impossible to sustain. It is a society which requires that the process of everyday living involves constant punishment and atonement, and in which even love does not come without a price.

The expression of love and of human feeling is inevitably accompanied by guilt. When Cal and Marcella first kiss, the primary response is not to continue.

'I'm a widow. With problems. You're a boy without ... Somebody might get hurt and regret it. I still feel guilty about Robert.' The kiss had broken the spell and she rose, saying that she'd better make a start on the dishes. (132.20)

As Cal declares his love, he realizes that his feelings for Marcella can never be straightforward.

'I love you,' he said. As he said it he felt a new danger. The more he loved her, the more friendly he became with her, the more afraid he was that he would tell her what he had done. It was the one thing he wanted to talk to her about, to have her console him. He wanted to share his guilt with the person he had wronged. To commune with her and be forgiven. (141.16)

And in the background, but never far from the surface of the narrative, are the words of the Preacher. These range from utterances heard in passing, to haunting inscriptions nailed to trees and posts and punctuating the rural and urban vistas through which Cal moves, seeming always to appear at some key point in the action – such as when Cal comes upon the cow accidentally mutilated by a landmine. The Preacher himself appears, pale and gaunt, at the very beginning of the novel, when Cal waits for his father at the abattoir, and towards the end, as Cal emerges from a shop bearing Christmas gifts for Lucy and Marcella.

Outside, the Preacher stood at the corner shouting at the top of his voice about God. He wore a black plastic apron with the words 'Repent ye; for

the Kingdom of Heaven is at hand'. There was no one listening to him . . .
He windmilled his arms and shouted as Cal passed him,

   'Without the shedding of blood there can be no forgiveness.' (142.30)

Religion provides no consolation for the people caught in the
private and public tragedies enacted in the novel. The words are
heard as only distantly meaningful. The sacrifices and shedding of
blood do not even begin to lead to redemption. The figure of Christ
which haunts the latter part of the novel is that of a painting by
Grünewald. It is not a calm, transcendental picture of suffering
prior to release, but a distorted figure, racked with unremitting
pain and unending suffering.

   The conclusion of the novel condenses many of the paradoxes,
contrasts and contradictions into a single paragraph.

The next morning, Christmas Eve, almost as if he expected it, the police
arrived to arrest him and he stood in a dead man's Y-fronts listening to
the charge, grateful that at last someone was going to beat him to within
an inch of his life.

It is a conclusion which echoes the final line of Chapter 3, the
mid-point of the novel.

He felt that he had a brand stamped in blood in the middle of his forehead
which would take him the rest of his life to purge.

Cal is above all a tragic novel, written with the compression and
understatement normally associated with a short story. The tragedy
of the novel lies in its recognition that, where loyalties are so
divided, guilt is perpetual and happiness has to be paid for by an
equal measure of suffering – they are the two faces of the same
coin.

Chronology

Bernard Mac Laverty's Life

1942   Bernard Mac Laverty born in Belfast, N. Ireland.

1960   He leaves school and works as a laboratory technician.

1970   He becomes a student of English Literature at Queen's University, Belfast, graduating in 1973.

1973–4   Mac Laverty moves to Scotland.
1977   His first collection of short stories, *Secrets and Other Stories*, is published, winning the Scottish Arts Council Fiction Award.

1980   *Lamb* is published.
1982   *A Time to Dance*, a second collection of stories, is published and also wins the Scottish Arts Council Fiction Award.

1983   *Cal* is published.
1984   A film of *Cal*, directed by David Puttnam and starring John Lynch and Helen Mirren, is released with a screenplay by Mac Laverty.
1985   A film of *Lamb*, starring Liam Neeson, is released, with a screenplay by Mac Laverty.

Bernard Mac Laverty's Times

1945 End of the Second World War.

1947 Britain grants independence to India, its largest colonial territory.

1968 August: first civil rights march held in N. Ireland. October: civil rights march in Derry, considered by many as the start of the recent 'troubles'.

1969 British soldiers sent to N. Ireland.

1970 Social and Democratic Labour Party (SDLP) established, with Gerry Fitt as leader and John Hume as deputy leader.

1971 Britain, under Conservative prime minister Edward Heath, joins the European Economic Community (EEC).

1979 Margaret Thatcher (head of the Conservative Party) is elected British prime minister.

1980 Beginning of hunger strikes by political prisoners.

1981 March: Bobby Sands, then leader of the Irish Republican Army (IRA), begins a new hunger strike. He dies in May, followed by nine other hunger strikers.

1985 The Anglo-Irish Agreement is signed by Margaret Thatcher and Garret FitzGerald (the Irish prime minister).

1997 *Grace Notes* is published and is shortlisted for the Booker Prize.

1987 During the annual Remembrance Day ceremony at Enniskillen, County Fermanagh, a bomb planted by the IRA kills 11 people and injures another 63.

1994 A ceasefire is agreed between opposing parties in N. Ireland and is then broken several times.

1995 Seamus Heaney wins the Nobel Prize for Literature.

1997 Tony Blair (head of New Labour) is elected British prime minister.

1998–9 US Senator Mitchell oversees plans for a ceasefire between opposing sides in the N. Irish conflict. New Scottish and Welsh assemblies meet for the first time. On 'Good Friday', 10 April 1998, an agreement (the Good Friday Agreement) is reached, in which a Northern Ireland Assembly is established and power devolved from the British government.

2000 With little progress in the decommissioning of paramilitary weapons, a condition of the Agreement, the British government proposes to suspend the Assembly and re-introduce 'direct rule'.

Cal

For my brother Peter

Chapter One

He stood at the back gateway of the abattoir, his hands thrust into
his pockets, his stomach rigid with the ache of want. Men in
white coats and baseball caps whistled and shouted as they moved
between the hanging carcases. He couldn't see his father, yet he
did not want to venture in. He knew the sweet warm nauseating   5
smell of the place and he had had no breakfast. Nor had he smoked
his first cigarette of the day. Smells were always so much more
intense then. At intervals the crack of the humane killer echoed
round the glass roof. Queuing beasts bellowed in the distance as if
they knew.   10

He saw the Preacher standing waiting with his glass. It was the
local doctor's prescription for any anaemic with a strong stomach.
The Preacher was tall and thin with the Adam's apple of a vulture
and skin that was made even paler, if that was possible, by the light
reflected from the white tiles. He cycled the countryside on his   15
breadcart of a bicycle with a small ladder strapped to the bar and
a clutter of tools in the saddle-bag, nailing tracts made from tin
lids to trees and telegraph-poles. 'The Wages of Sin is Death.
Romans 8:5' was on a sycamore tree on the Magherafelt road; and
further out 'I am the Resurrection and the Life. John 11:25'.   20

Crilly came over to the gateway to sharpen his knives.

'Hiya, Cal,' he said. Cal saw him press the blade on to the
carborundum stone with his fingers, heard it hiss.

'Is my Da about?'

Crilly looked up and stopped the movement. He nodded over   25
his shoulder.

'Will you tell him I want him,' said Cal.

'In a minute.' He squinted along the worn crescent of his blade and gave it an infinitesimal touch with the ball of his thumb. He caressed the stone lightly once or twice more, as if sweeping it clean, then moved back into the building.

5   'Shamie,' he yelled. 'Shamie.'

The humane killer cracked again and Cal saw the killing pen tip over and tumble a beast on to the floor, its legs stiff to the ceiling. It was immediately winched up by one of the hind shanks and its throat cut. The Preacher moved forward and held out his glass to
10 catch the spout of blood. Cal turned away.

His father appeared, holding two halves of a hanging carcase apart like a curtain. Seeing Cal, he went over to the gateway.

'What do you want?'

'You took the cigarettes with you.'

15   'Here,' he said, jutting out his hip. His hands were wet and slimy and he held them out as if he were to be body-searched by the Army. Cal lifted the tail of his father's white coat. It was japped all over with blood and stiff with cold fat. He put his hand in the trouser pocket and took out a packet of Embassy.

20   'Take a couple,' said his father. Cal took three and put the packet back. He fumbled in his own pocket for a match.

'See you,' he said, walking away. He struck the match, cupped it and lit one of the cigarettes, inhaling deeply. Almost immediately he felt the muscles of his stomach relax. Several more times while
25 standing still he drew the smoke to the bottom of his lungs and exhaled, each time with a sigh. He began to walk, the cigarette hanging from his mouth, his hands in his anorak pockets. It was an autumn morning, the air full of clear sounds. As he passed the pens of cattle he heard their nasal bawling and, when closer, the slow slap,
30 slap of their dung. He turned his face away and walked home to make himself a cup of tea and wait for his Giro to arrive in the post.

As he turned into his street he felt the eyes on him. He looked at the ground in front of him and walked. The eyes would be at the curtains or behind a hedge as a man paused in his digging. He
35 could not bear to look up and see the flutter of Union Jacks, and now the red and white cross of the Ulster flag with its red hand. Of

late there were more and more of these appearing in the estate. It
was a dangerous sign that the Loyalists were getting angry. The
flags should all have been down by now because the Twelfth of
July was long past. It was sheer cussedness that they were kept up.
Even looking at his feet Cal couldn't avoid the repulsion because   5
the kerbstones had been painted alternating red, white and blue.
Cal felt it was aimed at them, the Mc Cluskeys, because his father
and he were the only Catholic family left in the whole estate. Fear
had driven the others out but his father would not move. He was
stubborn at the best of times but if he thought pressure was being   10
applied to him he was ten times worse.

'No Loyalist bastard is going to force me out of my home. They
can kill me first.'

But it wasn't a single bastard that worried Cal, it was an accumu-
lation of them. The feeling of community that they managed to   15
create annoyed him and the stronger their sense of community
grew the more excluded and isolated the Mc Cluskeys felt. They
spoke to their near neighbours affably enough but beyond that
everyone else in the estate seemed threatening. The Radcliffs and
the Hendersons said they would stand by the Mc Cluskeys if it   20
ever came to an eviction.

Cal detested the condescension of some of the Protestant men
he met about the town.

'You're Shamie Mc Cluskey's boy? A good man, Shamie.' And
implied in everything they were saying was 'for a Catholic'. There   25
was faint affectionate amazement on their faces that there should
be a Catholic who was a good man, someone to equal them.

Cal turned in at the gate and walked up the path through his
father's neat garden. He let himself in at the front door with his
key. He took a mug of tea and a slice of toast up to his bedroom,   30
turning on the light rather than pulling back the curtains. He locked
the bedroom door with a small bolt he had recently bought in a
hardware shop. It was much against his father's wishes but he had
argued that he was nineteen years of age and had the right to some
sort of privacy. He put on an LP of the Rolling Stones to drown   35
the silence and sat on the bed with his back to the wall.

He put his head forward and sipped his tea. With his hair the length it was, he had had to develop some female gestures, like holding it back with his hand to prevent it getting in his cup. He had it parted in the middle so that it hung like curtains on each
5 side of his face. When he was by himself playing the guitar, almost as if it was a tic he would shake his head from side to side so that the hair would end up all over his face, screening him from the world. Within the tent of his hair with eyes shut he listened to the sounds his fingernails picked from the strings as he sang in an
10 American voice the things he'd heard on record. He could think of no good reason for this tic. It was like an attempt to rid himself of something, an overspill which resulted in spasmodic movement. He would also curse himself in pidgin French. He had learned very little French at school but he had retained enough of it to mutter
15 to himself, '*Cochon merde*', and twist his head. It was as if his mind had stuck. The phrase would come again and again. He even fretted as to whether or not it was grammatically correct. Not that it mattered because he even made up phrases of his own which were a mixture of French and English:
20 'Dirty *vache*. You big *crotte de chien*.'

In the morning he would wake with a ridiculous phrase like this in his mind and throughout the day it stayed with him like indigestion. Sometimes he wished that he knew more languages to curse himself more thoroughly. And yet at this thought he had
25 to smile.

He left his toast uneaten. The butter resolidified as it cooled. For the sake of the Movement he had tried to teach himself some Gaelic out of a book he had bought at a jumble sale but he never knew how to pronounce the written form of the words. How did
30 you say '*bh*' and '*dh*'? The words remained as printed symbols locked inside his head and he gave up the notion soon after. Some day he might go to a class and hear the words spoken.

He took out his second cigarette, straightened it with touches of his fingers and lit it. There was a slit in the curtains and a beam of
35 sunlight slanted into the room, making the smoke swirl flatly. When the record finished he moved to the window and peeped

out. The back garden led to a field of barley and beyond to the
smoky blue of the mountain of Slieve Gallon. Nothing moved. He
opened the window to let the smoke out but left the curtains closed
and when he sat down on the bed again they moved and unfurled
heavily in the slight breeze. With the window open he could hear   5
things going on. The monotonous cheeping of sparrows, a car
accelerating, children squealing distantly in the playground at
school. The quiet made him tense. He began to file his nails with
the sandpaper edge of his matchbox. The nails of his left hand were
closely trimmed, the fingertips hardened to leathery pads which   10
retained their scar of string long after they had ceased to press it,
while those of his right hand were as long as plectrums. He moved
the box away from himself in the direction of the growth of the
nail. To do it the other way – against the grain, as it were – gave
him a sensation he did not like. His smoking fingers were faintly   15
yellowed with nicotine. The silence made him want to play another
record. Then he heard a noise downstairs and stiffened. There
was someone outside. He unsnibbed his door and went quickly
to his father's room at the front of the house. Keeping to the side
of the window, he looked down and saw that it was only the   20
postman closing the gate. He went downstairs to find his Giro on
the mat.

2

Cal stood at the back of the queue in the post office. He wondered
why Mrs Doyle, who owned the place, didn't worry about security.
In the next town the post office had been modernized and the wire   25
grille replaced with bullet-proof glass. This would be an easy place
to do and there was plenty of money lying around. His stomach
tightened at the thought and he looked instead at a poster on the
wall urging him to prevent warble-fly.

When he got his money he bought a packet of cigarettes and   30
fumbled to find the red tab that would open the cellophane. On
the street he lit up and stood at the corner, his hands in his trouser
pockets. Arty Mc Glynn, smiling because he too had just got his
Giro money, joined him. They had been at school together.

'Hiya, Cal.'   35

7

'Hi.' Cal took out one hand to hold his cigarette and measured a long spit into the roadway.

'What are you doing with yourself this weather?' Cal considered this.

5   'Fondling,' he said. He spat again and walked away up Main Street to the library. It was a converted shop with a shop-front window displaying books. Inside a couple of old men browsed through the papers and a couple more were down among the shelves. It was warm and quiet and Cal had found it a good place
10 to pass some of the time. He had tickets which he used occasionally to borrow some cassette tapes but rarely, if ever, did he borrow books. He sat on a chair and flicked through *Time* magazine. There were pictures and an article about Northern Ireland and he felt strangely proud that the place where he lived was given so much
15 room in such an important magazine. When he was at school it was an occasion if anything from Northern Ireland got a mention on the news. He looked up from his magazine and noticed that there was a new woman behind the counter. She was small and dark-haired with very brown eyes. She seemed to match the wood
20 colours of the place. She was going through the index file, pulling out the small drawers and riffling through the cards. Over the top of the cabinet she briefly raised her eyes and solemnly looked at Cal. He stared back at her but she turned away to a customer, smiling at him and stamping his books with amazing speed. She
25 looked foreign, had that sallowness of skin which he associated with France. He tried to guess her age but couldn't. She wasn't young, perhaps somewhere in her late twenties.

The tapes were on a revolving stand near the desk and Cal went up to take a closer look at this woman. He turned the stand and
30 watched her file the tickets in a rank of them. Another old man came up with an armful of detective stories. He set his books down and hung his walking stick on the counter, and Cal watched it swing slowly to and fro. The old man leaned forward, resting his elbows on the desk-top, and the woman smiled and talked to him
35 as if she knew him. Cal turned the rack of tapes squeakily but continued to stare at her through them, willing her to look at him

again. She had a lovely mouth as well as eyes. It moved beautifully when she talked. She stamped the old man's books and took his tickets, slotting the books' cards inside them. When the transaction was complete he unhooked his walking stick and seemed embarrassed by the number of books he was borrowing. 5

'The best of luck anyway, Marcella,' he said.

Marcella.

'Oh Jesus,' Cal said into himself. Marcella. He put out his hand to move the rack again. It gave a faint screech as it turned and he saw his hand frozen in mid-air. At that moment she looked at him 10 and smiled. He moved his mouth to smile back but the muscles of his face would not respond properly. Marcella.

He left the library, stumbling on the old man's heels, and in the street he said it out loud.

'Oh Jesus.' He shook his head as if there were an insect crawling 15 in the porch of his ear.

It took him three matches to light another cigarette. He started out for home but stopped for a moment at the post office corner. There couldn't be many Marcellas around. He closed his eyes and leaned his head against the brick wall. Then he half ran, half walked 20 to his house. He stood in the middle of the bedroom floor, not knowing what to do. It must be her. He tried to recall the woman's face but could not. He sat on the bed, stood up to look out of the window but ended pacing the floor. Yet it might not be her. He might be able to tell from her face. If it was, could he ever go 25 back into the library? The more he thought of her, the more his fascination and curiosity grew. He felt a great need to recall her face. He could only summon up a bland set of features he knew were not hers. If he were ever to go back it would have to be now. He rooted in his drawer, rattling among useless lighters and Biros 30 that no longer worked, and produced two buff tickets. He walked quickly back to the library.

Once inside, he heard his loud breathing in the silence. The Marcella woman was having a cup of coffee. He studied her face, trying to read into it whether or not she was *the* Marcella. He could 35 not take his eyes off her, not because of what she was but because

of what he might have done to her. Her gestures, the way she raised
and rested the rim of the cup on her lip before sipping, every
movement of her face hypnotized him. He chose a Blues tape of
Muddy Waters and went up to the counter and waited. She took a
quick sip, set the cup down and came to him.

'Yes?'

He stared at her, moving his eyes over what he could see of her
above the counter. He had come to a library to borrow time. He
indicated the cassette and the ticket. Her nails were white and
unpainted and she wore a gold ring on her wedding finger. She
saw what she was looking for and moved lightly to it.

'Thank you, Mr Mc Cluskey,' she said and Cal looked up,
startled. Then he remembered that his name was on the ticket. She
set the cassette box on the counter and Cal watched the warm
prints of her fingers evaporate from the Perspex. *Merde. Crotte de
chien.* Merderer.

When Cal's father came home for his tea he smelt of the abattoir.
Cal tried not to breathe through his nose as they both moved about
the small kitchen. His father washed his huge hands and as far up
as his elbows with carbolic soap. Then he washed his face, making
loud spluttering noises, stooped over the sink.

'Towel,' he said, his eyes clenched tightly.

Cal gave it to him. The son was making a fry – eggs, bacon, black
puddings and some fried bread. When Shamie had dried his face
it looked shiny and red – as if he had sandpapered it rather than
washed it. He said,

'There's some yahoos outside.'

Cal left the pan to look between the slats of the venetian blind
in the front room. Four youths in denim were lounging against the
garden wall at the far side of the street. One of them, wearing a
red, white and blue scarf knotted at his neck, was looking over
at the Mc Cluskeys' house. He saw the slats move and pointed.
The others turned to look. The big one with clown-like black boots
and scarlet braces swung up his hand, giving Cal's eyes the two
fingers.

'Let them be,' shouted his father. 'These eggs are getting black lace edges.'

Cal rushed back to the pan and with a fish slice served the eggs on to plates. He put all the black puddings on his father's plate. He loathed them, made from blood, like cross-sections of large warts bound in black Sellotape.

They sat at the table and watched the news on television. The Army had shot a deaf mute, saying that he had been seen carrying a weapon, but by the time they had reached the dead man an accomplice had removed the gun. A Catholic father of three had been stabbed to death in a Belfast entry. The police said that there was no known motive for the killing. Gerry Fitt had had a steel door put on his house.

'Any jobs in the paper today?' asked his father.

Cal shook his head, his mouth full. When he had swallowed he said.

'A couple in Belfast.'

'You're safer away from the city.'

When they had finished, Cal cleared the table and washed the dishes while his father sat reading the paper. Cal spoke from the kitchen.

'There's a new woman in the library.'

'Hm-hm?'

'Called Marcella something.'

'That'll be Marcella Morton. I heard some of the lads saying that she'd taken a job to get away from the house.'

Cal closed his eyes. It *was* her. In the hot dishwater his nails had become soft and he trailed them across the metal bottom of the basin to find the last spoon. Oh Jesus. He dried it and put it in the drawer. In some way, he didn't know how, he would have to make it up to her. He cleared the tapes of the black puddings from the hole in the sink. They were limp and slimy and he shuddered as he threw them in the bucket. The water was like grey soup with tiny yellow grease circles. He poured it with a rush down the sink. A last teaspoon rattled out.

'There's always a sneaky bastard.'

He dried his hands and took three cigarettes from his packet and rolled them on to the mantelpiece for his father. Then he went to his bedroom to eat again the ashes of what he had done.

The next day Cal had to leave his room to go for more cigarettes. He
5 walked into the town centre, even though there was a tobacconist's at the far end of the street. The weather had changed and was threatening rain. The crows behind the church were making a racket and there had been a fly in his bedroom which had constantly landed on him, no matter how many times he scared it off with his hand.
10 According to his father both were sure signs of prolonged rain.

He bought his cigarettes and went to the library. Today she was dressed differently, a clean white blouse with a neck band which tied in a bow at the front. She looked up at him as he came in but glanced back at what she was writing on the counter as if he wasn't
15 there. He waited with his Muddy Waters tape in his hand. Ever since he had bought the cigarettes the tension in his stomach had increased. Now he felt as if he could bounce marbles off it. There were no smoking signs all over the place. A notice on the counter stated the hours of opening and closing. He looked at her again but
20 she was intent on what she was doing, her eyes cast down. Beneath the stuff of her blouse he could see a faint laciness where her body touched it on the inside. It was stupid coming in here to return a tape he had only borrowed the day before. It might be noticed. He wanted to reach out and touch her hand over the counter, to tell her that
25 everything would be all right. She took back his tape efficiently and beautifully, but not personally. He read magazines and looked at her until the want of a cigarette drove him out.

He went home and lay on his bed, smoking and listening to the radio until twenty-past five. When he went out it was raining
30 heavily, ringing a skin of rain which had not had time to run off the pavement. He put up the hood of his anorak, tucking his hair in at the sides. His front quickly became greeny-black as he walked into the rain. He stood dripping in a shop doorway opposite the library and waited until twenty to six.
35 She came out, putting on a cream-coloured mac, wrinkling her

face against the rain. Then she ran with a stiff-legged awkwardness towards the end of Main Street. Cal followed her, walking with long strides. She went into the car park outside the Control Zone and got into a yellow Anglia. As she drove past him he could not see her face because of the misted windows and the flapping windscreen wipers.

When he got home he was soaked. His father was rattling about in the kitchen making something to eat and by the quality of the noise Cal knew that he was angry.

'Where were you?'

'Out for a walk.'

'Jesus – you sit in that bloody room of yours the whole summer and the day it rains you decide to go for a walk.'

Cal hung up his anorak and began to dry the front of his hair with a towel.

'You might at least have put the spuds on before you went out. When I've a day's work behind me I don't want to be coming home and starting in to cooking. If you were working I could see through it. But you've bugger all to do all day except put on the dinner at five o'clock.'

'I was just going to,' said Cal. 'I got held up in the town.'

His father was setting the table. He filled a milk jug, held the empty bottle under the cold tap and ran a little water into it. He swirled it around and poured it into the jug.

'I wish you wouldn't do that,' said Cal.

'Waste not, want not.'

'It makes the milk taste funny.'

'Your arse.'

They watched the news on television while they were waiting for the potatoes to boil. No one had been killed because the first item was about redundancies in the Belfast shipyards. There had been three robberies at post offices throughout the province, netting a total of £15,000.

'Put the sausages on low,' said his father.

As they ate, Shamie told Cal that Crilly wanted him to call at nine o'clock.

13

'What for?'

'I don't know. He didn't say.'

'Can I have the van?'

Cal's father looked out of the window and said he could.

5 'There's something about that lad that I don't like,' he said. 'Too smart by half. I don't like you knocking around with him.'

Cal said nothing. His father went on,

'It sticks in my throat that he got the job that you gave up because you hadn't a strong enough stomach. Now he's got money to burn

10 and you're running about borrowing fags. Not to mention the embarrassment it caused me.'

Cal excused himself, leaving most of his dinner still on the plate.

'Leave the dishes. I'll do them later.'

'I've heard that one before.' He shouted after Cal, 'If you don't

15 eat you'll die.'

Cal lay on the bed smoking. What did Crilly want? He had hoped he'd been forgotten, passed over because he was useless. He felt sure that it was all going to start again.

He had been at school with Crilly and in one year, the third,

20 they had been in the same class together. It was wise to be on the right side of him because he could be nasty when he wanted, even then. He was a big lad for his age with large ears that stuck out at right angles from the side of his head. Somebody had once said that Crilly had ears like taxi doors and it had got back to him.

25 Even though the boy was much smaller than him, Crilly had no compunction about breaking two of his teeth. He also had a number of boys whom he had picked to borrow money from, boys with blazers and ties. When he saw them he'd admit politely that he owed them money and that they would get it back soon. But they

30 never did. A boy asked Crilly one day to pay him back and Crilly grabbed his tie and shirt front and screwed it into his bunched fist.

'Are you trying to say that I'm a thief?'

He put him up against the wall and drew back his other hand.

'You can wait for your money, son. But you've just put yourself

35 well down the queue, as of today.' He didn't punch him. He didn't need to.

Even the authorities recognized Crilly's ability to get things done. Some fourth-year boy had brought a series of pornographic contact prints into school and was showing them round. Cal and Crilly were still in the third year at the time. It was Father Durkin who let them know about it in the R.K. class. 5

'Lewd pictures, boys, destroy both the women in them and the men who look at them. If I could lay my hands on the gulpin who is poisoning the minds of the pupils of this school I'd flay him to within an inch of his life. There *is* such a thing as righteous anger.' 10

He seemed really angry and concerned. He was swishing his thin yellow cane in the air to emphasize his words as he walked up and down between the rows of desks.

'We know the boy is in fourth year, but it is such a serious offence that we can get no one to pass information on to us.' 15

He stopped directly in front of Crilly and said.

'An intelligent pupil could find out who was passing these detestable things around and,' he smiled a little, 'most of the staff would be looking the other way if anything happened. Do you think a worm like that is going to go home and say that he got his black 20 eyes for showing filthy photographs to juniors in the school?'

After R.K. Crilly went, as usual, for a smoke in the toilets. Cal saw him mix with the fourth year, asking questions, his head on a level with theirs. Then he got Cal to come with him and cornered a boy called Smicker. Crilly edged him into a lavatory cubicle. Cal 25 had to squeeze in before he could lock the door. Crilly grabbed Smicker by the shoulders and with a lightning dart of his head into Smicker's face, sat him down on the lavatory. Blood and stuff began pouring out of Smicker's nose. He wiped his hand across his upper lip and stared at the smear of red across the back of his 30 hand. Crilly started going through his pockets. He handed two photographs the size of large stamps over his shoulder to Cal. They had black edges with white sprocket holes.

'Where's the rest?'

'Gave them away.' Smicker was crying, holding his face. Crilly 35 went on searching his pockets.

'You fuckin' sold them,' he said and Cal heard the rattle of money disappearing into Crilly's pocket. Crilly then lifted the boy bodily off the lavatory seat and thumped his knee into his balls. Smicker bent over, unable to breathe, and Crilly cracked his fore-
5 head with his knee again. The boy slewed sideways and banged his ear and the side of his head on the partition as he fell. Cal heard a dull bone noise as Smicker's back crunched on the delft horseshoe of the lavatory bowl. Outside the cubicle boys were stamping and shouting 'Fight, fight, fight'. Some had climbed the partition and
10 were hanging over. Smicker was curled up in the corner, his knees to his chin, his hands between his thighs.

'Get out,' said Crilly to Cal, and they ran.

Afterwards Crilly had a look at the photographs and laughed. He showed them to Cal, who until that point had been afraid to
15 look at them. They were of slightly out-of-focus women whose eyes were reflecting the flash-gun. They were lying naked with their legs open, smiling sheepishly. They were on an ordinary sofa and behind them was ordinary wallpaper, very like the pattern Cal's father had put in their living room. To see them properly Cal had
20 to hold the picture a couple of inches from his face.

His legs were shaking and they were both full of nervous laughter after the fight. Crilly wanted praise and went over the incident many times.

'Did you see the look on his face when I got him in the balls?'
25 Cal nodded. As they talked, Crilly put the photographs in his pocket and Cal never saw them again.

Some weeks after that they were walking behind Smicker in the corridor when his pen fell out of a hole in the bottom of his bag. Crilly wanted to keep it but Cal had it in his hand and ran after the
30 fourth-year boy and gave it back to him.

'Crawler,' said Crilly when Cal came back red-faced.

If it was all to start again he would have to face up to Crilly; tell him he wanted nothing more to do with it. It was Crilly who was largely responsible for Cal's stomach having felt like a washboard
35 over the past year. Thinking of it made it worse.

★

He swung his legs off the bed and went downstairs to the kitchen, but his father had already done the dishes and was now snoring loudly in front of 'Nationwide'. Cal saw his uneaten dinner stored beneath a pot lid. Shamie would fry it up later rather than let it go to waste. He went to the window and looked out between the slats. 5
It was still raining heavily on an empty street. At least it meant there would be no aggro tonight. Rain kept the Protestants at home.

He took the keys of the van from the brass jug on the mantelpiece and went quietly out. He considered driving in the opposite direc- 10
tion from Crilly's house but then thought it might be better to get the whole thing over and done with.

When he called at the door Crilly himself answered it in bare feet.

'Mc Cluskey. What about ya?' 15

Crilly's mother came peeping into the hall to see who it was. She had no teeth and was wearing a jumper of bubble-gum pink. Cal couldn't see through the frizzed hair whether or not her ears stuck out.

'It's only Cal,' Crilly said to her. He led him into the carpeted 20
sitting room. Finbar Skeffington sat in an armchair beside the fireplace with his short legs straight out in front of him, looking at the high polish on his shoes. There was no fire in the grate. He looked at Cal, stood up and shook hands.

'*Go mbeannuigh Dia duit*,' he said. 25

'*Dia is Muire duit*,' answered Cal. That much he did know.

They all sat down, Crilly with his bare feet on the chair, holding himself round the ankles. Skeffington was small and round-faced with glasses – about thirty. He wore a sports jacket and a tie. On his lapel was a Pioneer Total Abstinence pin. His teeth reminded 30
Cal of a rabbit's, an impression which was intensified by his habit of wrinkling his face to adjust minutely the glasses on the bridge of his nose.

'How are you, Cahal?' he said.

'OK' 35

'And your father?'

'Oh, he's fine. Left him asleep in front of the TV.'

'Good. I suppose you've heard Gerry Burns and Peter Fitz-simmons were lifted last night?'

Cal nodded.

5   'We're losing too many good people. It's why we wanted to see you, Cahal.'

'Me? I had nothing to do with it.'

Skeffington smiled. 'No, I don't mean that. We need a driver.'

'Oh.'

10   'Yes, sonny boy,' said Crilly. 'The old hot tyres and squealing brakes.' He sucked the air back in his throat to imitate the sound.

'The call has come for money,' said Skeffington, knitting his fingers together. 'American money is tailing off. Internment is losing the edge it had for producing the dollars. Now we need to
15   gather some of our own.'

'How ?' asked Cal. Skeffington shrugged.

'People won't give it to you, that's for sure.'

'We've got to take it, sonny boy.' Crilly pointed his index finger at Cal and cocked his thumb. 'The Dick Turpin stunt, oul' Robin
20   Hood.'

'Speaking of Robin Hood, my father was telling me a great story of something that happened in Belfast. Did you hear about it?' asked Skeffington.

The others shook their heads.

25   'You'll enjoy this,' and when he laughed, baring his teeth, his rabbitness became more pronounced. 'It's about the rent strike. Well, many people were getting so far behind that they thought they'd *never* be able to catch up, so our lads decided to do a nice wee job on it. They appropriated some funds, a couple of places, I
30   think it was a supermarket and a bookie's, and went round the New Lodge Road giving every house what it needed to settle up the rent. Then somebody invited the rent man in and he went round every house and got paid in full. I believe his face was the picture of happiness, marking up his wee book. When he comes
35   out of the last house, our lads were waiting for him.' He mimicked Crilly's gesture with the pointed finger and the cocked thumb.

' "We'll have that," they said.' He exploded with laughter, slapping his thigh. 'Isn't that a good one? Everybody was up to date and the rent man hadn't a thing to show for it.'

'Boom-boom,' said Crilly.

'Stories like that are good for us. Even if they didn't happen we should make them up. Win the propaganda war and the rest will follow.'

'What about this money?' asked Crilly.

'We have to think of places that take in a lot. Petrol stations, off-licences, bookies'. Hit an off-licence late at night – a Friday night preferably.'

'Are you teaching your granny to suck eggs?' said Crilly.

Skeffington, ignoring him, went on.

'Get the money to me as soon as you can afterwards.'

Cal sat back in the chair and listened as they chose the best place. He lit a cigarette and flicked the match into the grate, empty except for some sweet papers. It was beginning to get dark outside. The wailing guitar sequence from 'The Dark Side of the Moon' came into his head and he listened to it, moving his fingers. Crilly got up and pulled the curtains.

'Cal, you are very quiet. Is there anything wrong?' asked Skeffington.

Cal took a deep draw on his cigarette. He said,

'I want out.' There was a silence. Crilly laughed.

'But you're not even fuckin' *in*.'

'Can't we do without that word, please?' Skeffington's face was wrinkled with distaste.

'I'm far enough in to want out,' said Cal. Skeffington considered this for a moment. He spoke with a polite electrical energy:

'Are you afraid?'

'Not really.'

'I've never known anybody who wasn't.'

'More tense than afraid.'

'Christ, who isn't?' said Crilly. He tucked his bare feet up and sat on them.

'What's the problem, Cahal?' Skeffington asked.

'I just don't like what's happening. That woman Marcella Morton has started in the library. I see her every day.'

'The problem with this kind of thing is that people get hurt.' Skeffington leaned forward. 'But compared with conventional war the numbers are small. I know that sounds callous but it's true. In Cyprus the dead hardly ran to three figures. That's cheap for freedom.'

'I have no stomach for it,' said Cal. His voice was tired.

'Do you think any of us have?' Skeffington stared at him. 'Anybody who enjoyed this kind of thing would have to be sick. But it has to be done – by somebody. Because we have committed ourselves, Cahal, it is our responsibility. *We* have to make the sacrifices. You just can't turn away and say you've no stomach for it.'

'But to kill a guy on his own doorstep?'

'He was a Reserve policeman – on of the enemy. This is war, Cahal.'

'He had it coming,' said Crilly. 'He would have done it to you and got a medal for it.'

Cal sharpened the ash on his cigarette against the side of the ashtray and lit another one from it. He stared up at the ceiling. Skeffington said,

'Others can ride on our coat-tails. The Gerry Fitts and the Humes. It's like a union. Some guys do all the work, others collect the pay rises without so much as a thank you. You have to steel yourself, Cahal. Think of the issues, not the people. Think of an Ireland free of the Brits. Would we ever achieve it through the politicians?'

'No.'

'Too damned right,' said Crilly.

There was a knock on the door and Mrs Crilly came in hesitantly, carrying a tray with tea things on it. Crilly jumped off his chair.

'Ma, I told you we didn't need tea.'

Skeffington stood up with his feet together and said,

'That is very kind of you, Mrs Crilly.'

'I'm afraid I've only got plain biscuits,' she said. It was a tiny tray and everything was rattling noisily. She looked around for help

and Skeffington pulled a small table into the centre of the floor. It
had spindly legs and under its glass top it had a view of a blue lake
and pine trees and snow-capped mountains.

'Thank you,' she said, setting down the tray. She reached for the
tea pot.

'We can do it ourselves,' said Crilly.

'Are you sure?' Mrs Crilly was smiling, focusing on the guests,
ignoring her son. She backed away from the table. Her pink jumper
drew attention to her breasts, which were small and sagging almost
to her waist. Cal thanked her.

'Isn't that a terrible night?' she said. 'For anybody on their
holidays.'

After she had left, Skeffington knelt on the floor and began to
pour the tea.

'Sugar?' he asked.

They sipped their tea in silence. Skeffington nibbled a biscuit
with his prominent teeth, swallowed and said,

'Your wanting to withdraw, Cahal, would make things very
awkward.'

'I'll drive if it's only for funds,' said Cal. 'Just this once. Then
you can think of getting somebody else.'

'Attaboy, Cal,' said Crilly.

At half-past five on Friday evening Cal waited on the street on the
same side as the post office so that she would have to pass him on
her way to the car park. He stood looking into a sweetshop window,
glancing to his right every so often. Then he noticed that the shop
window was at an oblique angle to the doorway and he could see
a reflection of the library without even turning his head.

She came out with a large cardboard box of groceries balanced
across her arms. The flaps of the box almost hid her face as she
walked quickly along the pavement, tilting her body backwards to
adjust to the weight. He let her pass, then turned and followed her.
She stopped at the kerb on the corner and looked awkwardly left
and right for traffic. Cal hesitated behind her. As she twisted to see
round her, a plastic carton of salt rolled off the top of her groceries

and clumped dully at her feet. She made a sound of exasperation but Cal, moving quickly, swooped and picked it up for her.

'Oh, thank you,' she said, turning her head to see who it was. She set the box on the pavement and squatted down beside it. 'It's
5 far too full.' She rearranged some of the items and wedged the salt upright between a packet of flour and the edge of the box. Cal saw as she crouched that she wore no stockings. Her legs were tanned and shining. She was wearing Dr Scholl's sandals.

'I hope you're not superstitious,' he said.
10 'It didn't spill.' She smiled up at him.

'Let me carry it for you.'

'Not at all.' She tried to put her fingers beneath the box.

'Please.'

Cal stooped over and lifted the box lightly by the hand-holes.
15 Like her he carried it on his forearms with his hands splayed at the front.

'Where to?'

'Thank you very much,' She seemed flustered. 'To the car park.'
20 They walked beside one another, she with her hands idle on her shoulder bag.

'Do you play the guitar?' she asked.

'A bit.'

'Your long nails.' She nodded to them.
25 'On the one hand some people say they are long,' he said, 'yet on the other hand they are not.'

She laughed and looked at him to see if he was conscious of the joke he'd made. He smiled at her unsureness, at her reluctance to make fun of him if it had just been a mistake.
30 'That's good. I like that,' she said.

Out from behind the counter she seemed much smaller.

'This is very kind of you,' she said.

'Not at all.'

There was an awkward silence between them. Even though he
35 was carrying the box, Cal stepped back to let her go through the gate to the car park first. He said,

'You're working in the library?'

'Yes, that's right.'

'I saw you today.'

'Of course. Over here,' she said, taking the car keys from her shoulder bag. She opened the boot of the car and when Cal set the box in, it sank on its axle. He blew out.

'It gets heavier the longer you carry it.'

She closed the boot with a bang. Again she smiled, not quite knowing what to say. Cal smiled back at her, shrugged and helped her by moving away.

'See you around,' he said.

'Thank you again.'

This time as she drove past him she waved and he waved back as casually as he could.

'I saw you today. *Merde*,' he said, spitting in the road.

That night when he got the door open after pushing against the heavy curtain which shrouded it on the inside he found a note folded and caught by the sprung metal tongue of the letterbox. He switched on the light in the hallway.

GET OUT YOU FENYAN SCUM OR WE'LL BURN YOU OUT. THIS IS YOUR 2ND WARNING. THERE WILL BE NO OTHER. UVF

Cal switched out the light and tiptoed into the darkness of the front room. He peered between the slats of the blind. The street was empty. The only movement was the rain slanting across the yellow halo of the sodium streetlamp outside the door. At the back everything was dark except for some pinpoints of light around the base of Slieve Gallon. As quietly as he could, he opened the window and listened. Water clinked and spluttered from the drainpipe. A curlew called once in the distance, then twice, very close. There was the steady slow pulse of his father's snoring from upstairs. He kept expecting the window to burst into a shower of glass and flame but he knew it wouldn't. It would be some night when they were both asleep. The panic of jumping from his window. He saw the ungainliness of his father's bulk crashing through the asbestos material of the shed roof. Would they be waiting outside to take pot-shots at the Fenians they had smoked out? This lot sounded a bit dramatic. 'THERE WILL BE NO OTHER.'

5 He went to the bathroom, using only the light from the curtained landing. It was the idea of people whose faces he did not know hating him that made his skin crawl. To be hated not for yourself but for what you were. He went into his father's bedroom and shook him gently.

10 'Shamie,' he whispered. 'Shamie.'

His father woke with a snorting noise.

'What?'

He switched on the bedside light and scratched his hair. 'What's up?'

15 'This.' Cal handed him the note. His father angled it to the light and read with squinting eyes, holding it a few inches from his face.

'The bastards.'

He got out of bed and knelt in the corner of the room. He had 20 been sleeping in his pyjama trousers only and Cal saw the puckered white flab of his back as he pulled back the carpet. He lifted a short floorboard by two nails which were not quite flush with the wood and brought a black polythene bag to the bed. He emptied a gun and some bullets on to the eiderdown. It was an old .38 and Shamie 25 loaded it, leaving the first chamber empty. The tiny clicking of the bullets as his father's fingers groped for them on the eiderdown made Cal think his teeth were covered in sand. He asked.

'Should we fill the bath?'

'Fill it but don't put in the blanket. It's a bugger to get dried.'

30 Cal half filled the bath and took an old mushroom-coloured blanket from the hot press and folded it over the side like a towel. When he came back into the bedroom Shamie was putting the gun beneath his pillow and climbing into bed. Cal said.

'Everything OK?'

35 'Are the doors all locked?' Cal nodded. 'Goodnight then.'

'Goodnight.'

'Isn't it a terrible thing,' said Shamie, 'that those bastards have us whispering in our own house.'

Cal thought about sleeping with his shoes on but instead set them together beside the bed, left on the left, right on the right. He checked by touch that his stick was beneath the bed, then in the dark he undressed to his jeans. Normally he slept in his underpants. He lit up and lay back. It was strange how much the room glowed red each time he took a draw. It was so quiet that he heard the faint hiss of burning tobacco.

He thought of the woman in the library. He wanted to put his arm about her – here and now – to lie with her and do nothing but absorb the silence. As he had followed her he had seen the slim shapeliness of her legs, how they had broadened at the calf when she had squatted by her box of groceries. Hairless and tanned, as if she had been to the Continent. Marcella was a Continental name. He shuddered.

He stubbed his cigarette out with more pressure than was required and turned over to go to sleep. But it was too quiet. Now and again he raised his head off the pillow and listened. Once a dog barked in the distance. Then another and another, from different farms. And just as suddenly they stopped and the silence returned. He listened so hard there was a kind of static in his ears – like listening to the sea in a shell. He expected whispering voices, the squeak of a rubber-soled shoe on their concrete path. He had heard on the radio once that the Universe had started with an unimaginable explosion and that static was its dying echoes a skillion years later. He lay on his back and listened to the echoes, waiting for his window to explode.

The first threat had been posted the same way and written in the same crude felt-tip printing. His father had been worried and angry and had told some of his workmates at the abattoir about it, including Crilly. The very same night Crilly had arrived at the house with a friend of his. Cal had been out at the time but later heard the story from his father. They had offered him a .38 for his own protection and he had accepted it. He was happy to know that

in the house he had the means to frighten off a mob that some
night he knew would march up to his door. Or to get a doorstep
killer before the killer got him. He was grateful to Crilly and his
friend for their promptness. Cal knew that in his father's mind it
5 was all a bit like the Westerns he so liked to watch on TV – that he
had right on his side and it was the baddies who would die. He
knew the old man felt safe with his notion and Cal did not want to
disillusion him.

He knew if somebody had marked you out it would all be over
10 in a blinding flash and a bang before you could take your hands
out of your pockets, and you would be bleeding into the carpet
when you thought you were still standing up. He knew too that if
the Brits were to search the house they would walk to the corner
of the bedroom, pull back the carpet and lift the floorboard. But
15 being in a Loyalist area saved them from that.

Some weeks after Crilly had brought the gun, he came back and
asked them if they would do him a favour. They said yes, of
course, and before they knew what had happened there were three
cardboard boxes full of stuff hidden in their roof space. Cal looked
20 in the boxes but everything was wrapped in sacking and black
polythene and he hadn't the will to look further. Those nights
when the stuff was in the house his bedroom ceiling seemed to
burn above him. The Mc Cluskeys' became a 'safe house' and
occasionally stuff would be moved in and a couple of days later
25 taken away again.

Then Crilly called one night and asked Cal to run him somewhere in the van. They moved something from one house to
another, Cal helping, taking one ear of the heavy sacks. He was
worried but he didn't say so. Crilly was always looking round him
30 as if his head was on a swivel. It became a regular thing that Cal
had to drive him, and they had had a couple of close calls.

One night after they had left off a load, the Army stopped the van.
Both of them had to get out and give their names and addresses. A
light was shone in their faces and they had to stand with their arms
35 extended while they were searched. The soldiers had screamed at
them, as they pulled up, to turn out the headlights of the van, but

from the reflected light of the torch Cal could see a man with a
blackened face crouched in the ditch with a rifle aimed straight at
Cal's head. The Army took about ten minutes to search the van –
inside the engine, the door linings, the seats. When they drove off
Crilly was on the verge of tears.   5

'Jesus Christ, why do we have to put up with that?' His teeth
were together and his fists clenched. 'Fuckin' scum from the back
streets of London and Glasgow pawing all over me. Did you see
the way they looked at you? As if they were touching turds.' He
smashed his fist on the dashboard in front of him and the glove   10
compartment fell open, lighting up inside.

'The bastards,' shouted Crilly. 'The day will come, Cal, the day
will come.'

'Thank God they didn't stop us half an hour ago.'

Cal heard his father turn in the bed and the scratch of a match   15
being lit. He got up, lifted his own cigarettes and went into the
front bedroom.

'Do you want a cup of tea?'

'What time is it?' said his father. He lifted the alarm clock off its
face and looked at it. It was twenty-past three. 'Why not?' he said.   20

Cal went downstairs and pulled the kitchen curtains before
turning on the light. As he waited for the kettle to boil he became
all gooseflesh, the light hairs on his folded arms standing up. The
summer was over.

When he got back to the bedroom his father was sitting up. He   25
wore an old bottle-green sweater with holes at both elbows. Part
of the crewneck had unravelled and his hair had become tousled
as he put the sweater on over his head.

'Thanks, Cal,' he said when he got his tea. He said it quietly
and Cal, for some reason, was moved. The bedside light shone   30
downwards, accentuating the shadows of Shamie's face, making
him look older than he was. Lying awake had sensitized them both.
Shamie looked at him and said.

'Put my jacket on or you'll freeze.'

Cal shivered as he put the jacket on, not used to the cold silk of   35

the lining next to his skin. He cradled his mug of tea in both hands
for the warmth, sitting on the bottom of the bed.

'You're very quiet these days, Cal. Is anything wrong?'

'No.'

5 'You go to that room of yours all the time. We don't talk any
more.'

'If I had a job it might be different.'

'You should never have left the abattoir.'

'The smell made me want to throw up all the time.'

10 'You'd have got used to that.'

Cal said nothing. They'd had this conversation many times
before, but never had it been spoken quietly. Shamie went on,

'I mean, do you know how embarrassing it was for me? I moved
heaven and earth to get you in there. There's few enough Catholics,

15 God knows. And you go and jack it in before the week's out. You
should have seen the look Mr Loudan gave me.'

'Crilly's a Catholic.'

'Crilly's not my son. But I'll say this for him, he does your job a
damned sight better than you ever did.'

20 Cal saw the tumble of purple and green and grey steaming
innards fall from the raised carcase and subside on to the ground
at his feet, the nervous flick and jig of movement in them. He could
smell them still.

'He's welcome to it.' He finished his tea and set the cup on the

25 floor. He offered his father a cigarette and, although they had
agreed to smoke their own, he accepted one. Shamie put his cup
on the bedside table and lay back on the pillows.

'Do you think we should move?' he said. 'I hate to let the bastards
get the better of me.'

30 'I don't know,' said Cal. 'I've been thinking about England.
Maybe get a job there.'

'England is rotten to the core.'

Cal smiled.

'I had a go over once when there was no work and precious little

35 dole here. I was never more miserable in all my life. Wolver-bloody-
hampton. In digs with pipes running head-high across a cupboard

of a room. Away from your mother. No thanks. If the dole keeps
you living you should stay here.'

'We'll see,' said Cal. He got up to go.

'What age were you when your mother died?'

'Eight – I think.'

Shamie pulled off his jumper and threw it on the floor. He settled
down for the night on the outside half of the double bed.

'I hope we get to sleep this time.'

'Goodnight,' said Cal.

But Cal could not sleep. When he overslept in the mornings it was
always worse at night. It was a cycle which he couldn't break. Tired
from insomnia, he couldn't wake. He lay with his hands clasped
behind his head. His mother had been called Gracie. He
remembered the janitor coming into the classroom and that he had
been amazed when the teacher, Mrs Mc Lean, looked straight at
him and said that he had to go to the office. His Aunt Mollie,
whom he hardly knew, was sitting crying on a straight chair outside
the headmaster's door. She said that his mother had collapsed in
her own kitchen with a brain haemorrhage and had been taken in
the ambulance with her apron still on.

For months afterwards, every time he thought of her when he
was alone Cal cried. Even to this day he could bring a lump to his
throat if he wanted to by thinking of her. He thought of her making
faces into the back of a soup spoon and laughing: of the day she
had lost her wedding ring and, as a last resort before his father
came home from work, how she had stood in the kitchen crumbling
into bits the wheaten loaf she had baked, and the wild whoop she
gave when her fingers hit hard gold. He could see her as if she were
alive sitting at the table by the window, with two cheap turquoise
combs holding back her hair, crying in absolute silence when she
got the telegram telling her of the death of Brendan, Cal's elder
brother, in a Baltimore car crash, knowing that it was not possible
to go to his funeral.

She went to mass and communion every morning and each night
she made them say the family rosary before the table was cleared.

29

She had a missal which bulged with memoriam cards, novenas and special prayers, and if people borrowed it they inevitably scattered the lot over the church floor. The little coloured strings for marking the place were worn past the point where they should have hung
5 out at the bottom of the page.

He wondered if the reason he loved her so much was because she had died before he had reached adolescence. He could not remember ever fighting with her or being beaten by her. From the age of fourteen onwards he had been constantly at war with his
10 father. Everything from the way he chewed his food to the number of cigarettes he smoked was the subject for a shouting match. And yet there were areas where Shamie was at a loss for words. Not long after Gracie's death Shamie had found a purple bruise mark in the crook of Cal's elbow. At night he gave himself love-bites,
15 sucking until he tasted the coppery blood coming through the skin. His father asked him what had happened. Not knowing why, Cal said that he had hurt his arm in school – in a fight with another boy. His father just said that he sometimes wished Cal's mother were alive still. She would have told him about it. At the mention
20 of his mother Cal cried and his father left the room.

Shamie never mentioned girls, and when anything to do with love-making came on the television he would either leave the room or become engrossed in the paper which was constantly on his lap. Unless the programme became really explicit – with nakedness –
25 he would not turn it off but mutter something about Britain being 'rotten to the core'.

(10)

With infinite slowness the window became visible behind its blue curtain. A bird sang a short burst and was followed by others. After the silence of the night it was now the noise of the birds which kept
30 him awake. Nothing would happen in the daylight. They would not have the courage to be seen. He could now sleep. Eventually, with a pillow folded about his head to muffle both his ears, he did. But only to dream his recurring dream about a young girl. Sometimes he saw her house from a bus, sometimes from a car.
35 Once he had a gun in his hand. She was naked and beautiful and

always in the upstairs bay window. She was always in a state of great agitation, which Cal knew was sexual, and flitted from one window of the bay to the other, touching herself, her breasts and her belly, against the blowing net curtains, as if she were dancing. He knew she needed his help, but when he sprang from the gate to her window-sill and into her room she showed stark terror on her lovely face. Then she burst out of the side window. The air was filled with her screaming and the shattering of glass. He looked out and as always she was below, skewered on some railings, screaming unceasingly.

Chapter Two

①

On the Sunday morning Cal woke and knew that he had slept in.
He grabbed at his watch and saw that it was ten-past ten. He leapt
out of bed and as he dressed he heard his father coming through
the front door.

5   'Why didn't you waken me?' Cal shouted, running down the
stairs, tucking in his shirt. His father was dressed in his good suit
and had a missal in his hand. Beneath his arm was a fat folded
bundle of Sunday papers.

'I did. I went in and told you the time and you answered me. I
10 thought you'd changed your mind about the match.'

'Were you at nine?'

'Yes.'

'Lend us the van and I'll go to half-ten in Magherafelt.'

'You'll never make it.'

15 Cal poured a dish of cornflakes and stood spooning them into
himself, his elbow held high for speed. He drank the last of the
sweet milk from the dish. Smoking his first cigarette of the day, he
pushed the van to its limits on the empty Sunday roads, driving
with the accelerator pressed to the floor. He got into the church
20 just as the readings were starting. Normally in his own church he
would have stayed at the back but as he hurried through the door
an usher in the middle aisle caught his eye and waved him forward
like a traffic policeman. Embarrassed, with his hair swinging,
Cal walked towards the altar and squeezed into the tiny space
25 the usher had spotted. He tried to make room for himself with
slight movements of his shoulders, easing his way back between
his neighbours. The second reading started but he couldn't

follow it at all. His eyes wandered round the bright church. It had been built fairly recently and he didn't like it. There was a painting on the wall of Christ crucified. It was in a modern style and designed to match the pale colour scheme of the building. He preferred dark stone churches – churches with a smell of age and leaded windows. 5

Several rows in front of him a child knelt up in the seat and looked back. She was beautiful, with large hazel eyes. Cal winked at her. She crouched shyly into her mother, then only slowly came up again. Cal repeated the wink. This time she crouched with a 10 smile. Her mother, wearing a black mantilla, eased the child round to face the front without turning.

The priest came up to the lectern and they all stood for the gospel. Cal made sure he was the first to sit down again so that the others had to adjust to him in the crush for space. He settled back 15 for the sermon. He liked this time. It was a time of comfort, of hearing but not listening. The noise of the words kept him from thinking his own black thoughts and yet the words themselves were not interesting enough to make him think of them. He was in a kind of warm limbo. He did not know the priest, who spoke simply 20 and in a voice which demanded attention. Cal tried to shut it out but it insisted. He wanted to drift but the voice constantly pulled him back. It told of Matt Talbot, who after a decade of drunkenness in Dublin turned to Christ. The rest of his life was spent in atonement for his early years. 25

'When he was discovered dead in his simple room and his friends were laying him out for burial, they found that his waist was lapped in chains. He had been wearing them for so long and had them so tightly tied about him that it was almost impossible to remove them from the mortified flesh of his body. Just as a staple or wire will 30 become absorbed by a living tree, so the body of Matt Talbot had invaded and become one with the links of his chains. Which of us, I ask you, would be willing to put himself through such suffering for the love of Jesus? Which of us would be willing to endure so much pain to right a wrong? The amazing thing was that Matt 35 Talbot was a working man like you or me. What separated him from the likes of us was his steel will and his enormous faith in the love of Jesus Christ.'

Afterwards Cal knelt with everyone else. He found it difficult to pray. The only prayer he could say with any sincerity was for the soul of his mother, and yet he believed her to be in heaven and in no need of his efforts. And the prayer always drifted from prayer to remembering her – snatches, scenes they had had together. She had a good voice and knew countless songs off by heart, rebel songs, and she would bounce him on her knee and sing with gusto:

As Roddy Mc Corley goes to die
On the bridge of Toome today.

And when he was older she would sing, instead of telling him a story at night, 'The Croppy Boy' or 'Father Murphy' with its slow, sad melody:

A rebel hand set the heather blazing.

The rest of his prayers consisted of telling himself how vile he was. If he was sick of himself, how would God react to him?

'*Merde. Dog-shit. Crotte de vache.*'

The communion came and the woman in the mantilla stood up. She tried to make the child stay in the seat while she went to the altar rails but the little girl refused to be left and followed her mother out in a small jigging panic. Cal, still on his knees, threaded his fingers into his hair and stared down at the chestnut-coloured knots in the seat bench in front of him. One was like a comet trailing a blood-red tail. Another had blacker densities, like eyes staring back at him.

When he looked up he saw that the woman in the black mantilla was Marcella. She was coming down the aisle, her hands joined, her head slightly bowed, followed by her little girl, who was walking and skipping. He had to look again to make sure it was Marcella because her black hair was severely scraped back and hidden beneath the mantilla. She turned into the seat, settled her child and bent over in prayer, her face in her hands. He had not thought of her as a Catholic. She was married to someone called Robert

Morton. The Mortons had been Protestant farmers for centuries. He looked hard at her bent back until the open-knitted texture of her dress glazed his eyes. In an attitude of prayer he pressed the knuckles of his thumbs into his eyes until colours leapt and spread and it began to hurt. Patterns merged into pain as he continued to press. He stayed like that until the mass was over, aware that his heart might be heard by his neighbours.

Yet he could not resist looking at her as she left her seat, shepherding her child in front of her in the crush of the crowd. Her eyes skimmed over Cal, not noticing him. She passed the end of his row and he left the seat. Someone stepped back to let him out and he stood aching and frightened behind Marcella. The packed church was slow to empty, the congregation inching its way down the aisle and out of the double doors. Cal's hands hung by his sides. He felt pushed forward by those behind him, taking short shuffling steps. The back of his hand brushed against the wool material of her dress. He saw through the black lace of her mantilla that her hair was gathered into a roll and held by a large wooden pin. Between her mantilla and the back of her dress he could see the slope of her neck and the pin-holes of her pores and the slight down of hair that furred her spine. He smelt perfume but could not be sure that it was hers. The pressure behind him increased and he was pushed up against her, the back of his hand against her firm haunch. He let it stay there for as long as he could, then pushed back in case she became suspicious. The touch of her echoed in his hand. She bent over to say something to her child and he felt her body brush against his. Oh Jesus. They were near the porch now and, escaping from the confines of the aisle, the crowd fanned out towards the doors. Marcella went to the right. Cal to the left. The firmness of her body still burned against the back of his hand and as he passed the holy water font he was taking out his cigarettes.

Standing smoking, he watched her thread her way through the cars, holding the mantilla on top of her head with one hand.

'Are you for the game, hi?' It was John Quinn.

'Aye,' said Cal.

'Do you think they will be any opposition?'

She opened the door and helped the little girl in. Then she went round the other side and unlocked the driver's door.

'Who?'

5 'Antrim. Fuck, how many teams is playing?'

'We'll eat them,' said Cal.

She took off her mantilla and glided into the seat. Cal's head turned and watched the yellow Anglia as it accelerated past. He looked down at his feet and saw a million cork tips mixed with the
10 grey gravel of the path by the wall.

2

Cal drove the sixty miles to Clones. Once over the Border he experienced the feeling of freedom he always got. This was Ireland – the real Ireland. He felt he had come out from under the weight and darkness of Protestant Ulster, with its neat stifled Sabbath
15 towns. On top of a tree a green, white and gold tricolour flickered in the wind.

The closer he got to Clones the thicker the traffic became. Derry buses with red and white scarves hanging out of the windows; cars from Antrim packed with people sitting on one another's knees.
20 Their colours were yellow and white and Cal thought of them as Papal flags. He had to park well away from Breffini Park and walk to the ground.

The teams came out and at their heels followed the umpires. They looked the same no matter where the match was played –
25 tubby balding men who stood at the side of the goal with their hands thrust in the pockets of their white coats. Abattoir men, fishmongers, laboratory assistants. Their flags were threaded into the side netting, a red one for a goal, a white one for a point. Mortal and venial sins. Red for sex and murder, white for working while
30 you were collecting the dole. He imagined the priest leaning out of the confession box with his flags.

He hadn't been to confession for over a year and never would go again. He shook his head and tried to concentrate on the game. He stood on his toes and yelled at the referee and for a time lost
35 himself. But the thing he had done was now a background to his

life, permanently there, like the hiss that echoed from the event which began the Universe.

At half time he queued for the toilet. From a distance the place reeked of urine but when he got inside the stink was overpowering. He stood staring at the black mildewed wall in front of him, holding his breath. The drain was overflowing, clogged with cigarette butts.

'And how's Cahal?' said a voice. Skeffington shouldered his way in beside him. 'It's nice to be winning the struggle.' Cal wasn't sure whether he was referring to the war or the football match. He noticed that Skeffington shielded his thing in his hand, like a boy smoking in school, and stared at the ceiling. Cal zipped himself up and turned away. Skeffington came after him.

'Adrian Mc Guckin is having a great game.'

Cal nodded. The ground after the rain was churned up into a black oily mass of muck and cinders.

'Is your father here, Cahal?'

'No, he said he had things to do in the garden.'

'Is Crilly here?'

'I doubt it.'

Skeffington smiled. They walked towards the back of the crowd, Skeffington almost tiptoeing to avoid getting the black mud on his polished shoes.

'There are not many aspects of our culture which interest Mr Crilly. But he's a useful man.'

Cal looked at him.

'Come now. Cahal. Practical things have to be done. If you've a burst pipe you send for a plumber. If you have a war on your hands you send for the Mr Crillys of this world. The hard men and the bandits are the real revolutionaries, if you see what I mean. They get things done, they punch the hole for us to get through later.'

'What do you want me for then?'

'A movement like ours needs all sorts. Crilly, you, me even.'

'I still want out.'

Skeffington put his hand on Cal's sleeve.

'That creates a big problem, Cahal. It would be out of my hands. I wouldn't like to see you hurt.'

A white-haired man carrying a half bottle of whiskey came slowly down the steps. There was a stupid smile on his face and he missed the last step, collapsing to the ground on his right side. He looked up at Cal and Skeffington, puzzled as to how he got there. The
5 whiskey bottle he held upright and safe. He saluted to them and muttered something. Cal pushed past Skeffington and with some difficulty managed to hoist the old man to his feet. His trouser leg and the side of his jacket were slabbered with the mud. There was also some on his hand with a red gleam of blood through it. Cal
10 aimed him at the toilets and he tottered off.

'Where do they get it on a Sunday?' said Skeffington. 'It makes me mad, Cahal, to think of some of the people we are fighting for.'

'It takes all sorts,' said Cal and smiled.

'Come down and I'll introduce you to my father.'

15 Cal refused, saying that he would meet him some other time, that he had to get back to his friends. Skeffington waved to him and shouted something in Irish, springing up the steps two at a time.

③

The next week Cal thought the longest of his life. He lay in his
20 room picking chords on his guitar, he played records and wished that he had some new ones, he smoked incessantly. Often he thought his watch was slow or had stopped. He went to the library three times; to go every day would be overdoing it. She did no more than nod to him with a slight smile of recognition for carrying
25 her groceries to the car. To see her when she was busy at work was useless. One evening he stood watching for her but she did not come out. He waited until ten to six, until he knew the potatoes would be burning, before running home.

What made it worse was waiting to hear from Crilly. Each night
30 his father came in and Cal would eat with him, or pretend to eat with him, watching the news on television, dreading hearing him say, 'Crilly wants you to call down.' But he didn't and every time he didn't it seemed like a reprieve. One night Cal did not sleep at all and it helped him because he got up early and went to bed the
35 next night at eleven o'clock and slept soundly.

Then at tea on Friday his father told him that he had been speaking to Pascal O'Hare. There were a couple of dead trees on O'Hare's land that were in his way and Shamie had bought them for next to nothing. He was really doing Pascal a favour. The two of them could do most of the big cutting after tea and Cal could   5
split the wood by himself during the day. They could borrow one of the abattoir lorries after hours and make a bit of money if Cal would sell the blocks around.

'Are you fit?'

Cal nodded.   10

'Then leave the dishes and come on.'

It was a calm evening, warm enough for them to take off their jackets as they worked. The first tree was a large elm, fallen from the edge of a copse years ago, its base up-ended and holding on to a dish of soil and roots. It lay across a ditch and some way out into   15
the field. With an axe Cal began to lop the smaller branches from the trunk. Shamie started the saw he had borrowed and it whined and girned, echoing round the small wood. Each time the old man cut into a branch the pitch of the saw rose to a scream and the white sawdust fountained on to the grass. Cal took comfort in the   20
noise, knowing that he did not have to speak.

When Shamie turned the saw off to jump the ditch Cal listened to the silence: a thrush singing from the copse, the distant moan of cattle from a lower field, then the demented motorbike of the saw would blot everything out again. They worked until dark and on   25
the way home they stopped off at the pub and Shamie bought pints of Guinness. As they drank they moved away from each other to different company.

The next day Cal took the van and drove to Pascal's place. He brought with him a sledge-hammer and a handful of iron wedges   30
his father kept in the shed, which over the years of being pounded had flowered at the top and become shaped like mushrooms. With these he split the cross sections, driving in one wedge and then another farther up the crack he had opened. The metal ring of the sledge on iron tinked back from the copse in echo. The sections   35
did not split easily but cracked and clicked under the strain, even

when he had ceased hammering. They opened whitely but fibres still gripped each halved section together and they had to be axed free. It was heavy work and Cal found that he was resting more frequently and for longer periods as the morning went on. The palms of his hands had become red and in an arc just beneath his fingers was a row of blisters which had burst and were now loose skin lying flat. But the pile of blocks was growing. There would soon be enough to fill a lorry. He sat astride the tree, smoking a cigarette. He knew where he would take the first load, if he had the courage. They couldn't get the lorry until after six but that was the point. It meant that she would be at home.

He jumped from the tree and took the sledge in his stinging hands and swung it, bisecting the block cleanly for once. He began to chant a negro work song in a thick American accent, striking the wedge at the end of each line.

Take this hamm – or
Carry it to the cap – tain.

But before he reached the third verse he had to stop for another rest.

Even though the lorry had been thoroughly hosed down, the cab still stank of the abattoir. Cal rolled both windows down, hoping the smell would be flushed out as he drove. Shamie had helped him load the wood but Cal had said that there was no need for him to trek round the doors and dropped him off at the house to put his feet up.

He knew the road, had travelled it many times in his mind, hating every twist and turn of it. The lorry was difficult to handle and he had to press hard on the stiff clutch. His left knee shook when he rested his foot on the floor. He went over in his head what he should say.

The lane to the farm was unmetalled and filled with ruts. The lorry bucked slowly and swayed from side to side. Easing through the gates, he saw a weal of red paint still on the cement gatepost. He stopped at the front door and left the engine running.

A moment after he had rung the bell the heavily patterned net curtain twitched. The door opened and instead of Marcella a tall grey-haired woman with glasses stood there.

'Yes?'

'Would you like some blocks?'

'How much?'

Cal told her what he thought was a fair price. The frames of the woman's glasses were shaped like wings. She looked him up and down. Her mouth was a tight businesslike line.

'Let me see them.'

Cal led her round to the back of the lorry and eased the tailboard down a bit. The woman looked at the wood, then at him.

'Is it dry?'

'Reasonably. It'll dry out if it's stacked.'

'They're very big. They mightn't fit in the Rayburn.'

Cal shrugged. His eyes were straying to the front door but nobody had followed the woman out. The windows all had net curtains drawn.

'Could you split some of the bigger ones?'

'Oh yes. They're easy chopped.'

'That would be very kind of you. I'll take the lot then.'

Cal hesitated.

'I didn't mean *I* would do it. I meant it was possible . . .'

The woman smiled and it transformed her severe face.

'I'll take the lot anyway,' she said.

'Where do you want them?'

The woman pointed to the side of the house.

'They would be dry enough there.'

Cal reversed the lorry to where she had pointed and tipped the load off with a dull rumbling. She came out of the house with her cheque book in her hand.

'Could I have cash, please?'

'Oh, it's like that is it? I'm afraid I don't have that much cash in the house at the moment. Can you come back tomorrow?'

Cal looked at the pyramid of logs on the ground and shrugged. The woman smiled again.

'We're a bit short-handed at the minute,' she said. 'If you would stack them up for me I would pay extra. And more again if you split the bigger ones.'

Cal looked all around the yard. He could hear a child crying somewhere.

'Do you have an axe?'

She pointed to what she called the tool shed and said that he would find one behind the door. She watched him until he came out again with the axe, then she went back into the house.

Cal began stacking the wood against the gable-end, throwing aside the larger chunks. A chicken came round the corner, bowing and making long, slow clockwork noises. Several others followed it, stopping in mid-stride. They proceeded past, ignoring him. He hadn't seen the yellow Anglia anywhere, so perhaps she was out. The Mrs Morton woman must be baby-sitting. His hands were so sore now that he used only his fingers to make the stack of wood. It was as if his palms had been scalded. He could not bear to touch the axe again. He could come back tomorrow for his money and split the big ones then. It would be another chance.

He straightened his back and looked around him. The house was facing west and there was a livid sunset, not an array of scarlet clouds, but the single red orb of the sun descending into autumn greyness. He knocked on the door again without much hope. Mrs Morton opened it.

'I've stacked the most of them for you,' he said. 'I'll be back tomorrow night to do the rest – and collect the money.'

'Very good. Did you put the axe back?'

'Yes.'

Leaving the lorry at the abattoir meant that he had to walk the long way through the estate. He was alert, watching gardens, moving slightly out into the roadway when there was a blind wall at a corner. Away ahead of him on the far side of the road he could just make out three figures. It was now dusk moving into darkness and the street lights were glowing bright red before becoming yellow. Cal kept his head down and continued to walk at the same pace.

He flicked his eyes up to check on the group. All three were now standing. They were the crowd in denim he had seen outside his house. His stomach tightened as he saw them move slowly across to the side of the road he was walking on. As casually as he could he looked over his shoulder. The street was empty. He veered 5 across the road, walking at the same pace to the other pavement. Their crossing might just have been a coincidence, but now they hesitated and moved back. Cal began deep breathing. He was either going to have to run or fight. He searched his pockets for anything that might help him, but there was nothing except ciga- 10 rettes and some loose change. His only bit of luck was that he had put on heavy boots that morning for going out to Pascal's farm. The three of them stood across the pavement, barring his way. They were about Cal's age and he knew their faces but not their names.

'When are you getting out,' said the biggest one in the middle, 15 'to let somebody decent into that house?'

'We're not,' said Cal, moving into the road to pass them. His voice embarrassed him by shaking too much.

'Would you live in it after them?' said the small one.

'Fenian bastard.' The big one lunged and grabbed Cal by the 20 front of his jacket. Cal half jumped, half butted and caught him on the nose. Snot suddenly appeared on the big one's upper lip and he staggered back, his face in his hands. Cal kicked hard with his boots at the others and felt himself being kicked. It was all in his head. Pain was for later. His fear had become a kind of anaesthetic 25 and he smashed at anything with his fists and feet. Somebody clubbed him in the mouth and his head jerked back. The big one had recovered sufficiently to join in again and was hitting with something very hard across Cal's shoulders. As yet Cal had not gone down but he knew he would if he stayed. He leapt a garden 30 hedge, half breaking it down, and ran. In the semi-dark another hedge appeared and he burrowed and jumped through it. It scratched his face and there was something hard in its middle which deadened his knee cap. He ran limping down the margin of a stubble field, listening over his shoulder to hear if they were 35 following him. They were shouting.

'We'll get you the next time.'

'Fuckin' bastard.'

The trouble was he knew they would. It had been a chance encounter, fists and feet. Next time it would be clubs, pickhandles, 5 knives or worse. He did not slow down but ran the whole way in case they should make it to his home before he did and be waiting.

Once inside, he bolted the back door. He had to sit down even before turning on the light. His breath was coming harsh and fast like sawing. His legs were jelly, so much so that he wouldn't trust 10 them to walk to the other room. Then he noticed that he was crying, not with fear but with something else. He fantasized about having Shamie's gun, went again through the lead-up to the incident, only this time he produced the revolver and blew the big one's head apart.

15 'Is that you, Cal?' His father's voice rose above the television.

'Yeah.'

He went to the bathroom and stood trembling at the mirror. His face was the colour of wax. There were some scratches from the hedge and both his lips were beginning to swell visibly. He pursed 20 them out and spoke to his image in a negro voice. He spat blood and saliva into the washbasin and dashed water into his face. He checked his teeth between his finger and thumb. They were all still firm. The knuckles of both hands were skinned and bleeding. He turned his hands over, looking at the blisters on one side and the 25 scars on the other. He snorted and went downstairs. His father did not look up from the television when he came in.

'I think you'd better get our friend out again tonight.'

'Why?'

'I got a hammering on my way home.'

30 His father looked up.

'Jesus, Mary and Joseph.' He stood scrutinizing his son's face. 'Who was it?'

'I don't know. The crowd from the other end.'

Shamie was about to touch the scratches with his fingers but Cal 35 twisted his head away.

'Don't fuss. I'm OK.' He still heard the tremor in his own voice.

Shamie moved to the sideboard and rattled among the bottles. He poured a tumbler full of sherry and handed it to Cal.

'That's all there is,' he said. Cal drank it off, disliking its cloying sweetness, and shakily held out his glass for more. Shamie filled it again.

'I think we should consider moving,' said Cal. He eased himself into the armchair and propped his stiff leg out in front of him. His old man remained silent, then poured himself a sherry. 'Their blood is up. Next time they'll really have a go. Guns maybe.'

'Where would we go?'

'They have to house you if you are homeless.'

Inside him the sherry acted quickly to warm him. The shaking began to fade away. He laughed.

'A big bastard with a short haircut. I got him a nice one on the nose.'

He mimed the head-butt for Shamie but his father did not laugh.

'Maybe you should go away for a week or two,' said Shamie. 'To your Aunt Betty's.'

'I'll just be careful.'

The national anthem came on the television over a picture of the Queen in full uniform seated on a black horse. Shamie snapped it off without looking at it.

'And they say it's a free bloody country.'

Cal watched the square picture shrink to an intense dot of light – then fade. He rose unsteadily.

'Pints of sherry'd be all right,' he said.

'Oh, what about the blocks?'

'Sold the lot.'

His father whistled and put out his hand.

'Fifty per cent.'

'Tomorrow.'

Cal slept late the next day. When eventually he did get up his body was so sore from the kicking and the previous day's hard work that he could barely move. His head ached so that every time he bent over it thumped. Whether it was from the sherry or a reaction to

45

the beating he didn't know. He leaned on the dressing table and looked at the image of himself staring back naked. The swelling in his mouth had gone down a bit but the lower half of his body was covered in blue-black bruises. He turned, looking over his shoulder.

5 They were on his buttocks and thighs, distinct marks the size of toe-caps, and on the fleshy parts of his shoulders there were longer welts. He turned round again and covered his wrinkled penis with his hand.

'Thank God they didn't get you, son.'

10 He switched on the water heater and later had a bath, lying in it for almost half an hour before he attempted to soap himself. He washed his hair while sitting in the bath, pouring jugfuls of water over his head. With his eyes closed against soap and cascading water he felt very vulnerable. What if someone were to burst into

15 the bathroom now? How easy a target he would be, stark naked, blinded, groping with outstretched arms for a towel. It was a feeling he had had ever since childhood. The things he was afraid of then were unknown to him. He had never seen what he was afraid of. But there were times when he experienced fear more than others;

20 the dark of his bedroom after his mother and father had gone to bed and turned off the landing light, thinking him asleep; bowed over the washbasin with his face soaped; the moments just before sleep when the blanket at his cheek, normally a woolly texture, became hard and pitted like the surface of the moon while at the

25 same time it was soft and repulsive like tripe. There were nights he tried to count to a million. The enormity of the number filled him with awe. To go to hell for all eternity. He remembered standing by the kitchen table, his chin on a level with its surface, as his mother baked, and seeing a red tin of Royal Baking Powder. The

30 label was a picture of a tin of Royal Baking Powder which in turn had a picture of a tin of Royal Baking Powder on it. The tins spiralled into smallness, into the vertigo of infinity. He put his eye very close to the tin but all he could see were tiny dots of paint. When his mother died he thought of her dead for all eternity. In

35 heaven she would know if he committed any sins. Sometimes when he was bad he was afraid that the devil would come to him, but

even worse was the thought that when he did something good Our
Lady would appear to him half-way up the dark of his bedroom
wall.

'My child,' she would say.

But now that the fear was specific – the big one with the short 5
hair kicking the bathroom door down – it was less intense. He
could take precautions against it, like locking all the doors, whereas
for a child a locked door kept nothing out.

After tea Cal borrowed the van and drove out to the Mortons'
farm. As he bounced over the potholes in the track he saw the 10
yellow Anglia parked between some cars outside the front door.
When he was eleven Cal had secretly fancied a beautiful girl in the
church choir, Moira Erskine, who sang the *Adeste fideles* solo at
Christmas. One day after mass, in the churchyard, for some reason
or other she called him over and he was so embarrassed that he 15
just turned and ran away as hard as he could. Now he should be
doing the same thing but instead he was doing the opposite. He
was trying to get close to the one person he should be continents
away from.

He parked the van near the gable-end and went up to the door. 20
Again it was Mrs Morton who answered it.

'I've come to split the rest of the wood – and collect the money.'

'Yes, dear,' she said. 'Call in again when you've finished. You
know where the axe is?'

'I'll not need it.' 25

Cal went to the van and took the sledge-hammer and the metal
wedges out of the back. His hands were still raw to the touch and
he spat on them to begin work.

After a while he heard someone squelching through the mud.
He looked up and saw Cyril Dunlop coming across the yard. He 30
was the same age as Cal's father and they knew each other from
about the town. They would stand for hours on end chatting at the
street corner and then Shamie would come home and say. 'That
Cyril Dunlop was in every Orange march that ever there was. And
believe me, Cal, that Orange Order is rotten to the core. They 35
wouldn't give you daylight if they could keep it off you.'

Cyril wore his cap tilted almost on to his nose.

'What about ye, young lad,' he said, 'what brings you round these parts?'

Cal nodded to the pile of wood. 'My Da bought a tree and I'm just splitting this load for them.'

Cyril bent down and picked up a piece, weighing it in his hand.

'It'll make good burning when it dries out.'

'I didn't know you worked here.'

'Six years or more now,' said Cyril. 'Well, I'll be off for my tea.' He saluted goodbye to Cal and climbed into one of the cars. He drove off at speed, flouncing brown water from the puddles of the lane into the hedge.

The clink of the wedge and the ripping crack of the wood hypnotized Cal as he worked on block after block. He was almost finished when he heard a child's voice at the front of the house. It was the little girl and she came running round the corner, not expecting to see anyone. She was the toddler he had seen in church but now she was smothered in a woollen hat and scarf. She stopped and stared at him.

'Hello.' The word hurt his throat coming up.

She turned and ran. A moment later Marcella, dressed in a sheepskin jacket and green wellingtons, appeared. The child pointed to Cal. She nodded politely to him, then, recognizing him as the boy who had carried her groceries, said hello, her voice lifting in surprise. Cal stopped working and rested the sledge-head on the ground.

'Hello, that's a nice evening.' He heard the chat he had scorned from his father coming out of his own mouth.

'Yes, we're just coming out for a breath of air.' She put her hand down to her daughter's head. 'I'm trying to tire this one out before she goes to bed.' The child was nuzzling into her skirt, not looking at Cal. 'Mrs Morton warned me there was someone here but I didn't realize it was you.'

'You got home all right the other day?' Cal said. She looked confused.

'Sorry?'

'With your groceries.'

'Oh, yes. Thank you again.'

Then she noticed the wedge half driven into the wood opening up a crack.

'That's smart,' she said, pointing. 'I've never seen it done that way before.'

'That's an old trick of my father's.'

She smiled and moved the toe of the boot on the pivot of her heel. Cal explained to her how the second wedge opened the crack further until the first one dropped out.

'It's a bit like "Give me a big enough lever and I'll move the world". Give me a big enough wedge and I'll split it.'

She laughed. 'That's nice,' she said. Her teeth were very white. The child began to tug at her skirt, wanting to go. 'Just a minute, love.'

Cal was sweating from his exertion and his shirt was open to the waist showing his lean, hairless chest. He began to close it. She said,

'That was my first week back at work. Everything went wrong. I felt that day that the world was out to get me. And then you arrived to help.'

'The Girl Guides awarded me a gold star.'

The child continued to tug at her mother's skirt and she had begun to whinge. Marcella hadn't heard his joke or else she didn't think it funny. Her face was serious.

'I must go. All right, all right, Lucy, we're going now.' She turned away. 'Good to see you,' she said.

Cal watched them stepping through the pocked mud until they disappeared behind the barn. He swung his sledge high over his head and brought it sweeping down. He missed the wedge completely and left what looked like a hoof mark in the white rings of wood. He stopped for a cigarette, fearing that he might fracture his leg if he went on. He sat on the tail-board of the van with his feet on the ground. The match flared and he spun it away from him, hearing it whirr and hiss into a puddle.

In the distance on the main road he watched the box shape of a

police Land Rover moving between the hedges. He tensed every
time he saw one. It turned into the Mortons' lane and Cal stood
up. It came lurching up the lane towards the house. No one could
know he was here. But maybe the old woman had phoned them.
5 Could somebody have recognized him? He set the burning cigarette
on the tailboard and moved just out of sight behind the gable-end.
He heard the Land Rover stop, heard voices. They were calm
voices, laughing. Cal moved back to his cigarette. One RUC man
was standing at the door. He wore a canvas-green bullet-proof bib
10 over his black uniform. In the Land Rover Cal could just make out
another policeman behind the heavy wire grille on the windscreen.
A sickle of light showed the shiny peak of his black cap. Cal felt he
was being stared at. He took a drag of his cigarette and set it down
again, then swung the hammer, driving in another wedge. He heard
15 Mrs Morton open the door. The voices faded and the door closed.
Cal worked on, feeling the eyes of the other RUC man on his neck.
He moved out of sight round the gable-end and began stacking the
wood. If Mrs Morton's son had been in the RUC Reserve it was
perfectly natural for them to call. A message, business, or maybe a
20 friend of her son's.

The wood pile was almost complete when he heard voices again.
The Land Rover started up and Mrs Morton waved as they drove
away. Cal went over to her.

'I'm nearly finished now.'

25 'That's good. Let me see.'

She came round with him to inspect the job.

'Very neat,' she said. 'How long will it take to dry?'

'You could leave it a week or so. The tree's been dead for over a
year so really you could use it any time.'

30 'Come and I'll get you your money.'

Cal followed her to the door of the house and hesitated.

'Would you like a beer?' she said over her shoulder. Cal nodded.
'Well, come in then.'

'My boots are filthy.' He took them off and left them in the
35 porch. There were no holes in his socks but the heels had gone as
thin as muslin. He followed her into the large kitchen and sat down

on a stool at the table. She took a can of beer from a cupboard and jerked the ring-pull. She was looking around for a glass.

'It'll do in the can,' said Cal.

But she insisted on pouring it shakily into a glass. The glass was clean but not clean enough. The beer appeared flat and bubbled 5 like lemonade, forming no head. Even so, Cal was glad of it.

'Do you do this all the time?' she asked.

'What?'

'Work at the blocks?'

'No, my Dad bought a tree and I'm just helping him out. I'm on 10 the dole.'

'Like plenty of others.'

To the right of the cooker was a tea-caddy with a picture of the Queen on its side. Mrs Morton took a wallet from her bag and began counting out the money in uncreased notes. She made a fan 15 and handed it to him. Again he noticed the shake in her hand – like a slow shudder – as she reached the money to him.

'We'll be lifting potatoes the day after next if you'd like to come along. The money's not great but it's better than nothing.'

'Thanks,' he said, taking the money. She had given him a fiver 20 extra for the work he'd done. It was not enough but it was not so little that he felt he could complain while drinking her beer.

'Well?'

'Yes, that would be OK.'

'We start at eight.' 25

'There'll be no complications about the dole or anything?'

'I shouldn't think so. That part of it is up to you.' She stood with her arms folded, waiting for him to finish his beer.

'A lorry will pick everybody up at half-past seven at the post office corner if you're interested.' 30

Cal said he was and stood up to drain his glass. Mrs Morton was seeing him out in the hallway when he heard a terrible bout of coughing coming from the room opposite. Immediately Mrs Morton left him standing and went into the room. With the door open Cal could hear the coughing even more clearly. It sounded 35 wet and bubbling – like death throes – and it went hacking on and

on and on, taking no pause for breath. Cal stared at his stockinged feet and felt his gorge rise. Mrs Morton's voice comforted around the awful noise. It seemed that the person must die or turn inside out if the fit did not stop. He tried to block off his sense of hearing
5 by staring intensely at the wall. They had put on a new wallpaper of blue flowers. He thought of going out himself to get away from the sound, then it stopped. Mrs Morton's voice was left consoling and crooning on its own. Then she said.

'I'll be right back.'

10 She appeared in the doorway to finish leaving Cal out.

'My husband was badly injured that time. One got him in the larynx and the other here in the lungs.' She pointed to her chest and neck to indicate precisely where. She spoke to Cal as if he knew all about it and he found that unnerving. He nodded sympath-
15 etically, pausing long enough to put on his boots but not to tie them, and left. By the time he reached the tail-board of the van the laces were gritty with mud and soaking wet. Tying them up left black welts all over his hands.

(7)

It was a cold grey morning and Cal nodded sleepily as he joined
20 the others at the post office corner. Some were of his own age but the majority were boys and girls taking the day off school to make some money. In his time Cal himself had done the same thing. Everyone was dressed in shabby clothes and wore wellington boots. There was an air of jokiness and high spirits as they stood on the
25 back of the lorry driving out to the farm. Cal's hair blew straight out in the wind and some of the younger ones laughed at the sight. Suddenly a police Land Rover with its hee-haw siren blaring swung into the main road behind them with a squeal of tyres. It roared along and overtook them so fast its body tilted at an angle to the
30 chassis.

Someone said, 'Jesus, they'll sell no ice-cream going at that speed.'

But as the day wore on the laughter died. A fine drizzle of rain came on, turning the ground from soil to muck. It clogged behind
35 Cal's guitar nails and continually he had to sweep his wet hair back

with his dirty hands so that it and his forehead became dirty too. After a time his fingers became like sausages with the cold. The tractor, driven by Cyril Dunlop, came round, wheeling up the soil and potatoes with an inevitability which he hated. The only colour in the landscape was the red and blue of the plastic baskets they were collecting into. Everything else was the drab hue of potatoes, from their clothes to the field itself with its withered buff potato tops lying flat on the ground. Occasionally he would come across a potato split by the tractor and its whiteness and cleanness was a relief to the eye.

It was a humped field and beyond and above stood the Morton farmhouse. As lunchtime neared the potato gatherers looked up at it more frequently. It seemed that Cyril would never call a halt, but finally he did, by stopping the tractor and whistling with two clean, dry fingers.

Mrs Morton fed them all in the large kitchen with newspapers covering the floor. Cabbage and bacon and mashed potatoes moistened with bacon gravy. In the field there was no pleasure in smoking, his hands were in such a state, and after eating Cal smoked three cigarettes, lighting them from one another. He sat on a stool, his back aching, and it seemed like only five minutes before Cyril called on them to start again. Everyone groaned and protested.

The afternoon crawled through the slow drizzle. Cal found that his mind was going blank for long periods with the repetitiveness of the work, and when he became aware of this he enjoyed it in retrospect. It was not often these days that he could remain switched off for any length of time.

For three days, although he ended up each day physically filthy, work had a cleansing effect on him. It was as if idleness had allowed dirt to accumulate on his soul, to clog his mind, and work moved him through it untouched. At night after a bath he watched in the mirror the progress of his bruises and saw them turn from blue-black to a jaundiced yellow. His plectrum nails were broken and filled with mud. They looked disgusting and he decided to cut them. They fell in black crescent moons on the coverlet and afterwards he gathered up the five of them and threw them out of the window. With the money he earned he could buy finger picks. To be able to keep long nails was one of the few advantages of being unemployed. Work made him tired at night so that he slept immediately he lay down.

5 And although the work of potato gathering was mindless he liked to be praised. Once or twice over the three days Cyril would shout as he drove past on the tractor.

'You're doing a grand job, son.'

Twice a day a big kettle of tea was brought to the field, bouncing
10 on the back of a trailer, and they sat on sacks by the wet ditch, drinking from white enamel cups. Cal talked to Cyril over the tea breaks and found him affable enough for an Orangeman. Then when the job was finished and Mrs Morton was paying them from the big table in the kitchen she asked Cal to wait behind. Saying
15 that they were still short-handed, she offered him a job on the farm.

'But no dole, if you please.' She adjusted her glasses by the wing-tip with her shaking finger and thumb. 'See Cyril Dunlop, my foreman, and he'll tell you what to do. Can you start on Monday?'

20 Although he had not thought of it, Cal knew it was what he had been waiting for and accepted immediately.

Chapter Three

On Friday afternoon the lorry dropped him at the safer end of the
street and he walked the rest, head down, tensed against the cold.
He had to wait until after tea for the water to heat sufficiently for a
bath. They had finished early and he was in long before his father.
When Shamie came through the door Cal had the dinner ready to   5
serve and was singing in the kitchen, drumming on the draining
board with two pliable knives. He wanted to keep the good news
of his job until they were sitting eating. It would be something to
talk about. A children's programme was turned low as they waited
for the news. When they sat down at the table Cal said,   10

'I got offered a job.'

'Good man yourself.' Shamie clapped him on the shoulder, the
only part of Cal he could reach from where he sat. 'Doing what?'

'Morton's farm. Where the potato picking was.'

'What's the money like?'   15

'I don't know. But it's bound to be better than the dole.'

'Cheers anyway,' said his father, raising his cup of milk to him.
'Oh, big Crilly says you've to call down after tea.'

Cal paused in the toast. Would that bastard never leave him
alone? The mashed potato in his mouth turned to cotton wool and   20
he found difficulty in swallowing it. The news came on. As Shamie
stood and bent to turn up the sound Cal lifted his plate and carried
it into the kitchen. He scraped the food into the pedal-bin, listening
to the calm voice of the news reader giving the headlines of the
day's events. Two hooded bodies had been found on the outskirts   25
of Belfast; bombs had gone off in Strabane and Derry and Newry
but no one had been hurt; there was another rise in coal prices;

and finally there was the elephant in Belle Vue Zoo that had to have his teeth filed.

'I'm going to have a bath,' said Cal. Shamie did not raise his eyes from the screen.

5   Feeling clean on the outside, with his hair held back in a tail by an elastic band, Cal drove the van to Crilly's place. Crilly himself came to the door chewing and put him in the front room, switching on one bar of the electric fire. He said he would be with him in a minute. Cal sat slumped in an armchair, looking round him. The
10 muted waves of unreal laughter from some show on the television rose and fell in the next room. There was a picture on the wall of a ragged child with one glistening teardrop standing on his dirty cheek. Beside it was a plaque of wood and burned into it with a needle were the words MADE IN LONG KESH CONCENTRATION
15 CAMP. It had a badly drawn clenched fist surrounded by barbed wire and the words IRELAND UNFREE SHALL NEVER BE AT PEACE.

There was a brass picture hammered out in some way so that the words and the figure were raised up from its surface. The figure was of an old woman sitting sideways wearing a bonnet and beneath
20 her was a poem called 'A Mother'. It told of all the good things a mother ever did and ended with the line 'The only bad thing she ever does is to die and leave you'. Cal thought of Crilly's mother with her sagging breasts and her tight pink jumper the colour of her gums. He thought of his own mother and had to turn away and
25 look at something else. He saw himself in a mirror above the fireplace. The edges of the mirror were laced with red and yellow roses. He turned his lip up in a sneer.

Crilly came in with a cup of tea and a slice of bread and jam. He sat down opposite Cal, folded the bread over and bit a half moon
30 out of it. There were ticks of jam at the corners of his mouth. His voice was muffled with bread.

'Well?' he said.

'Well what?'

'Are you ready for tonight?'

35 'What are we doing?'

'You're driving, that's what. An off-licence in Magherafelt.'

'Guns?'

'Protection.'

Crilly finished his bread and jam and threw the hard crust into the empty fire-grate.

'Don't worry, Cal. It'll be easy.'   5

'What about a car?'

'I think I've that arranged. You like the Cortinas?'

Cal nodded.

'But there's no need to rush. The later we leave it the more takings there'll be.'   10

The door opened and Crilly's mother put her head in. There was something different about her.

'You never asked Cal if he wanted any tea,' she said to her son.

'No thanks, I'm just after some,' said Cal.

Mrs Crilly came right into the room and did a twirl in the middle   15
of the floor, holding out her dress like a model.

'Do you like my new teeth?' she said. Then she smiled as if she was biting through steel. Cal said he thought they were lovely while her son sat and rolled his eyes to the ceiling.

At nine o'clock Crilly and Cal went out. Cal drove the van to an   20
address at the other end of town. He stood with his back to the pebble-dash wall to one side of the door while Crilly rang the bell.

'Is your Dad in?'

Crilly turned and winked at Cal. A man's voice said,

'Oh, it's you, *a chara*.'   25

There was a jingle of keys and Cal saw a hand pass them out.

'Remember you didn't notice it gone until after eleven.'

'OK'

'If you do I'll break your legs, and if I don't somebody else will.'

The man laughed and Crilly smiled at him.   30

When the door was shut Cal moved down the path and got into the van. Crilly led in the white Cortina. Just outside Magherafelt Crilly indicated and turned off the road into a forestry plantation. The trees were black in the red brake lights. Crilly got out and began counting trees, then dodged in between the saplings. Lean-   35
ing against the white car, Cal lit a cigarette. He held it between his

lips as he pulled on a pair of thin leather gloves. His hands were shaking. He could hear the sound of Crilly thrashing and crackling about among the trees. Then he came out with a parcel. Cal slid behind the steering wheel of the Cortina and Crilly got in the other
5 side.

'One for you and one for me,' he said.

'I don't want one,' said Cal. 'I'm driving.'

Crilly loaded his gun by the light coming from the open glove compartment. Cal pushed his aching back into the upholstery and
10 adjusted his seat to suit his leg length.

'Do you wear stilts when you're driving?' he asked.

'I'll load yours just in case.'

'I'd only shoot myself.'

Crilly was wearing stylish driving gloves with holes in the backs
15 of them. Cal wheeled the car round, the headlights probing deep into the dry brown forest floor. On the road there was no talk between them but Crilly hummed and clicked his tongue. Cal felt like screaming at him to stop it. He tried the car out for speed and handling and it responded well. As they drove towards Magherafelt
20 he said,

'For Christ's sake, Crilly, don't use that thing.'

'It persuades people to hurry up.'

To get to the off-licence they did not need to pass through the security gates which blocked off the town centre. Cal parked on
25 the opposite side of the road and they sat watching. A customer came out carrying a polythene bag in both arms. They could not tell whether the shop was empty or not because of its frosted-glass door.

'Do you know what it's like inside?' Cal asked.

30 'I've been in twice this week.'

Cal indicated and moved across the road, double parking directly in front of the shop. Crilly put on a pair of sunglasses and got out.

'Keep that engine running,' he said.

Cal turned up the collar of his coat. Crilly stood on tiptoe,
35 looking over the dulled and lettered half of the door. Cal saw him flip up the hood of his anorak and pull his scarf over his mouth.

He pushed the door open with his foot and stepped in. The door swung shut after him on its spring but in the instant that it was open, as if it was the shutter of a camera, Cal saw two women customers look up in fright. The door stayed shut and Cal began to count. Fourteen, fifteen, sixteen. He knew that to count accurate 5 seconds he should say one thousand and seventeen, one thousand and eighteen. A man came round the corner and began walking towards the car. Was it the law? No double parking allowed here, sir. But the man had a dog on a lead. It kept stopping and sniffing at the bottoms of walls. After each bout of sniffing it lifted its hind 10 leg and peed over the leavings of some other dog. One thousand and forty, forty-one, forty-two. He looked down at the tray beside the gear stick and to his horror saw that the pistol Crilly had left him was nakedly visible in the street lights. He covered it with a dirty cloth from the glove compartment. The man was now almost 15 level with the car. Cal turned his head away, pretending to look for something in the back seat. Where the fuck was Crilly? Was he choosing a wine? The man stopped patiently for his dog again then moved off into the pool of the next street light. Cal rolled the window down to see if he could hear anything. A record on a 20 jukebox played faintly farther along the street. Cal watched the door, trying not to blink, until his eyes felt dry. Where was the big bastard? Was it a thousand and ninety? He gave up the idea of counting. Crilly had been in there two or three minutes. Then suddenly the door sprang open and in its shutter-instant Cal saw 25 the two women lying face down on the floor. He stuck the car in first and revved. Crilly, carrying a Harp polythene bag, thumped his shins and cursed getting between the two cars at the kerb. He jumped into the passenger seat. The gun was still in his hand. They were moving before he had time to shut the door. 30

'What kept you?' shouted Cal.

'I was like lightning.'

'What did you do to those women?'

'I told them to lie on the floor.'

'Jesus, I thought you'd killed them.' 35

Trying not to draw attention by squealing the tyres, Cal drove as fast as he could round the corner and out into the main road.

'It was easy – a cinch,' said Crilly. 'They were shaking in their fuckin' high-heel shoes. Couldn't get the money into the bag quick enough.' He was laughing, but Cal put it down to nerves. He
5 leaned forward and noticed the waft of nervous sweat – like onions – from beneath his own coat. He heard Crilly click the legs of his sunglasses shut and put them in his pocket.

'Sink the boot, Cal boy.'

But Cal already had his boot to the floor.

10 They dumped the car at the forestry plantation and got into the van.

'Are you sure you have everything?' said Cal. He turned the key in the starter. 'Oh Jesus, the other gun.' He leapt out and took the pistol from beneath the dirty rag and handed it through the window
15 to Crilly. They drove off at speed as Crilly re-wrapped the guns.

'We'll drop them at the manor house,' he said.

'The sooner the better,' said Cal.

An estate wall ran for some five or six miles along the right-hand side of the road. At several points it had become dilapidated and
20 fallen down. Cal stopped when told at the first gap beyond the small bridge where they had turned off the main road. Crilly looked around and, seeing no headlights, left the van with his parcel. He returned almost immediately, staggering and laughing.

'What's up with you?' said Cal.

25 'I'm just remembering.'

'What?'

'The woman behind the counter. At first she refuses and I points the gun at her. Then she says, "Who's it for anyway?" As if it made any difference which side was robbing her.'

30 'You should have told her it was in aid of the Black Babies,' said Cal.

Crilly was still laughing quietly as they neared home, then Cal heard him scuffling in the Harp bag. He turned on the overhead light and sorted through the bundle of notes. Cal objected that he
35 couldn't see to drive. Crilly switched the light out and put some of the money in his pocket.

'Do you want any fag money?' he asked. Cal said he didn't but Crilly threw some notes on his lap.

'You deserve it.' said Crilly. 'The Cause can afford it.'

He told Crilly that it didn't feel right, but when he stopped the van outside Skeffington's house he felt between his legs and put the money in his pocket.

'Are the pubs still open?' Crilly looked at his watch and nodded. 'Hurry up then.'

Skeffington lived in a big house with a gravelled driveway and as Crilly crunched his way up to the front door there was a frantic barking from inside. The door opened a slit. Cal saw Crilly hand over the Harp bag then turn and wave to the van. He cursed and got out.

'Cahal, *a chara*, come in, come in,' called Skeffington.

'We were just off to the pub.'

'Sure, I'll give you a drink here.'

Crilly seemed to have gone dumb. Skeffington held an Alsatian by its collar and motioned them in. Cal hesitated but then followed Crilly. The house was luxurious, full of gilt mirrors and flock wallpaper.

'Besides, I'd like you to meet my father,' said Skeffington.

The Alsatian was snuffling at the crotch of Cal's jeans. Skeffington smacked its nose, showed them into a room and led the dog away.

'Why didn't you tell him we were going to the pub?' said Cal.

'I didn't like to.'

'Arse-licker.'

They stood awkwardly in the centre of the room, uneasy about sitting in the white armchairs. The door opened and old Skeffington came in, followed by his son.

'This is my father, Cal. The man I've told you so much about.'

They were all introduced. He was small and bald, but the image of his son. He even had the same facial tic, wrinkling his nose to adjust his glasses. He wore a tweed sports jacket that looked too big for him and Cal could see that the waistband of his trousers was as high as his nipples. The old man nodded during the introductions but said nothing.

Finbar insisted that they all sit down and busied himself getting the drinks. The old man seemed to disappear when he sat in the chair. His son talked incessantly.

'Daddy was just telling me a great story before you came in.' Old
5 Skeffington nodded and smiled faintly. 'About going through the barriers today. The transistor has been fading recently. Whiskey, Cal? Some water? And Daddy was down getting some batteries. He got them outside the security gates in Hanna's, and had to go on into town. What about yourself, Daddy?' His father indicated
10 with an almost closed finger and thumb how much whiskey he wanted. 'And this young Brit frisked him. He says, "What are those?" about the lumps in Daddy's pockets and Daddy says, "Batteries," and, says your man, "Very good. On you go." '

Because he was a Pioneer and used to orange squash, Finbar
15 poured very large whiskeys. They were in Waterford crystal tumblers. He handed the drinks around and poured himself a tonic. Cal was still waiting for the punchline of the story. 'You could have a bomb up your coat and provided you declared it, I think they'd let you through. I'm a teacher, Cal, and I know that in England it
20 is no different. It's all the boys at the runt-end of the school who are going to end up in the Army. The idiots, the psychopaths – the one class of people who *shouldn't* be given a gun.' Finbar sat down on the arm of the sofa with his drink. 'Daddy can spin a great yarn when he gets going.'

25 The old man smiled and sipped his drink.

'Do you remember the story, Daddy, of Dev in O'Connell Street?' His father nodded again. There was a long silence. 'Or the one about Patsy Gribben?' His father nodded yet again. Finbar turned to the other two. 'Patsy Gribben was this old boy who used
30 to hang around my father's shop. Every day he'd be in betting. But the drink was his real problem. And then one day you decided to trust him, isn't that the way of it, Daddy?' His father agreed that that was the way of it. 'So you gave him – wasn't it a thousand pounds – to put in the bank. Well, Patsy Gribben didn't come back
35 that day. Not surprisingly. This will make you laugh, Cal. He was picked up off the Embankment in Belfast, totally and utterly drunk.

And do you know this, the police recovered nine hundred and ninety-seven pounds from his pocket. Poor Patsy.'

Old Skeffington finished his drink and smiled. He began to extricate himself from the chair. Finbar put one hand under his armpit to help him up. His father whispered something to him and then waved goodnight to Cal and Crilly. His son led him out, holding lightly on to his elbow.

'The wit is off to his pit,' said Cal.

'What?' Crilly leaned forward but Skeffington returned almost immediately. Cal looked at the clock and saw that the pubs had closed ten minutes ago.

'He says he's a bit tired tonight,' said Skeffington. 'But hasn't he such a wonderful fund of stories.'

The other two laughed politely. Skeffington slid down on to the seat of the sofa and asked,

'How much was there?' Cal shrugged. Crilly said that he hadn't counted it.

'Let's do that now then.'

Skeffington poured the contents of the bag on to the table and the others helped him sort the notes into piles. During the silence of counting Cal felt it on the tip of his tongue to say that he had got himself a job but he knew that the next question would be 'Where?' and he did not want to tell them. If Crilly knew that Cal was hanging around Morton's farm he might want to break his legs – not only want to but might well do it. Skeffington might want to do worse. When they had finished counting there was seven hundred and twenty-two pounds. Skeffington congratulated them.

'I think, unofficially, we should slip a few quid of this to Gerry Burns's wife. He has four kids and things must be difficult.'

'What about Peter Fitzsimmons?' asked Crilly.

'His wife works.'

'Fair's fair.'

'OK, let me think about it.' Skeffington stacked the different denominations of notes one on top of the other and folded them neatly into the bag. 'Well, Cahal, do you feel any better after tonight?'

'No.'

'Do you still want to – refuse to help?'

'I'm afraid so.'

'Not to act – you know – *is* to act.' Crilly looked confused. 'By not doing anything you are helping to keep the Brits here.'

Crilly nodded his head vigorously and said.

'If you're not part of the solution, you're part of the problem.'

'But it all seems so pointless,' said Cal.

Skeffington paused and looked at him. He spoke distinctly, as if addressing one of his primary classes.

'It's like sitting in a chair that squeaks. Eventually they will become so annoyed they'll get up and sit somewhere else.'

'How can you compare blowing somebody's brains out to a squeaking chair?' said Cal.

Skeffington shrugged his shoulders. 'That's the way it will look in a hundred years' time.'

'You have no feelings.'

'How dare you? How presumptuous of you, Cahal. You have no idea what feelings I have.' His voice calmed and he asked. 'Do you know Pearse's poem "Mother"?' Both the young men shook their heads. Skeffington began to recite.

'I do not grudge them: Lord, I do not grudge
My two strong sons that I have seen go out
To break their strength and die, they and a few,
In bloody protest for a glorious thing . . .

'That poem ends, Cahal,

'And yet I have my joy:
My sons were faithful and they fought.

'Unlike you, Cahal.'

'But it is not like 1916.'

'It wasn't like 1916 in 1916.'

There was a long silence.

'Have you got an ashtray?' Cal asked.

Skeffington got up and looked around.

'There should be one in the house somewhere.' He left the room and Cal said,

'Let's get out of here.'

'In a minute.'

Skeffington came back in with a clean ashtray which he set on the arm of Cal's chair.

'What was it you were saying, Cahal?'

'It was you that was doing the talking.' Skeffington touched his finger to the bridge of his glasses and smiled weakly. Cal said quietly.

'We were talking about my replacement.'

'We don't want replacements. It's recruits we want. And the more the better. If only they would let the Paras loose in Derry again . . .'

'The bastards,' said Crilly.

'You wouldn't say that if you were one of the thirteen murdered.'

'Probably not.'

'You leave out the shit and the guts and the tears.'

Skeffington took a tiny sip of his tonic.

'We must be strong enough, Cahal, to ignore that. It is not a part of history.' He stared at Cal as he spoke. 'I know what you're thinking. But I was in Derry that day. They had us cowering behind a wall. There was an old man lying in the open. In the rush one of his shoes had come off and was lying on its side. There was a big hole in the heel of his sock. Can you believe that? Will that be recorded in the history books? I could hear him dying, Cahal, I could see the blood running out of him over the paving stones. Then a priest came, waving a white hanky, and gave him the Last Rites.' Skeffington continued to stare at Cal as he talked. His bottom lip dropped, showing his lower teeth. Cal looked away but heard him say, 'And we were all Irishmen living in our own country. *They* were the trespassers.'

On the Monday morning Cal started work on the farm. He was embarrassed at his lack of knowledge about almost everything. Although he had lived all his life in a country town he had had no

contact with the kind of work which kept it going, except his brief
week in the abattoir, where he was too busy trying not to throw up
to learn anything. He seemed to stand about all that first morning
with his hands in his pockets and his feet aching as Dunlop showed
5 him round. Dunlop knew everything inside out but was a poor
teacher. He raced through the instructions for cleaning the
milk filters at such a speed that Cal was afraid to interrupt him.
At the end he had no idea how to dismantle one, never mind put
it back together. He heard words he had never heard in his life
10 before. Brown stomach, lungworm, black scour, bankrupt worm.
He knew that Dunlop was showing off but he had no way of
countering it.

He found the reek of living cattle much more acceptable than
the smell of the abattoir and after a while grew to like it. The
15 animals had a soft milky smell on their breath and the dung smell
that hung around them was not unpleasant.

Later in the day Dunlop told Cal to muck out the byre and
because it was something he could do he went at it with a will. As
he scraped and shovelled the slabbery dung he remembered: 'For
20 too long the Catholics of Ulster have been the hewers of wood and
the drawers of water.' Father Brolley was addressing the whole
school in the chapel at a time when Civil Rights was on the go. Cal
remembered nothing more of the sermon and he would not have
remembered that particular bit had they not made a joke of it
25 afterwards. 'The *hoors* of wood and the *drawers* of water.' Another
thing he remembered was the sunlight coming through the stained-
glass windows and how one purple stain spasmodically lit up the
priest's white surplice as he swayed backwards and forwards in
the passion of his preaching. Then Dunlop came in and seemed
30 surprised and annoyed that Cal hadn't got very far with the mucking out. Cal felt the man was testing him, making sure he knew
who was boss. In defence he said it was hard work.

It seemed to give Dunlop too much pleasure when he caught
Cal slacking. One windy day Cal had been coming up from the
35 lower field and felt he needed a smoke in peace. Just off the lane to
the house, and parallel with it, was a derelict cottage. Cal stopped

and lit a cigarette in the shelter of the crumbling glass porch. He
stood smoking, enjoying the cigarette despite his cold hands. The
wind cuffed the panes of glass but no draughts got in, even though
much of the putty had fallen away in dried segments. He looked
through the letterbox of the inner door and saw dimly that there 5
was lino on the floor and a sideboard in the hallway. He didn't try
the door because he could see that it was locked with a horseshoe
of a padlock. Just then Dunlop came round the corner.

'Mc Cluskey,' he shouted. 'What the hell are you doing?'

Cal turned. 10

'Just looking.' He dropped his cigarette and twisted his boot on
it.

'I'm standing waiting on you. I sent you to *that* lower field,' he
said pointing, 'not one twenty miles away.' The look on Dunlop's
face was one of anger but Cal could see that he was pleased to have 15
caught him sneaking a cigarette.

All that week Dunlop gave him a lift to and from town, morning
and evening. Several times Cal saw the yellow Anglia pass in the
opposite direction and followed it with his eyes. During the day he
occasionally saw Marcella's child playing in the back garden or 20
heard her prattling from another room when he was standing
having a cup of tea in the kitchen. He also heard again the stomach-
churning bubble of coughing from somewhere in the house.

In the morning Dunlop had little or nothing to say and in the
evening Cal was aware that the other man was choosing things to 25
talk about which had no connection with religion or politics. They
were politely wary of each other. Then one evening he said.

'You were lucky to get that job, son,' Cal nodded. 'Don't get me
wrong, but you're only the second one of your sort they've taken
on.' 30

'My sort?'

'You know what I mean. I've nothing against Catholic people.
It's the religion itself I don't like. I put in a good word for you when
old Mrs Morton asked about you – on account of your father. A
good man, Shamie.' 35

'Thanks,' said Cal. 'Who was your first Catholic?'

'He was an out-and-out scoundrel. They didn't know he was a
Catholic until after he left. John Harnett was his name and you
couldn't tell anything from that. This was long before the troubles
started – long before your so-called Civil Rights was ever heard of.
5 But he was an out-and-out layabout and when he started turning
up in the mornings smelling of drink I got Mr Morton to give him
his cards.'

'How did you know he was a Catholic?'

'He gave himself away one day pulling out a hanky and his
10 rosaries fell on the lino.'

'So you knew before he got the sack?'

'I suppose so. But he was a layabout of the first water.'

'Why did she hire me then?'

'I've no idea – especially after what happened. You'd have
15 thought that would have put her off for the rest of her natural. But
she's as odd as two left feet.'

A police patrol car was drawn up at the side of the road and a
policeman in a flak-jacket waved them down. Behind the car
another policeman balanced a Sten on his hip. Cal crossed his legs
20 and lowered himself imperceptibly in the seat. Dunlop slowed the
car and rolled down the window at the same time. They drew level
with the policeman, who stooped to look in.

'Och, it's yourself, Cyril,' he said. 'I didn't recognize the car.'

'How are you, Bill?'

25 'On you go, Cyril.'

The policeman rapped the still moving car on its roof with the
flat of his hand.

Each time the yellow Anglia passed them on the road Cal's
frustration grew. He had taken a job and hoped – for what he did
30 not know. But without a job he would have been able to go to the
library and watch her, maybe speak to her if there wasn't a queue.
Now he had to be content with a glimpse of her as she drove past,
her eyes riveted to her own side of the white line.

On Sunday he borrowed the van and went again to ten-thirty
35 mass in Magherafelt. He told Shamie that he liked the way the
priest preached, but when asked who was it he had to admit that

he didn't know the name. Marcella wasn't there and he drove home in the rain to spend the day reading a damp *Sunday Independent* in his bedroom.

On Thursday the library stayed open late, until seven-thirty. Cal shaved and washed and went out immediately after tea, knowing there was a one in three chance that she would be on duty. It was dark and cold with a wind which whipped his hair into his face. The library window was the only one lit up in a row of dark shops. As he approached he could see it was her and he felt a surge of elation. He stopped outside and watched her in the lighted room. She walked from behind her desk, carrying a pile of books back to the shelves, moving with grace.

Inside, the library was warm and Cal undid his parka. He moved to the magazine shelves near the desk and picked up a copy of *Punch*. A number of women were browsing among the shelves and he heard an old man cough. He sat down on a plastic chair and flicked open the magazine but did not read. As he settled in the chair his trousers and the surface made a fart-like noise in the silence so he moved again several times in case it should be misinterpreted. The floor was covered in large green carpet tiles. One at Cal's foot had a grey coin of recent chewing-gum stuck to it. Through the open shelves he could see Marcella coming – at least he could see her legs. She walked into the shelved alcove next to him and he looked at her heels. She was again wearing Scholls. She rose on her toes to reach a shelf and he could see the arched insoles of her dark stockings. She came round the corner to his alcove.

'Hello.' She smiled, seeing him, and his insides went to water.

'Hi.' He stood up, the magazine flopping in his hand.

She had unloaded all her pile of books except one, which she held flat to her breast. She turned sideways to Cal, scanning the shelf. The profile of her breast had become a plateau touched at its tip by the book. Cal wanted to close his eyes. To make a shutter-image of it, just as he had made one of the two women sprawled face down on the floor of the off-licence. She slotted the book into its rightful place and, her arms now empty, she folded them and turned to him.

'Well, how are things?'

'Fine,' said Cal. He felt himself begin to blush and fought it helplessly. The redness invaded his face and neck and his ears burned. Jesus, to be almost twenty and still blushing. To be out of
his own control. It hadn't happened to him for years. He looked down, hoping to hide the worst effects of it behind the curtain of his hair.

'What are you reading?'

Cal's watering eyes looked down at the magazine.

'*Punch*. I got a job.'

'So I heard. My mother-in-law was telling me about it.'

'I see your little girl sometimes during the day.'

Marcella smiled and folded her arms a little tighter. She wore a medallion over a thin, black polo-neck.

'She's lovely.'

Marcella nodded, agreeing without the slightest hint of pride. Cal's embarrassment at their conversation grew. She spoke in a normal voice and everything she said could be heard in the silence. When it came to his turn to speak his voice was a whisper and yet
because she talked loudly he felt he should speak at the same volume.

'Yes, that's one of the things I miss most about working, not being home with her. Especially Thursdays. She's asleep in bed by the time I get back.'

'You can go in and look at her in the cot – like a Hollywood movie.'

Marcella laughed and began straightening the magazines on the display board.

'Is it only tapes you take out?' she asked.

'Yes. I don't read much.'

She angled him over to the wall and much to Cal's relief she lowered her voice.

'It's part of our job, you know, to encourage the public to read.'

She put her hands on her hips – a little like a school mistress – and was about to take a step back on to the chewing-gum spot when Cal reached out and touched her elbow, guiding her sideways. He showed her the danger and she thanked him. School had been in, she said. The touch of her was still in his fingertips.

'What kind of thing would you be interested in?'

Cal shrugged. 'I don't know. Maybe . . . lots of things.'

'Do you read novels?' 5

He thought. At school they had read something called *Under the Greenwood Tree*.

'No,' he said.

'I wish I was like that. It would mean that I could start all over again and it would all be new to me.' 10

Cal wondered if she was taking the piss out of him or not. He felt uneasy. He set his copy of *Punch* on the rack and stepped sideways.

'I'll have a look,' he said. 'Maybe I'll try it again. School put me off.' 15

Marcella took this as an end to the conversation and smiling retreated to sit behind her desk. Cal walked down among the shelves of books. From the very outside of the Irish History section he could see her from between the shelves and, all except for his eyes, he could remain hidden from her. 20

He stood watching her stamp books for one of the women. Her quick movements, the neatness of her gestures, her upturned face with its open smile when the transaction was completed made him feel weak. He wanted to lie down here among the warmth and the books and never get up until she came with her pale decorated 25 hands and raised him to life again. Her desk was open-fronted and after the woman had gone Marcella crossed her legs. Her Scholl hung from her tilted right foot. Her eyes looked up and Cal thought they met his, so he looked away and moved out of sight deeper between the shelves. 30

He touched the spines of some books and went so far as to take one out and flick through it. There were pictures of Sir Edward Carson, Sir James Craig and the Reverend Ian Paisley, all on the one page. For sheer physical ugliness they were hard to beat. Three men with battering-ram blunt faces whose political fighting had 35 left them looking like old boxers. There was a picture of Padric

Pearse in profile. He had heard somewhere that Pearse never looked directly at the camera because he had the most God-awful squint. Cal read on the opposite page what Pearse had said, that the heart of Ireland would be refreshed by the red wine of the
5 battlefields, that Ireland needed its bloody sacrifice. He closed the book and slid it back among the others. A siren hee-hawed its way through the town at speed. An old man looked up, then bent over his book again.

Cal moved to the fiction section. It might please her if he were
10 to take a novel out. Tilting his head so that one curtain of his hair hung down straight, he read the titles on the spines. He looked at one called *Women in Love* but thought the title too pointed to get past without Marcella noticing. He finally settled for a fat red book because he knew its title and because he had heard that it was
15 highly intellectual. He had also watched two episodes of it on television. He waited until there was no one at the desk then carried his book to her. It was impressively heavy. She stamped it and said,

'You'll be back for Part Two tomorrow.'

Cal laughed and said yes, he would be. The old man came up
20 behind him with a pile of books he wanted to take out.

'Did you see it when it was on TV?' Cal asked her.

No, she hadn't. But she had read it and thought it great.

'Don't let the names put you off,' she said. He watched her fingers skim the cards until they slowed to a walk. She extracted
25 his card.

'Cal Mc Cluskey,' she said and although he hated his name, the way she said it was clean and beautiful.

Cal walked into the street and stood for a while on the dark side, watching her through the window, then turned for home. The
30 book felt the size of a lunchbox under his arm. He might even try to read it. It would be good to walk into the library the next week and say casually, 'I enjoyed that very much. Very intellectual.' And she would say, 'Cal Mc Cluskey.'

It was not until the end of Main Street that he began to sense
35 that something was wrong. There was a glow above the houses of the estate but at first he thought it was the street lights. Then he

noticed that the glow was billowing with smoke. When he saw the blue pulse of a warning light he began to run. The street was full of people and a fire engine and a police car were pulled up on the pavement. He knew it was his house and he fought his way through the crowd. There were flames gushing from the front room window 5 and glass crashed and tinkled as it broke in the heat. A crackling loudspeaker voice came above the noise from the cabin of the fire engine. Cal shouted to one of the firemen,

'Is my father in there?' His voice was almost a scream.

The fireman wrestled with the hose and Cal couldn't hear what 10 he said. Cal went as close as he could until the heat was scorching the skin of his face and he had to turn his head away. The firemen were pumping a white column of water through the front room window and it seemed to be having no effect. Small explosions and cracks continued. Cal could see flickerings beginning to come from 15 upstairs.

He moved back into the crowd to try and find out if anyone knew about his father. Then he saw him. Someone had brought a dining-room chair on to the pavement and Shamie was sitting on it, his head in his hands, crying. He was still in his shirt-sleeves. 20 When he heard Cal's voice he looked up and said. 'Thank God, thank God.' He stood up and shook hands with his son. Cal thought it a completely daft thing to do.

'I wasn't sure whether you were in the bedroom or not,' said Shamie. He held on to Cal's hand for a long time with both hands 25 and Cal felt him shaking. He pulled Cal closer and for one terrible moment Cal thought he was going to kiss him in front of the crowd, but he whispered in his ear.

'The gun. They'll find it afterwards.'

'Sit down. Don't worry.' 30

A woman neighbour brought an overcoat and she made Shamie put it on, saying,

'It makes you ashamed to be a Protestant.' She too was crying.

'Just so long as Cal's safe,' said Shamie. 'I thought you'd be upstairs with your room locked. I couldn't remember you going 35 out.'

Cal lit a cigarette and gave it to his father. Shamie inhaled,
shivering. A voice roared from the other side of the crowd 'Fenian
bastards'. And the loudspeaker voice crackled and said things
which nobody could quite catch. A policeman in a flak-jacket edged
his way through to where Shamie was sitting on the chair and,
squatting to be on a level with him, began to ask him questions.

Shamie, still wearing the borrowed overcoat and in a state of shock,
was led by Cal into Dermot Ryan's small kitchen. Dermot, one of
Shamie's cousins, lived in a pensioner's bungalow at Ardview and
although Shamie had had offers of a bed from almost everyone
who spoke to him he had insisted that he come here, to keep trouble
in the family. Old Dermot, when he heard about the fire, had to
take two extra blood-pressure tablets.

After the fuss of the street they sat drinking tea and Shamie told
them as much as he could. The petrol bomb – if it was a petrol
bomb; for all Shamie knew they could have poured the stuff
through the letterbox and set fire to it – must have come through
the front door. Shamie had been having his usual sleep in the
armchair and had heard nothing. The first thing that warned him
was the smell. He woke up and could hardly see across the room.
When he opened the door the hall and the stairs were a blazing
inferno. He just ran out of the back door and started shouting up
at Cal's window, but got no answer.

The excitement was too much for Dermot Ryan and he shuffled
off to the lavatory. Shamie whispered to Cal,

'I'd been expecting this and I'd taken the gun out. It's lying on
the bedside table.'

'Jesus.'

'Will they search the house?'

'If they haven't already.'

Cal immediately went back to the estate, running all the way.
The crowd had dispersed now and the house was in darkness. In
the street lights he could see black scorched crescents, like some
kind of eye-shadow, above the windows. The fire brigade was still
there in case anything should flare up again. They had knocked

74

the front door down and were tramping heavily through the débris and broken glass. Cal explained who he was and that he wanted to get up to the bedroom. They pointed out that the stairs had collapsed. Cal said that his father needed his blood-pressure tablets or he would be seriously ill. The firemen shrugged and said that if he went in the risk would be his. They could not stop him going on to his own property. As yet they hadn't checked the safety of the floors upstairs. Cal borrowed a torch from them and used the small window-cleaner's ladder Shamie kept at the back. The windows were broken and once in his own bedroom he stood on a large pane of glass which cracked and rang, echoing strangely. The stink was awful. He directed the beam around the room. The flames had not got this far but everything was black. His tape cassettes were warped lumps. The plastic lampshade had become a stalactite hanging from the ceiling. He had to kick the door open to get into Shamie's room and the floor groaned and creaked when he put his weight on it. The gun lay on the bedside table and he put it in his inside pocket after making sure that the safety catch was on.

In his own room he paused and picked out his guitar with the torch. The tuning knobs had melted. He picked the instrument up and the back banged away from the top with a faint grating chord, the way the sole of a shoe splits from its upper.

'Aw Jesus no.'

He threw the guitar on to the floor, where it boomed and repeated the chord thinly, and he eased himself out of the window.

He was breathless when he got back to Dermot Ryan's place. Shamie looked up at him anxiously and Cal winked to assure him that everything was all right. In his absence they had fixed up the sleeping arrangements. Dermot would sleep in his usual place and Shamie could use the sofa. The floor was all that was left for Cal and a pillow and some blankets were piled on the sideboard for him. They had more tea and then Dermot said that if he didn't go to bed he would pay for it the next day with his blood pressure, so he said goodnight and went out. Cal took the gun from his inside pocket and hissed to draw Shamie's attention.

'Now that the house is gone, you've no need of this.'

Shamie nodded.

'I'll get rid of it for you.' Cal started wrapping it in a brown paper bag but he froze when Dermot came back in wearing striped pyjamas and a Fair Isle pullover. He had not yet taken his cap off.

'The clock,' he said. 'Goodnight.'

When he had gone Cal slipped the gun into the inside pocket of his jacket. He made up his bed on the floor and Shamie lay down on the couch.

'Were we insured?' asked Cal.

'I haven't paid it for years. Not since your mother died.'

Cal took off his shirt and got into the envelope of blankets he had made himself.

'That's great.'

'I'm useless at running a house.'

'Maybe the Government will pay compensation,' said Cal. 'It was no accident.'

'I'll go and see about it tomorrow.'

They lay back and lit cigarettes. Cal for the first time in years felt safe. No one knew he was in this pensioner's house. He was sure he would sleep. If only he could get away from himself as well. He supposed that was what sleep was. But that too could be ruined by dreams. The hearth began to hurt his neck through the pillow and he moved a bit closer to the sofa. The door opened again and Dermot stood there. He still wore the cap.

'Sorry,' he said. 'For the pills.' He hurried into the kitchen and came back with a glass of water. 'Goodnight.'

'Dermot,' said Shamie. 'Thanks for everything.'

'They're old that knows their fate.'

Dermot went out, closing the door after him gently.

'You wouldn't want to be doing anything too secret after Dermot goes to bed,' said Cal. 'He's in and out like the wee weather-man. Who's going to turn out the light?'

Father and son argued a bit as to who would. Eventually Shamie, for having the advantage of the sofa, did it. In the darkness the fire

still glowed. Cal threw his cigarette over his shoulder into it. He
loved sleeping in a room with a fire. He had been ill once in their
first house in Clanchatten Street and they had moved his bed down
beside the range. The fire door was usually kept open at night to
keep the room warm and he would lie listening to his mother's
voice talking to a neighbour or his father, feeling the heat from the
fire on his face. The voices would become indistinct, mixed with
the rattle of teacups or the creak of a chair, and for a long time he
would be half asleep, half awake – listening not to what was said
but to the enveloping sound of their saying.

Shamie sat up on the sofa.

'Cal?'

'What?'

'I forgot to tell you. Crilly said he wants to see you.'

'When?'

'Saturday lunchtime.'

'OK'

Cal put his hands behind his head. The floor seemed to be
getting harder the longer he lay. He thought of Matt Talbot, of
saints who slept on boards.

'I can't stay here,' he said. 'There's no room.'

'Where will you go?'

Suddenly Cal thought of a place. If he stayed there it might solve
a lot of problems.

'Have you told anybody about my job?'

'I'm sure I have.'

'Did you tell Crilly where it was?'

'No, I've only talked to him once this week.'

Cal struck a match in the dark and lit another cigarette. Shamie
refused one, his face looking old in the light from the flame.

'Do me a favour, Shamie.'

'What?'

'Don't tell him. Say I left after the fire and you don't know where
I am.'

'Why?'

'Just a favour. Don't ask me why. If anybody's looking for me, just say I've gone. Tell them England if you like. But you just don't know.'

There was a long silence. The coals in the fire collapsed and ticked. In the dark Shamie's voice sounded frightened.

5 'Are you in any trouble?'

'No, nothing like that.'

'That bloody Crilly one. I never liked him.'

'Will you do that for me?'

'If it's what you want. But where will you go?'

10 Cal inhaled and blew out the smoke without seeing it.

'It's better if you don't know,' he said. 'I'll come and see you here.'

He heard his father turn and try to get comfortable.

'Cal? You would tell me if you were in any trouble, wouldn't
15 you?'

'Yes.'

'I don't like the sound of it, Cal.'

'I'll tell you someday. OK?'

'OK'

20 Soon Shamie's breathing deepened and became regular. Cal had made him take two of Dermot's sleeping pills to calm him. He thought about Marcella and tried to recall his shutter-image of her with the book touching the point of her breast. Then he wondered where in all the confusion he had left his own library book, the one
25 the size of a lunchbox.

④ The next morning, feeling drained rather than restored by his shallow sleep, Cal stood at the corner, as always, waiting for Cyril Dunlop. He did not like this being at the same place at the same time. Every day Catholics were being shot dead for no apparent
30 reason, as the police said. Were they *so* stupid? It wasn't the thought of being killed that frightened him, it was the fear that he would lose his dignity if they tortured him. Men had been castrated before they were killed – one bloke had had his head put between the jaws of a vice and the vice tightened until his skull cracked; and a
35 Catholic butcher was murdered and hung up on a meat hook in

his own shop like a side of beef. They were the actions of men with sick minds.

He kept moving his eyes, scanning the road both ways, expecting to see two blokes on a motorbike. They would slow down and draw level, then the guy on the pillion would point something at him 5 and Cal would be dead. Once that first week he did see two people on a motorbike and he stepped closer to the wall but it roared past. If it happened this morning he would be ready for them. Then he thought of reaching into his inside pocket, taking out the paper bag, unfolding it, removing the gun, releasing the safety catch and 10 aiming it. Then firing. Cal smiled. His killers would be in Belfast having a cup of tea by that time if they had anything above second gear. If somebody wanted to get you they would get you. Having a gun was no help.

Dunlop's car came along and pulled in to the side. Cal got in. 15

'I didn't expect to see you today,' said Cyril.

'You heard then?'

'It was all over the town. What happened? Was it accidental?'

Cal laughed at his question.

'We were burned out.' 20

Cyril shook his head in disbelief and pursed his mouth.

'I'll have to admit, Cal, there's bad bastards on both sides.'

'Thanks.'

Cal was conscious of the hardness of the gun pressing into the left side of his chest. If they were stopped and searched this morn- 25 ing, what would the police make of it? A staunch Orangeman and a Republican with a gun in the same car. Then he remembered with relief that Cyril Dunlop was never stopped. When they recognized him they waved him on. It was funny, Cal thought, how Protestants were 'staunch' and Catholics were 'fervent'. 30

All that day he spent mucking out the byre again and carrying in winter feed. Dunlop told him that now the cattle were in most of the time this had to be done every day. Cal worked on his own and the noise of the beasts was a comfort to him. They snuffled and breathed, chewed and ground their teeth. One would occasionally 35 low for no reason at all. He wondered why children were taught that a cow said 'moo'. It was the last word to describe the kind of nasal moan that they made. They had such white eyelashes, such huge eyes that they turned on him when he came near. Cal talked to them as he worked among their skidding, hoofed feet. The task 5 of mucking out was so mindless that he had too much time to think. He wondered if anything could be salvaged from his bedroom. The guitar was certainly a goner – and all his tapes. His tape deck might still work. He felt sorry for Shamie, losing all the things he had gathered over a lifetime. But in a way for himself it could be a clean 10 start. Like burning a wound to cleanse it.

At lunchtime he took a walk to the derelict cottage. He made sure that nobody was around and went into the glass porch. He had brought a small iron bar with him, but he didn't need it because when he tugged at the padlock it snapped open in his hand. He 15 drew the bolt back and stepped quickly inside. The room to the right was filled with a pyramid of mouldering furniture with chair legs sticking out at all angles. There were tins of paint piled in one corner and someone had cleaned brushes with different colours on the wall. On the shelf by the door there was a bottle of purple 20 meths with a label 'Not to be taken'. Someone had added in Biro 'seriously'. The room to the left was empty but had lino covering the floor. Two panes of the window were broken and someone had nailed a square of hardboard over the bottom of the frame. He pulled back a corner of the lino and with the crowbar eased up a 25 floorboard. The nails screeched dryly as he put his whole weight on it. Give me a big enough lever and I'll move the world. He tucked the paper bag containing the gun under the floor and jumped on the board to flatten it.

That afternoon he told Dunlop that he would not need transport. 30 He had a mate who was picking him up and that same mate would leave him out in the mornings. Dunlop shrugged. He seemed disgruntled that Cal was no longer dependent on him.

'OK, if that's the way you want it,' he said.

At six he passed Cal sheltering from the wind and rain at the 35 gable wall.

'He's always late,' said Cal.

After Dunlop's car had turned on to the main road Cal headed
down the lane. About a mile and a half farther along the Toome
road was a pub, the Stray Inn, and he walked to it to pass the time
until dark. He sat in the warmth sipping a pint and spoke to no
one. When he saw the lights come on in the car park, Cal set off
back to Morton's farm. He got to the cottage, opened the door and
went in. By now it was completely black and he moved slowly,
waving his arms in front of him like antennae. He located the
sideboard in the hall, went into the empty room and hunkered
down on the floor. 'I'm squatting,' he thought, smiling in the dark.
He had planned this whole thing very badly. He should have got
himself a torch and something to sleep on. Tomorrow he could get
them. When he was in the kitchen for a tea break in the afternoon
he had nicked a couple of rolls from the breadbin. There had been
a pile of them so two wouldn't be missed. The coat pocket of his
jacket swung heavily with a can of beer – the last of six he had
bought himself on Tuesday. He chugged open the ring-pull and
the beer hissed in the dark. He covered the foam with his mouth
to stop it spilling. He ate the rolls slowly to make them last and
kept some of the beer for later. His eyes were becoming used to
the dark and when he struck a match to light his cigarette it briefly
lit up the room like daylight. He smoked while walking up and
down, his feet crunching over fragmented glass.

From the back window he could see the Morton farmhouse and
he was close enough to the lane to hear the Anglia drive past. He
watched but only saw an instant of her framed in the light of the
doorway as she went in. He leaned his forehead against the window.
In the total darkness he was sensitive to minute changes of light
and aware immediately a lamp went on upstairs in the farmhouse.
He looked up. Marcella came to the window and with a gesture
like a priestess pulled the heavy curtains together. At least now he
knew which was her bedroom.

He thought of himself as a menial at the gate-lodge to the house
of his mistress. If his guitar had not broken he could have stood
beneath her window and serenaded her. Again he smiled sourly in
the darkness. Then gradually as the evening dragged by, minute

by slow minute, he became depressed. He thought of himself as a monk in his cell not only deprived of light and comfort but, in the mood he was in, deprived of God. He had ceased to believe in the one thing that dignified his suffering. Matt Talbot lived with
5 chains embedded in him for the love of God. What if he had not believed in God and yet had continued with his pain? What if he had suffered for another person? To suffer for something which didn't exist, that was like Ireland. People were dying every day, men and women were being crippled and turned into vegetables
10 in the name of Ireland. An Ireland which never was and never would be. It was the people of Ulster who were heroic, caught between the jaws of two opposing ideals trying to grind each other out of existence.

His sin clawed at him, demanding attention. He fought it for as
15 long as he could but there was little to distract him except the cold. In the pitch darkness his eyes, with nothing to do, naturally turned inside himself. Tired of pacing, he lay down on the floor with his knees to his chest for warmth. He lay inert on broken glass, his eyes open to the night, and saw again the terrible thing that he had
20 done.

It was almost a year ago to the day that he had called for Crilly in the van. He had felt sick in his stomach because when Crilly had met him in the street earlier he had said that this was the big one. They drove to the town hall to a dance. The band was tuning up
25 and there were two or three girls, embarrassed by being early, standing in the darkness at the back of the hall. The place was so empty Cal could hear doors closing.

Crilly and he had gone to the bar and then retired to a corner with their drinks.

30 'Well, what's the big one?'

'A cop – the Police Reserve.'

'What about him?'

'We do him – that's what.'

The muscles of Cal's stomach went rigid and he felt his palms
35 sweaty. He rubbed his hands slowly together.

'Is he coming here?'

'No. We'll be seen here. We'll do it, then come back.'

'I see.'

' "Where were you last night?" Answer: "At a dance."
Boom-boom.'

Cal bought two more pints.

'Don't worry, Cal. This guy is the greatest bastard unhung,
Skeffington says that we've got to squeeze the Police Reserve and
the UDR Maybe put people off joining them. So he picked this
guy, this real turd who lives outside Magherafelt. And tonight we
do him.' Cal said nothing. He cleaned the condensation from the
outside of his pint with one finger. 'He planted a gun on two totally
innocent guys about a month ago,' Crilly went on. 'They are up in
Crumlin Road jail now. Not only that, but he had his mates give
them a kicking to end all kickings and said that they had resisted
arrest. He knew them too – two Catholic lads from the town – the
big fucker.'

'I'm just driving,' said Cal.

'That's all we're asking you to do.'

After his second pint Crilly warned him that he could have no
more. They shouldn't be drinking at all before a job. Cal had to
drive straight. The band began to play and gradually the hall filled.
Crilly bought a half bottle of whiskey over the counter and slipped
it into his pocket. They danced with three girls each – 'Someone
who knows you well,' said Crilly. Cal was incapable of conversation
with any of them. During a fast number the keys in his pocket
chinked and he thought they might give him away.

Crilly looked at his watch and said that he had some hardware
to pick up and he would see him in the car park in fifteen minutes.

'By that time you should have wheels for us.'

Cal loathed Crilly's Hollywood turn of phrase. On nights like
this Crilly thought he was in the big picture. Cal gritted his jaw
and followed him. They had the date in purple ink stamped on the
backs of their hands so they could come back in again.

'I feel like a library book,' said Crilly, going down the stairs.

'Don't be stupid,' said Cal. 'They closed ages ago.' He felt guilty
making a laugh but he was nervous.

Cal slipped on a pair of thin leather gloves and walked around the dark end of the car park. There were two Cortinas among the ranks of cars. He tried the doors of one and they were locked. In the other, a red one, he noticed that the lock button of the back door was up. He was in and quickly over into the front seat. He pulled the string of Ford keys from his pocket and began to work through them systematically. Crilly had got them from a bloke in a garage in return for not burning it down. 'He was a good mate of mine, anyway,' he'd said. Eight keys tried and still no luck. The eleventh key clicked and the starter fired. He was expecting it so much that the sudden noise made him jump. He turned on the lights and edged the car out between the others and down the aisle. When the attendant waved a casual goodnight Cal made sure he was looking the other way. He parked, waiting for Crilly, the engine running. He should have gone to the lavatory after two pints. He rubbed his stomach and belched quietly. Nerves gave him wind. It was ten minutes before Crilly appeared from a side street with a Spar carrier bag. When he got into the car Cal smelt petrol but didn't say anything.

'Nice one, Cal,' he said, looking round him. 'Enough juice?'

'Three-quarters.'

They drove on to the main Magherafelt road. Crilly navigated and checked his gun at the same time. The tiny clicking of bullets set Cal's teeth on edge.

'I love the weight of an automatic,' Crilly said. 'You wee beauty.' He held it up for Cal to see. 'The only thing is, they're liable to jam.'

Cal did not look at it but kept his eyes on the road. Undipped headlights glared in his driving mirror and he slowed down. With relief he saw the car pass him and its tail lights draw away. Crilly slipped the gun into his pocket. From the other pocket he took the half bottle and opened it with a tearing click. He tilted it to his mouth and after swallowing gasped.

'Oh fuck – that's good stuff. Left here.'

Cal had missed the turn and had to reverse back to it. His voice was thin and tight.

'You didn't give me enough warning. Keep your eyes on the road.'

'Oh-ho. Cal's nervous. Getting jumpy, eh?'

Crilly gave him plenty of warning for the farm lane on the right. Cal slowed and the car bumped and swayed through the potholes. They passed a dilapidated cottage on the right and then pulled into a farmyard. It was a big cream house. Dogs in an outhouse somewhere started up a frantic barking. Crilly took another swig from his bottle.

'Keep her running, Cal. This won't take long.'

Cal pulled the car up close to the front door and Crilly got out. Cal waited. He badly needed a piss. He held on tight to the steering wheel. He ran his fingers round the back of it. For some reason it reminded him of the ridges on the roof of his mouth. He curled his tongue and touched them with its tip, counting. Five or six. Like the hard sand of the sea-shore. He wanted a cigarette but he knew it would be in his way if they had to take off fast. The idling engine missed a beat and Cal touched the accelerator lightly to keep it going. The thought of a stall at this stage made him weak.

He didn't hear the bell when Crilly pressed the button. It was dark but there was a light somewhere in the house. Cal tried to burp. The beer and his nerves combined to make him feel he had swallowed lead. He didn't want to watch but he felt compelled to. He tried to get beneath the wind by swallowing air but just managed to belch the pockets of air which he had swallowed. A light came on in the hall, lighting up the area of the front door. Cal felt his bladder on the point of bursting. Crilly waited, one hand in his pocket. The net curtain twitched, then the door opened. Still the dogs kept up their incessant barking.

Cal saw the man smile. Then he looked confused. Crilly pulled the gun from his pocket and the man froze. He was in carpet slippers. Crilly shot him twice in the chest. The gun sounded unreal – like a child's cap gun. The man very slowly genuflected. He shouted as if he'd been punched in the stomach.

'Mar-cell-a.'

It was a kind of animal roar. Cal heard a click and Crilly saying fuck. With both hands he snapped the gun and cleared the jam.

'Marcella,' the man roared again. Then Crilly fired a shot through his head, the gun only inches from it. Stuff came out on the wallpaper behind him. Crilly fired three more shots up the
5 hallway then turned and ran. He jumped into the car shouting.

'Go like fuck.'

Cal heard the tyres scream as they sprayed muck and stones before they finally gripped. He swung at the gateway, going too fast in first gear. The car slewed sideways in the mud and thumped
10 off the cement gatepost with a metallic clang.

'Keep her going, keep her going,' screamed Crilly.

Cal bounced the car into the lane and drove at speed. He did not stop at the turn on to the main road but blazed out, hoping there was nothing coming.

15 'What did I tell you,' shouted Crilly, 'the fuckin' thing jammed.'

Cal felt sick. He wanted to let all his functions go at once.

'This wee bastard puts his head round the corner of the hall. So I let him have it too.'

'Who?'

20 'I don't know who he was. But he was too nosey for his own good.'

They did the return journey in half the time. Crilly talked non-stop, dressing-room talk, none of which Cal heard, and finished his half bottle which he put in the Spar bag. He directed Cal to
25 park behind some sheds on wasteground. They got out and Crilly took a can from the bag and poured it over the upholstery of the car.

'Have you got a match?'

Cal gave him a box of matches and could wait no longer. He
30 opened his trousers and urinated in a gush against the side of a corrugated-iron shed. It drummed like stampeding animals. Crilly struck a match and threw it on the seat. The match went out and he cursed. He struck another one. Cal's stream seemed endless and he pushed to get it out quicker. This time the car exploded
35 with a dull whumph – blue at first, turning to yellow flame. Crilly started to run.

'Jesus, will you come on.'

Cal still had not finished but he stopped his stream and zipped himself up at the run. On the street they stopped running. Crilly saying it was too suspicious.

'You go back to the dance. I'll get rid of these,' he said.   5

Cal climbed the stairs to the hall with his knees trembling. He wanted to burst out crying like a child. He held out his hand to the man sitting at the entrance table to show him his stamp. His hand was shaking badly. He went to the lavatory to finish emptying his bladder and saw himself chalk-white in the mirror. He felt physi-   10
cally sick looking at himself and yet he continued to stare, his hands holding the sides of the wash-basin. But he did not vomit.

He went into the hall and straight to the bar. The place was hot now and smelt of sweat and perfume. It throbbed with noise. The band in matching powder-blue uniforms were moving in unison.   15

'I see a face,' sang the vocalist, 'a smiling face . . .'

Cal could feel the pulse of the maple floor in his feet. He ordered a large whiskey and drank it straight off and ordered another one. There was a mirror behind the bar so he eased himself off the stool and found a corner. He saw Crilly barging his way through the   20
crowd. He winked at Cal when he came up.

'OK, kid?'

Cal nodded.

'Right, we've got to dance. Be seen.'

He took Cal by the arm and thrust him towards a group of girls.   25
Cal stopped in front of one with ginger hair and pale eyelashes. He asked her to dance by holding out his hand to her. She came with him on to the floor. The tempo had slowed and everybody seemed to be doing old-fashioned ballroom dancing. Cal put one hand on her back and held her fingers with his other hand. She was not fat   30
but he felt the indentation her bra strap made in her back. She danced, afraid to meet his eyes, staring into the distance humming the tune. She was warm to the touch and her hand was damp. Cal guided her inexpertly round the floor, conscious of the living movement of her body under his hand. He saw the man genuflect   35
again, his heel coming away from his slipper, the astonishment in

his eyes. Marcella. The name roared in his ears, drowning out the band. The ginger girl was chewing gum, not constantly or he would have noticed it before now, but occasionally she would move it around her mouth, give a few chews and then rest. She had a dark
5 mole beneath her chin with a tiny blonde hair curling from it. The quick whiskeys made him unsure of his feet. It was the first dance of a set of three but when the band stopped the girl gave a quick chew.

  'Thanks,' she said and walked off the floor back to her friends.
10 In the bar he flinched seeing a woman raising a tomato juice to her mouth. Crilly was still on the floor, his shoulders swaying, both hands low on his partner's back. He was talking furiously. Cal waited until Crilly danced to the edge of the floor and shouted to him,

15 'I'm away home.'

  He did not wait for a reply but shouldered and elbowed his way towards the door in such a way that people looked after him in annoyance. He felt that he had a brand stamped in blood in the middle of his forehead which would take him the rest of his life to
20 purge.

Chapter Four

①

Cal continued to live in the cottage, appearing early in the mornings before Dunlop and hanging around at night, as if for his lift, until Dunlop went. On Wednesday Dunlop drove into town for some tractor spares and Cal went to the cottage. He sorted among the piles of furniture and found three square seat cushions on a battered 5 sofa. These he lined up in the corner of his own room for a bed. He covered them with two thin, grey blankets which draped a pair of better-looking dining-room chairs set aside from the main pile. He borrowed a small hand-brush from the tool shed and swept the glass and dirt off the floor into the hallway. He thought of borrowing 10 the torch that sat on the shelf but realized that if he could see the house anyone in the house could see him. Instead he began to know his way in the dark.

After a week he had to accept that he was growing a black beard, not because he wanted one, but because he could think of no way 15 of shaving. There was a jaw-box in the tiny kitchen but no taps. Several nights he walked to the Stray Inn to get cigarettes. The place also sold pub grub and Cal would eat because he knew that if he did not, eventually he would become ill. The clientele was not local but the sheepskin-coat brigade who drove out from various 20 towns for somewhere different to go. He thought it unlikely that any of them would know him.

He got the feeling that the house was the earth and the cottage the moon orbiting it. At night sometimes when the wind was in the right direction he could hear the distant rattle of dishes. He would 25 keep a kind of vigil and see the lights come on in different rooms and wonder whether it was Marcella or not. Although she was light

years away from him he felt the enormous pull of her. And yet, like the moon and the earth, he knew that, because of what he had done, they could never come together. His sin kept them apart as surely as cold space. All that was left to him was to watch her. He
5 had heard Father Brolley say once that sin was outlawing yourself from God. After death God did not point the finger and say, 'Depart from me, ye accursed'. You realized your sinfulness and remained outside. A man damned himself.

One night Cal saw Marcella come to her window and, with a
10 sweep of her arms, draw the curtains. Then a light came on at the side of the house above the kitchen extension. If he had barred himself by his action the least he could do was look. He slipped out of the cottage and walked across the farmyard. The window where the light had come on was bubbled glass and he could see
15 the vaguest movement of her through it, rippling backwards and forwards. The dogs in the outhouse began to bark but Cal clicked his tongue and they knew the sound and settled down again. He stood watching the square of light, imagining her and what she was doing. Then she came and opened the small top pane of the
20 window, fastening it open by the window catch. Steam began to form in the cold outside air. There was a tank of diesel oil at the side wall of the extension and, loathing himself for doing it, Cal climbed quickly from it on to the flat roof. He did not dare go nearer. If she saw him – oh sweet Jesus, if she saw him. He stood
25 at the end of the roof watching the clear pillar-box sized slit in the misting window. Her arms came up and struggled to pull a black jumper over her head. He could hear the constant plummeting of the bath taps. She had her hair tied up in a top-knot with what looked like one of her daughter's green ribbons. He ached to see
30 more of her. He loved the way her eyes were averted, the way she was intent on what she was so busily doing, the way her head kept ducking in and out of his vision. The fact that she was totally unaware of his spying presence made him shake. He stood on tiptoe to try to see more of her and the tremble in his legs became
35 exaggerated. She straightened up and he saw the bare nape of her neck, tanned, with the black hair scraped up and away from it.

Through the bubbled glass he could only guess at the rest of her movements, stooping, bending, walking. He took several steps closer to the window and hesitated. He rose up on his toes again. She walked to the bathroom door and took down a towel and as she reached up one of her breasts came into his line of vision. White and shielded, unlike the brown of her shoulders – not heavy but with reaching up, raised. He tried to fix the picture, to snap the shutter. The noise of the rushing taps stopped. He heard her begin to hum a tune and it made him feel like the biggest shit on earth. She disappeared from the bubbled glass into the bath and he heard her swirl the water. If he moved any closer there was a possibility that she would look out and see his burning eyes at the slit. How would she feel then? Everything would go – the job, all his planning, the chance to be near her. He could never show his face in the library, never speak to her again. He climbed awkwardly down on to the diesel tank and ran doubled to the cottage like a thief. *Merde. Crotte de chien*. Shit Mc Cluskey.

He lay on his cushions with the smell of mildew in his nose and, thinking of her, he relieved the tautness in himself. The true hopelessness of his position came to him in the gloom that followed. He was in love with the one woman in the world who was forbidden him. He was suffering for something which could not exist. Apart from her age – what widow would look at a long-haired boy ten years younger than herself – by his action he had outlawed himself from her. She was an unattainable idea because he had helped kill her husband. And every one of his actions distanced him a little more – touching her in church, spying on her in her bathroom. He snorted a laugh. If touching her thigh with the back of his hand in church was an extra inch between them then slaying her husband put him on the outer edge of the galaxy.

He lit a cigarette and the room flared yellow for a moment. Despite the impossibility of his situation he could not leave the cottage. There were Skeffington and Crilly to contend with now that he had made the break from them. So far as he knew he was safe here and the gun beneath the floor was for the day Crilly came looking for him. They shot deserters – even deserters who protested that they had never joined in the first place. But Crilly would never think of looking for him here.

He could not sleep and smoked two more cigarettes. It was cold and he put his anorak on top of the two thin blankets. His only change for bed was to take off his shoes. He smelt himself, his feet and his shirt and knew that the time was long since past when he needed a bath and a complete change of clothing. He had been wearing these things for a fortnight now and he was beginning to feel and smell like a tramp. One day he had gone without socks and underpants and washed them under the tap in the byre with a block of yellow carbolic soap and left them to dry, weighted on the mantelpiece with three stones. But they had not dried overnight and rather than endure again the chafing of his boots and the vulnerability of his genitals he had put them on damp and let them dry by the heat of his body. He would have to see Shamie about a bath and ask him to get him some shirts and socks and things. Preferably hair shirts. He wondered if hermits had worn hair Y-fronts how long they would have put up with it. One of the things he missed most was washing his teeth. The first couple of days he was conscious of an extra layer each time he ran his tongue over them. Although he couldn't see, he felt they were yellow. He remembered a recipe of his mother's and nicked some cooking salt from the kitchen and mixed it with soot from the cottage chimney – the black and the white together. The powder didn't go grey but remained as grains of black and white. Each morning he scrubbed his teeth with a finger coated in the mixture and rinsed his mouth out, rationing himself to one gulp of water from the Cow and Gate tin he had filled from the yard tap. He threw his cigarette butt into the fireplace and watched the glow fade gradually. He settled to try and sleep.

Suddenly the room was filled with a blue-white light and the outside door exploded open. There was yelling and the thunder of heavy feet. The inner door was kicked and sprang back against the wall. Cal was half-way out of his bed and running doubled over when a voice screamed 'Freeze'. He saw rifles pointed at him. A light blinded him and he was kicked on the side of the head. He fell back against the fireplace. He was yelling his head off and so

were the people in the room. As he was hoisted to his feet he saw
a negro face. They spread-eagled him against the wall and hands
probed his body from top to bottom. The negro said,

'What you doing here, cock?'

The other soldiers were turning over his bed, shaking out his 5
smelling blankets. The negro took Cal by the hair and turned his
head, shining the light into his face.

'I said, what you doing here?'

Another voice said, 'All right, Sergeant.' Cal remained against
the wall, his arms and legs spread out. Warm stuff trickled into his 10
eye and he realized that his head was bleeding. The last voice that
spoke was high-class. It spoke again.

'Do you have an explanation for your presence here?'

'This is where I work,' said Cal.

'Where?' 15

'On Morton's farm.'

'It was they who telephoned us.'

'They don't know I'm here.'

'We want to know *why* you're here.'

Cal tried to take his arms down and turn and have a reasonable 20
conversation with this man but the moment he moved another
voice screamed 'Freeze', and Cal heard the rattle of a rifle being
aimed and froze. He bore his weight on the heels of his hands. His
arms were beginning to drain and tire.

'I was burned out of my own house a fortnight ago. I had nowhere 25
else to go.'

'What was the address?'

Cal told the man and he clumped out of the room. A radio set
crackled and spoke from outside. The posh voice came back in again.

'You say you work here?' 30

'Yes.'

'Come this way.'

The negro used the barrel of his rifle to wave him towards the
door. Two other white soldiers with their faces blackened had their
guns trained on him. Cal led the way past the Land Rover with its 35
glaring searchlight up the lane to the farmhouse. He stepped in an

ice-cold puddle and realized that he was still in his stocking feet.
He was shivering uncontrollably and held himself in his arms to
try to keep steady and warm. He walked jerkily, tiptoeing as stones
bit into his feet. There was another Land Rover with a crackling
5 radio at the front door of the house. The high-class voice went
inside. He seemed to take ages. Cal's feet ached with the cold and
the sharp stones. Still the rifles were trained on his chest. A soldier
had a brief conversation on the Land Rover radio and then went
into the house. The high-class voice came out with Marcella. She
10 was wearing a lemon towelling dressing-gown and had her hair still
in a top-knot tied with the childish bow. She stared at Cal and her
face was creased with concern.

'Yes it is. I'm terribly sorry about this,' she said to the officer,
'but after what's happened . . . Cal, come inside.'

15 'Just one moment, Mam.'

They asked Cal his name and his address and a lot of other
questions. Then they asked him to sign something. He looked over
his shoulder and saw lights and figures moving about in the cottage.
If they found the gun he was well and truly fucked. He knew they
20 would get the murder out of him if they hurt him badly enough.
Shakily he wrote his name on the paper. The soldiers piled into the
Land Rover and drove down the lane.

'You'd better come in,' said Marcella.

Cal watched the cottage. The lights went out and both vehicles,
25 their red tail lights waving, bumped away towards the main road.
He turned and followed her. Mrs Morton was sitting in the kitchen
also in her dressing-gown. She wore a hairnet and her face was pale
and sick. She looked up when he came in.

'You are a stupid boy, Mc Cluskey,' she said. 'Do you realize
30 the trouble you have caused?'

'I'm sorry,' said Cal.

'When I saw matches being lit in that cottage I was terrified out
of my mind.' Her glasses were catching the fluorescent strip and
shining white.

35 'Let me do something about that head of yours,' said Marcella.
Cal moved off the spot where he'd been standing and saw the

damp outlines, not only of his socks but his toes through his socks. She sat him down on a chair.

'My husband wakened with the fuss and was beside himself with fear. When this kind of thing has happened to you once you can never forget it.'

Cal tried to explain but Mrs Morton cut him short.

'Why didn't you *tell* us you were burned out of your home? That way we could have done something to help. But oh no, you knew better.'

'We'd heard there had been some families burned out,' said Marcella, 'but we'd no idea it was you.' She brought a Pyrex bowl of warm water to the table and clouded it white with some Dettol. She detached Cal's long hair from the wound and bathed it with a cotton wool swab. The tips of her fingers touched his face lightly here and there as she moved his head.

'I don't think it needs stitching. It's a graze and a bruise rather than a clean cut.'

'I've a good mind to pay you off here and now,' said Mrs Morton. 'I mean to say, you're working here a fortnight and you break into our property and scare the living daylights out of us.'

'I'm sorry. I'm really sorry,' said Cal. 'But I didn't know what else to do.' He closed his eyes and thought that she might *not* be going to pay him off if she were speaking that way. The soft stuff of the sleeve of Marcella's dressing-gown brushed his cheek and he could smell the talc she must have used after her bath.

'The Army say,' Mrs Morton went on, 'that we'll have to get that place bricked up now. It's a security risk without anyone living in it. That means we've lost a store because of you.'

'Gran, would you put the kettle on? I think we all need a cup of tea.'

'I'll not sleep if I drink tea at this time of night – but I suppose I'll not sleep anyway after all this.' She got up and put the kettle on. Marcella, squeezing a fresh cotton wool ball to dampness between the fingers of one hand, dried the wound.

'There,' she said. She smiled at him. 'I'll get a plaster for that.' She lifted an Oxo tin from a shelf and took out a large Elastoplast.

She removed one half of the paper backing and stuck the plaster beside the wound. She pulled it taut and at the same time removed the other half of the backing, smoothing it out with pressure from her thumbs.

Mrs Morton had stopped talking and they drank tea in an embarrassed silence.

'Where will you go now?' Marcella asked.

'I don't know.'

'You can sleep on the couch,' said Mrs Morton, not looking at Cal. 'I wouldn't have it said of me that I put somebody out on to the roads at this time of night.' The cup rattled on its saucer with the tremor in her hand.

'And tomorrow?' said Marcella. Cal shrugged and looked at his tea. 'Gran, could I have a word with you?' Both women got up and went into the other room. Cal sat waiting, staring at the Queen's simpering smile on the side of the tea-caddy.

When they came back in again it was Mrs Morton who did the talking. She stood with her arms folded, her slippered feet splayed flatly at right angles. Her legs were blue-veined and as white as candles.

'My daughter-in-law has suggested that we compromise. In order to prevent the Army coming back and bricking up the cottage we shall make you a tenant. You can fix the place up the best you can – but, as I'm sure you know by now, there are no facilities. I will charge you no rent.'

'I would like to pay something,' said Cal.

'This is not generosity on my part. If you paid rent you could complain. This way you have no legal rights. You go when I say you go.'

'I'll pay in some way.'

'I'll take it out of you in work,' said Mrs Morton and came as near to smiling as she had done that night.

He was awakened in the morning by the sound of a radio in the kitchen next door. He got up and was about to go back to the cottage when Mrs Morton rapped on the door.

'There's tea made if you would like a cup.'

He went into the kitchen, muttering thanks. Mrs Morton looked at his tousled appearance and directed him to the bathroom. At the speed at which he would steal something Cal washed himself all over with soap and hot water, standing in the bath, and dried himself with the moss green towel he had seen Marcella use the previous night. In the mirror he was startled by his beard and saw the Elastoplast with the raw redness at its edge. There was a slight dark coloration round his eye. He scrubbed his teeth with toothpaste, using somebody else's brush, and the cleanness of his mouth felt exhilarating. He tried to take as short a time as possible in case they thought he was really dirty. Putting on his socks again he found that they had gone crisp and hard with mud. He rolled them up and put them in his pocket. At least his feet were now clean.

He drank his tea and said again and again how sorry he was for the night before.

'Once you've been through a tragedy you're scared of it ever after,' Mrs Morton said. 'It seems like only yesterday that Robert was killed. He was such a kind boy – and very popular. Even though she's a different religion, he and Marcella were well suited. He was so good to her too.' She shook her head in disbelief.

Cal saw the sludge of tea leaves appearing at the bottom of his cup. He did not know whether to stall and see if Marcella would come down or to rush and be away from Mrs Morton.

'Later on, see my daughter-in-law and she'll try and fix you up with some furniture. She's taking a lie-in. It's her day off today.' It was enough to know that he would see her later that day. He thanked Mrs Morton for everything and said that he must go. Dunlop would be waiting for him. Seeing his bare toes gripped round the rung of the stool Mrs Morton offered him a selection of wellies from the kitchen cupboard to walk to the cottage.

It took him until lunchtime to muck out the byre and when he had finished he went up to the house and knocked on the kitchen door. Mrs Morton brought him in and called for Marcella. Her child came first, cocking her head to see who it was, and Marcella followed.

'Can we take the small bed from the back room? Anything in the attic is liable to be damp.'

'Take whatever you need. You're in charge. It was your idea.'

Cal and Marcella went up the stairs and the child followed
shouting, 'He's a stinky-poo.'

Marcella shushed her and Cal reddened because he knew it was probably a fact.

He carried the mesh frame of the bed to the cottage on his bowed back and she accompanied him with armfuls of blankets
and blue-striped pillows. Lucy carried several folded pillow slips and splashed deliberately through the centres of puddles. They went in and out of the house all afternoon, ferrying stuff to the cottage. Curtains, a Tilley lamp, a camping stove, a kettle, a card table covered with moth-eaten green baize. They took two chairs
from the other room of the cottage itself – the two good ones that had been covered up. Cal noticed that in the house with Mrs Morton Marcella was serious and reserved but each time she left the front door her mood seemed to change.

On the first trip she said,

'Right, we're under way,' and grinned at him crouching beneath the bed-frame, his fingers threaded in its mesh. 'Operation Stable. There being no room at the inn.' When she saw the place she said that it was better than she had remembered it. She lit a fire with paper and kindling and a cornflake carton full of coal. Cal wheel-
barrowed some of the blocks he himself had cut to keep it going. When they had moved all they could think of, including a mat for him to step out of bed on to, Cal suggested that they have a cup of tea. He lit the camping stove and lifted the kettle. He paused and said,

'We have all the accommodation for making tea, except water and tea and milk and sugar.'

'No tea pot, no cups,' said Marcella.

'Where do you think you are, a hotel?'

When they went to the house Mrs Morton threatened to take
the price of the items off his wages. She made him uneasy, not knowing when she was joking or serious. She also told him that if

he looked hard enough he would find a pump in the back yard of the cottage. Whether or not it was working after all these years she didn't know.

In the cottage they sat waiting for the kettle to boil. Little Lucy was in the hall talking to herself and the blocks on the fire were spitting and hissing.

'This reminds me of playing house,' said Marcella, 'when I was wee.'

'Where was that?'

Marcella told him something of her upbringing in Portstewart. She was of an Italian family, the D'Agostinos, who had a café business on the sea-front – cream walls with quadrants gouged in soft plaster. They had sent her to the nuns at Portstewart Convent for her education, a great Elsinore of a place built on a cliff overlooking the Atlantic. As a matter of fact she and Lucy had just been to Rome in the summer for a holiday. It wasn't really a holiday but something to get her mind off what had happened here. Had he heard about the awful thing they had done to her husband? Cal nodded, then pretended that the fire needed nursing and crouched at it with his back to her. All he could say was 'Hm-hm', like someone on the phone, as she told him. He felt that he might seem too callous so once or twice he steeled himself to look over his shoulder and meet her eyes. He tried to change the conversation.

'Was it in Rome you got the tan?'

She told him how guilty she felt lying in the sun, aware of the irony that her only concession to widow's weeds was her black bikini. Her Mama had given her the money for the flight and a long list of addresses. She had seen hundreds of aunts and uncles and cousins whom she couldn't understand because she had let her Italian slip badly and they were unwilling or unable to reduce the speed of their speech. But they had spoiled Lucy rotten when she was there and had hugged Marcella for herself, the knowledge of her tragedy in their dark eyes.

She drank her tea from a mug, sitting like a yogi on the bed. Cal sat up on a straight-backed chair in a kind of trance listening to her. He had imagined her as very quiet.

'There's something missing,' she said and ticked off the various items in the room on her fingers. 'I know what it is, and what's more I know where to get one.'

'What?'

5   'A chest of drawers. There's one in the next room.'

She leapt from the bed and Cal helped her carry the small chest into his room. The drawers stuck when she tried to pull them out and the whole thing shook so that the handles, like small brass door knockers, rattled.

10   'My mother used to rub candles on the runners to free them,' she said.

'Thanks very much,' said Cal laughing, 'but I've got nothing to put in them.' Marcella stopped – again she looked serious and concerned.

15   'Of course. You were burned out. Did you lose everything?'

Cal nodded. 'I only went back once. Everything was ruined.'

'And you've been wearing those things since?'

Cal began to blush.

'Stinky-poo,' she said and he laughed with her. She became
20 serious again and sat on the bed nursing her cup. She pursed her mouth and looked at him.

'Are you easily offended, Cal?'

'No.'

'Would you accept some second-hand clothes?'

25   'Sure.'

'What size?' she asked him.

'Almost any size of second-hand clothing will fit me,' said Cal.

She laughed and said, 'Good. Let me just go and see. I've been meaning to give all Robert's stuff to a jumble sale but I've never
30 got round to it.' She hesitated at the door. 'You've no objection to wearing a dead man's things?'

Cal sat on the creaking chair, looked down at the floor. He had to say,

'No, none at all.'

35   In the hallway he heard her say, 'Come along, Lucy, another trip to Granny's.'

He was still sitting in exactly the same position when she came back carrying a red leather suitcase with an airline label looped to the handle. She clicked the case open on the bed.

'I've been thinking,' she said. 'I didn't want to give you anything Gran would recognize. She's a bit funny that way. Her son and all that. So you don't get suits or fancy pullovers. Come and see if you like anything.'

Cal heaved himself up to look into the suitcase. There were ironed shirts of pale RUC green, two pairs of flannel trousers, nondescript pullovers, assorted colours of socks and underpants.

'I wonder will they fit?' she said, holding up a pair of trousers. 'You're about the same height but Robert had a well-developed middle-age spread. Try them on.'

Cal took a pair of trousers into the small kitchen and Lucy followed him. He put her out as gently as he could. Getting into them, he thought of the monks and hermits with their hair shirts designed to cause suffering. The trousers were the right length but large at the waist. He took his own belt and threaded it through the loops and tightened it to the well-worn last notch. They didn't look too bad. A bit like pictures of Dutchmen he had seen in his primary reader. He went back into the room.

'They'll be all right if I get pregnant,' he said.

'Oh, Cal.' She was stifling a laugh and looking sorry for him at the same time.

'They'll do until I wash my own jeans.'

'Why don't you give everything to me and I'll do it in the machine.'

'No.'

'Why not? Do you not think I'm a woman of the world?'

'They're . . .' He paused, looking for the right word. 'They wouldn't pass the test.'

'What do you mean?'

'This guy I know made up a test. If you throw your drawers at the wall and they slide down – they'll do you another day. If they stick you need clean ones. I need clean ones.'

Marcella laughed loudly, her face twisted in disgust. Cal said.

'Let me steep them first.'

'But how and in what?'

He thought for a moment and his face lit up. 'The pump,' he said. He changed back into his own trousers and all three of them went out to the back of the cottage. There was a roughstone wall which was covered in brambles and whin bushes.

'It must be in there somewhere.'

Marcella picked a fat blackberry and popped it into Lucy's mouth. The child chewed and disliked it, then spat it out all over her chin. Her mother tut-tutted and cleaned her with her hand and then wiped her hands on the grass. Cal was stooping, looking into the thicket of brambles. He stepped into it, crushing the lattice-work down with his boot. Marcella could now see underneath the canopy.

'There it is,' she said.

Cal went up to the tool shed and got a rake and an implement like a butcher's meat cleaver on the end of a pole. He hacked a way through to the pump and tried to clear a space around it while Marcella raked back the long tendrils of bramble. They became living things like snakes which caught round the legs of her jeans and curled and whipped as she tugged to get them away. She made the child stand back in case she got scratched. Cal rested to get his breath back and watched Marcella. She ignored him and went on working. Each time she stretched forward her jumper rode up and bared a small crescent of the flesh of her back. As she bent like that he could see the nodes of her spine. She straightened up, pulled down her jumper and smiled breathlessly at him.

'It's not like stamping library books,' she said.

Eventually they had an area round the pump cleared and it stood, a squat grey thing with fluted sides and an iron helmet.

'The question is, does it work?' said Cal.

Marcella went behind it and began to move the handle up and down. It clanked and screeched with rust and nothing happened.

'Don't give up,' said Cal.

She continued to work the monkey's tail of a handle. Cal listened at the spout and heard gulps and wheezes.

'Come on, put your back into it, Marcella.' He realized that he had said her name for the first time and it was like meat in his mouth. She was panting with the effort. A little rusted water squirted out and slapped on to the stone font. They both cheered and Lucy came forward to stare.

'Keep her going,' shouted Cal. Soon the water came in clear gulps every time the handle was depressed. Cal straightened up and said her name for the pleasure of it.

'Good on you, Marcella.'

She hawed on her fingers and rubbed an imaginary lapel. He had forgotten all about that. They had done it at primary school when they got their sums right. Maybe she wasn't that much older than him after all.

'Why don't we go brambling some day? Before they all die off,' said Marcella.

'Yeah,' said Cal.

Then Lucy began to cry. Her thick woollen tights had become snagged on a briar and she was dancing around to get rid of it but was getting more entangled with each step. She put her hand down to pluck it away and screamed as she was pricked. Marcella ran to her and picked her up, making comforting noises. The child held up her thumb with the bubble of blood on it and squealed. Marcella hugged Lucy to her and Cal watched. The mother leaned back from the child to see her whole face but they remained snugly together at the waist.

'Oh, I think we'll have to get a bandage for that.' But still the child cried. Marcella turned to Cal.

'I think she's tired. I'd better go.'

Again he wanted to freeze the moment, of her turning to him, some of her hair straggled across her face, locking the weeping child to her hips with both arms. As she chose her steps through the cut briars she shouted,

'You'll not forget to send me your washing?'

Cal waved.

When he was alone he could hardly believe that it had happened. They had been together for nearly three hours, they had talked, he

had made her laugh. In a way they had made a date – to pick
blackberries; two dates, the other one to hand in his washing. He
had to go into the cottage to have a seat and smoke a cigarette.

Afterwards he ran up to the byre and borrowed a bucket. When
5 it was filled the water was a faint cool green against the white of
the enamel. Cal carried it from the pump, one arm horizontal, the
other down and steady to keep the water from spilling. Hewers of
wood and drawers of water, right enough. He poured the contents
of the bucket into the jaw-box and undressed, dropping each item
10 into the water as he took it off. He approached the pile of dead
man's clothes totally naked. To get it over with he dressed quickly,
trying not to think. The drawers were slack but not loose enough
to fall down; the socks and shoes were perfect. When he was fully
dressed he plunged his dirty clothes up and down in the water and,
15 after wringing them out, sniffed them. They were presentable,
clean enough to be washed.

He went to the house and knocked at the kitchen door. Marcella
opened it and took the wet clothes from him as he stood on the
step. She was businesslike and brief and had closed the door before
20 Cal could think of anything else to say.

That night he lit the Tilley lamp and sat by the fire looking
around at his place. Marcella's curtness at the kitchen door had
taken the edge off the day. He felt as if he had made the rest of it
up or at least interpreted it wrongly. He wondered where he had
25 left his fat library book. It would come in handy now with the
whole night ahead of him. He had nothing to do but sit. It was like
watching television except that someone had taken the set away.

He put his feet up on the mantelpiece and leaned back in the
chair. He thought about how things happened to him but he
30 brought nothing about. What he needed was self-discipline. His
mother had ruled her own life with a hand of iron. She did everything she should do, getting up at seven and walking a mile to mass
every day no matter what the weather; if she wanted one thing
badly she did without others: if what she wanted was spiritual she
35 denied her body. In Lent she took black tea and weighed her
morsels of food on scales and for six weeks wouldn't let a sweet

cross her lips although she loved them. She sent money abroad to her working sisters while at night she sat with a wooden mushroom darning her stockings with a criss-cross of brown thread. She worked so her family would not want and Cal had never wanted while she was alive.

Once as a child he had had an ear-ache – he had never felt pain like it before or since – and as he lay in bed with his throbbing head on a hot water bottle wrapped in a towel she had stroked his hair and said,

'Just offer it up.'

It was her answer to everything, to turn pain and sorrow into a gift for God.

Cal was unsure of God but it came to him that the gift of suffering might work without Him. To offer it not up but *for* someone. 'I suffer for you, you suffer for me.' And that person might never know, that was the beauty of it. That way it was even more selfless.

He got a sense of a new life, a new start now that he had officially moved into the cottage. He would discipline himself. He felt a surge of his own power to direct his life into whatever path he wanted. There were six cigarettes left in his packet and he lit one and smoked it with a decadent pleasure, knowing it to be his last. The rest he threw in the fire.

An hour later he decided to go to bed, partly to enjoy the luxury of a mattress and pillows and partly because he had no cigarettes left. Not long after he fell asleep he had another terrible nightmare. They were becoming more frequent and more vivid. Now that he felt safe from the world outside he was being attacked from within his own head.

He dreamt that he was in a railway station in Rome and was waiting for someone to come off the train. All the people moving about on the platform were dressed as if they were in the school production of *Julius Caesar*. Only gradually did Cal notice that they had no eyes but instead domed seamless lids like Roman statues, yet they appeared to know where they were going. He looked across to the other side of the platform and saw Marcella dressed the same way. She had eyes that saw him, and she inclined her head

to let him know that she recognized him. She was looking down
into the tracks and Cal followed her gaze. There was a man in a
blue boiler suit lying between the lines face downwards in the shape
of a crucifix, his body pointing in the same direction as the track. His
5 wrists lay limply over each shining rail. The train was approaching
slowly, the driver hanging far out from the cab. Cal signalled
frantically to Marcella but she didn't seem interested in the plight
of the man. She smiled. Cal had to turn away as the train inched
forward. Although he did not look, he experienced himself the
10 flange of the wheel and the hawser-straight track catching the
gristle of the wrists between them. Blood fountained and gushed
from the wounds and shot high into the ceiling of the station.
The black steel girders, the curved Victorian glass roof dripped
blood-drops like the start of a thunderstorm. They japped and
15 streaked the white togas of the crowd with slashes of red. But the
crowd did not seem to mind. Cal yelled at them, he screamed and
screamed until he woke. He didn't know where he was until the
barking of one of the dogs reminded him. He was too scared to
attempt to sleep again so he sat up and ached for a cigarette.

20 The next night Marcella came to him to return his clothes.

'Come in,' said Cal, taking them from her. His shirt was still
warm from the iron.

'I've brought you some books,' she said. In her hands she held a
small wooden rack shaped like a cradle with several paperbacks on
25 it. 'I don't think a place looks furnished without books.'

'Thank you. Have a seat.' The magnesium-white flame of the
Tilley lamp created large shadows on the wall when anyone moved.
Cal put the book rack on top of the chest of drawers. Marcella sat
on the edge of a chair.

30 'Are you settling in?'

'Yes. It's great.'

There was an awkward silence. Cal coughed. The lamp made a
faint but constant hiss as it burned.

'Did you ever read the *Crime and Punishment*?' she asked.

35 'No, it was burnt in the fire.'

'Oh yes.'

Again Cal felt the silence. He frantically tried to think of something to talk about – to keep her there. She sat with her empty
hands joined tightly. She said quietly,

'At night after I've put Lucy to bed I get so depressed. I feel I've   5
just got to get out of that house.'

He wanted to put his arms round her, to apologize to her. Then
with a little surge of excitement he realized that he didn't need to
strive to keep her there. She had come of her own free will. But the
excitement died immediately. She hadn't come to *him*, she had   10
come to get away from something. It would have been the same
no matter who lived in the cottage. Cal raked the fire and put
another block on it.

'I can't stand to hear Grandad coughing. I hate watching people
suffer. I get so annoyed with them. I'd have made a terrible nurse.'   15

'You put a good patch on me,' said Cal. She smiled and
unclenched her hands. Outside the wind threshed the trees.

'I think it would have been better for him to have died at the
time. This way he is half alive and creates misery for everybody
around him. He was such an active man for his age.'   20

'Is there any way I can help?'

'No,' she said. Her eyes became glassy and she tucked her chin
into her neck. He heard her sniffle and went over to touch her
shoulder with his hand. She struggled to find a handkerchief in her
pocket and blew her nose surprisingly loudly.   25

'I'm so callous it worries me sometimes. Here I am crying and
I'm crying for myself. Sometimes I think – they're not related to
me. Why should any of it be *my* responsibility? There are days
when I just want to take Lucy and go.'

'Why don't you?'   30

'I don't know. Perhaps I will do a disappearing trick one day.
Everything's happened so quickly. Mrs Morton doesn't exactly
help. She's not the easiest to live with. She's got Parkinson's
disease. It's not too bad now but it will get worse and she knows
it. I feel it's a great pity for both of them. Robert was an only   35
child.'

Cal

Cal took his hand from her shoulder because it felt awkward and sat down on the edge of the hearth at her feet.

'That was probably the main reason why I went out to work – to get out of that house. It was a kind of compromise. I said I'd go on living here provided they allowed me to get out to a job.'

'I wish there was some way I could help.'

'You're listening to me. That helps.' She stood up abruptly. 'But now I must go.'

'Are you sure you're all right?'

'I'm fine now.'

'A cup of tea or something?'

'What's the something?'

'Nothing.'

She reached out her hand and touched his arm through the sleeve of his shirt and smiled weakly.

'Thanks, Cal. Oh, that was the other thing.'

'What?'

'Do you want a lift to mass on Sunday?'

'I hadn't thought that far ahead.'

But he said yes. He saw her to the door and watched her running through the night, her hands in her pockets, her head down into the wind. When he came back in he stood there patting each pocket in turn looking for his cigarettes until he remembered that he no longer smoked. He walked to the Stray Inn to buy himself a packet, cursing himself all the way in made-up French.

On Sunday she allowed Lucy to sound the horn and Cal came running to the lane. Without saying anything he knew that he should not sit with them in church. He was also wary of being seen so he sat well away from the back where all the 'boys' were gathered round the door. It was unlikely that Crilly would come this far to mass but he might have friends.

Going back, she asked him if he liked the church. He said that it was too clean and bright – too much like a supermarket.

'What do you think of the mural?'

'What?'

'The crucifixion.'

It was in keeping with the cleanness of the church; everything was simplified, ruled black lines, pastel colours.

'It's all right.'

'Oh, Cal, I think it's awful. It's deodorized.'

Cal shrugged. He was always getting things wrong. She said,   5

'We went on a school trip down the Rhine one summer and I saw a crucifixion that made all others pale for me.'

'The things people get up to on school trips.'

'No, be serious. It was a painting. And it was the first thing like that which had any effect on me. It was by a man called Grünewald.   10 Do you know the one?' Cal said he didn't. 'I stood and stared at it for so long the teachers lost me and had to come back for me. The pain in it is terrible. Not like our Walt Disney mural. Are you interested in painting?'

'I liked looking at the art books in school. Everybody said I was   15 looking at the nudes.' From the back seat Lucy said.

'Noods, noods.' Marcella looked over her shoulder and laughed. In the lane with the engine running she told Cal that she would pick him up for mass every Sunday, if he wanted, and give him a lift after the library if he was going in to see his father.   20

One wet Thursday night Cal took a set of clean clothes in a polythene bag and asked Dunlop for a lift into town. The man muttered and grudgingly said OK Cal felt Dunlop was mad about the way he had managed to insinuate himself into the cottage. Because this was a one-off occasion Dunlop spoke his mind. The   25 de-mister in the car had broken and Dunlop kept swabbing a clear porthole on the windscreen. Cal could see the rain slanting across the beams of the undipped headlights.

'This whole bloody business would be cleared up overnight if they brought back hanging. If only they would give the Army a bit   30 of freedom. But no, they can't do this or they can't do that or they'll find *themselves* up in court. Even a rat, Cal, will suck eggs in the presence of a chain dog. Let the chain off. Beat the shite out of the bastards.'

'But how do you know who they are?'   35

'They know damn well. And even if they do tramp on a few innocent toes, isn't it better that way than giving the IRA the freedom of the country? Root them out, that's what I say.' He groped again for his rag to wipe the windscreen. Cal felt himself
5 shrug in the dark.

'Do you know what I'd do if I was in charge?' said Dunlop. He waited until Cal was forced to say no. 'Long Kesh is full of known IRA prisoners, isn't it?' Again he waited until Cal replied, to give the appearance of logical steps in his argument. 'Well, every time
10 a policeman or soldier is shot I would put *two* of those bastards up against the wall and blow their brains out.'

'That's nice.'

'This is a war, son. I don't think you understand that. Sometimes I think Hitler had the right idea. He had the wrong cause, mind
15 you, but he knew how to fight a war. What harm did Robert Morton ever do anybody? A nicer man you couldn't meet and now he's dead.'

'Would you do the same to the Loyalist prisoners every time a Catholic was murdered?'

20 'Maybe. But it's not the same thing. That's the lunatic fringe. They get mad seeing good men shot down day after day. So would you. When you're fed up shadow-boxing you sometimes turn and hit the referee.'

'What's so terrible about a united Ireland anyway? One island,
25 one country.'

'And be ruled from Rome? A state told what to do by priests and nuns. Sheer voodoo, Cal. Mumbo-jumbo. Ulstermen would die rather than live under the yoke of Roman Catholicism. Not an inch. It's a good saying.'

30 Cal leaned forward and wiped his half of the windscreen clear with back of his hand.

'I'm serious, Cal. I would *die* rather than let that happen.'

Cal believed him and settled down to silence.

 The minute Cal saw his father he knew there had been a terrible
35 change in him. The man had aged twenty years in a couple of

weeks. He sat in Dermot Ryan's chair, his arms lying limply on the arm-rests. The flesh of his face had almost disappeared and what was left seemed to have slipped and sagged. He did not even smile when Cal came in.

'How are you, Shamie?'   5

'Not so good.'

'What's up?'

'Ach, I don't know. I don't know whether I'm coming or going.' He began to cry, his face tight like a fist. 'I never knew how much I loved that house, that garden.'   10

Cal stood, not knowing what to do. Dermot Ryan was washing up some dishes in the kitchenette. Cal left his father sobbing.

'How long has this been going on?' he asked Dermot.

'It started just a couple of days after the house went up. He's driving me round the bend.'   15

'Is he like this all the time?'

'Mostly.'

'Has he been to a doctor?'

'He says he's not sick. He goes to his work every day.'

Cal went out to his father.   20

'Shamie, you're a sick man. Go to the doctor. It's free.'

'I know what he'll say,' said Shamie. Even his voice had changed, had lost all its strength. It wavered like the voice of an old woman feeling sorry for herself. 'Snap out of it, he'll say, but I can't. I've lost interest in everything, Cal.'   25

'He'll give you pills, make you feel better. Any word of them housing you?'

'No. I think they'll wait until I'm a pensioner and then they'll tell me I can stay here.' He had stopped crying.

'You see, you're making jokes already,' said Cal. 'Go to the   30 doctor tomorrow, will you?'

'What'll I tell him is wrong with me?'

'Say you're depressed.'

'Who isn't, these days.'

'Will you go? For me?'   35

Shamie nodded abjectly. Cal asked Dermot if he could have a

bath and offered money for heating the water, but Dermot said he wouldn't take it. Cal gave his father a cigarette and they smoked together. Cal asked him,

'How are things at work?'

5 'Same as ever.'

'Do you see Crilly?'

'Every time I see him he wants to know where you are. And that doesn't help, Cal. I'm worried about you.'

'What did you tell him?'

10 'Nothing. I don't know a thing. Neither I do. Where are you, Cal?'

'It's better kept quiet. I don't particularly want to see Crilly at the moment.'

Ash fell off the end of Shamie's cigarette but he did not bother
15 to brush it from his lap.

'Don't tell him you saw me tonight.'

'There was also a man called here looking for you,' said Dermot. 'What was his name, now? Hetherington or something. A school teacher with glasses.'

20 'Skeffington?'

'That's him. A very nice man.'

In the bathroom Cal trimmed round his black beard with Dermot's razor. It was probably the first time in weeks he had seen a mirror and he was surprised at himself. He thought the beard
25 suited him. People had always said that he was a good-looking boy and now, seeing himself, he could almost believe them. He must take after his mother because Shamie was no oil painting.

Lying in the bath he worried about his father. He would have to risk it and come back and see him more often. The Valium might
30 help, if Shamie were to go to the doctor's. He wondered how many people had cracked up like Shamie as a result of the troubles. Shaking remnants of themselves. The bastards who had burned them out would rejoice if they knew they had broken Shamie's spirit as well. Cal put on his clean clothes, combed his wet hair and
35 felt guiltily good. He had a cup of tea with the two old men before he left with his bag full of dirty washing.

'When will I see you again?' asked Shamie.

'Soon. But you go to the doctor tomorrow, you hear?'

'Yes,' said Shamie. He began to cry again silently. 'I will. I can't put up with this much longer.'

Cal left, tight-lipped and worried. He kept to the side streets and put up the hood of his anorak. Although it was raining he didn't dare go in and stand in the brightness of the library with its plate-glass windows. He waited for Marcella to turn out the lights and lock up before he moved out of the shadows.

'Oh, there you are,' she said. 'I thought you weren't coming.'

'Sorry I'm late but my father wasn't well.'

He told her of the change in Shamie as they walked to the car. She said she knew exactly how he felt. The rain had stopped and the sky was becoming clear of cloud.

She drove and Cal watched her watching the road. He retained enough memory of Shamie's misery to feel guilty about being happy with her. He told himself his father would get over it when he went to the doctor. There was no sense in worrying. He saw her ringed hand move the car smoothly through its gears. Although he was dying for a cigarette he controlled himself, not wanting to pollute the atmosphere which was sweet with her perfume. She was quiet and Cal asked her why. She said it was the thought of going back to the house without Lucy awake to greet her.

'Would you like to go for a drink?' Cal asked.

At first she refused, saying that she was expected home soon after the library closed. She didn't have to be home but they would worry if she was late. Then she relented, saying to hell, she would have time for a quick one.

They drove to the Stray Inn and Cal thought how well she fitted her surroundings, hugging her sheepskin jacket around her even though they were near the artificial log fire which flapped yellow flames. She said she would drink a Martini and Cal made a mental note to get a bottle for the cottage. He himself had a pint and a whiskey. She said 'Cheers' and he '*Slainte*'.

'I feel guilty doing this – like skipping school,' she said.

'Why?'

'Mrs Morton treats me like a schoolgirl, I suppose. I fight back but she always has the last word.'

'She's an odd woman.'

'You can say that again. You don't know the half of it.'

5 'Why did she take me on?'

'I don't know. They always thought of themselves as liberal Protestants – they didn't even object too much to Robert marrying me. As a matter of fact the big fight there was with *my* parents.' She began to mimic: '"Why for in Catholic Ireland you want to 10 marry a Protestant boy?" Then after Robert was killed it was so typical of his mother to want to employ a Catholic. To prove to the world that she was not bigoted.'

Marcella had a glass in front of her with just a slice of lemon in it.

15 'God, that was quick,' said Cal and tried to buy her another but she insisted that it was her round.

'Did you ever mitch school?' he asked.

'No. But I think this is what it would feel like.'

'I'll bet you were a genius at school.'

20 Marcella denied it, but probing her further he found out that she had been to university in Glasgow to do a library course. She had worked for a year and then married. She had been married for over five years before Robert was killed. Cal calculated a rough age for her and found there was an impossible nine years' difference 25 between them. She looked at him with her lovely eyes and seemed to guess what he was thinking.

'You are good for me, Cal. You make me feel younger. Really, I should get out a bit more.'

Cal was on the point of asking her to come out with him but 30 couldn't find the words. She looked up at the clock.

'Look at the time,' she said, lifting her bag.

'Take it easy. You're a big grown-up person. Let your hair down for a change.'

'It's funny you should say that. Lucy's favourite story at the 35 minute is Rapunzel. I have to read it to her every night. Do you know it?'

'No.'

'It's about Rapunzel being trapped in a tower and the only way her lover can get in is by climbing up this enormous pigtail she has. He arrives every night and shouts,' she cupped her hand to the side of her mouth, ' "Rapunzel, Rapunzel, let down your hair." Every time I read it I think it means – go daft, do something wild, for God's sake. I say to myself, that's me.'

'Why don't you?'

'There's nothing worse than the sight of people *trying* to enjoy themselves. For years I watched them in Portstewart: families with their plastic macs and their fixed grins. Really, Cal, we'd better go.'

In the dark car park, away from the lights of the pub, Marcella looked up at the clear sky. They had taken their drinks so quickly that both of them felt heady.

'What a beautiful night it is now,' she said. 'It's the sort of night you could lie on your back and count the stars.'

Cal looked up. 'And not worry whether you got it right or not.'

She laughed at his silliness almost the whole way home. Cal said that with two Martinis she made a great audience.

The good weather held and on Saturday afternoon it was cold sunshine in a winter-blue sky. The trees were nearly bare now and outside starlings made electric chirps and a noise that Cal could only think of as a whistled 'phew'. He was crouched at the window of the cottage replacing the hardboard with glass and putty when he heard voices. Marcella's distinctly, a child's less so. He stopped working to listen. They were coming the long way round past the brambled wall and he heard Marcella's mothering talk, her crooning seriousness. Lucy said something and made her laugh. Cal looked out from the broken pane and saw the child balanced on the wall and the mother, arms outstretched, waiting for her to jump. When she did Marcella whirled her round once and set her on the ground. They held hands and began to pick their way through the brambles, still talking to one another. They were not yet aware of Cal and they stopped. Marcella reached out and

pressed Lucy's nose with her index finger and made a sound like a buzzer. The child laughed, a high-pitched giggle. Cal felt the same way as he had on the roof that night outside the bathroom window. This was something he shouldn't see, should have no part of. He
5 turned away from the window and sat down, the pane of glass in his hands. It was remarkable how clear it was, yet the cut sides were dark green. The difference between a bucket of sea and the sea itself.

'Cal?' Marcella's voice spoke from the empty window frame and
10 then her head poked through. 'Are you decent?'

'I try to be,' said Cal.

'Cal?' The child's voice squeaked in imitation of her mother's as she was lifted to put her head through the other gap.

'Hiya,' said Cal.

15 'It's a lovely day. Are you too busy to gather some blackberries?'

'Give me a minute until I putty these windows in.'

'What strange grammar.'

'What do you mean?'

'You "put" things in, not "putty" them in.'

20 'It's my coarse accent and your ignorance about windows.'

Lucy smelt the stuff and said,

'Stinky-poo.'

'I'll get some containers and I'll see you at the house.'

'OK'

25 And they walked away, Marcella bending at the waist, listening to what her child had to say, until their voices disappeared behind the wall.

They went over the fields to a long lane which separated the Mortons' farm from its neighbour. The child was sufficiently used
30 to Cal now and walked between them, holding a hand of each. In her other hand Marcella carried a Tupperware box. Lucy sometimes lifted her feet and they carried her like a laughing frog.

'This is the kind of day I love,' said Marcella. 'Crisp. It's as if you're seeing everything through a lens.' Cal nodded. The view
35 when they reached the top of the field stretched for miles.

'Isn't this place beautiful?' Again Cal nodded. 'You are just agreeing with me. Does looking at that not do something for you?' The countryside, a deep winter green, fell away to the blue mountains of Slieve Gallon. It was crossed by dark random lines of trees and hedges. Here and there a red barn or a white gable stood out and far off a window shone like a diamond. Cows all facing in the same direction grazed their way across a field.

'Not really. I was born here. I've looked at it all my life,' said Cal. 'It's too much like a growing factory. It's all so much money. I like the look of Donegal where nothing grows. Beaches, bogs and mountains.'

He climbed a gate and took the child from Marcella's hands, then held out his hand to her as she climbed over. There was a little vibration of strain as she jumped down.

'I'd like to go and live in Italy,' she said.

'Because of the troubles?'

'No, not really that. It's just such a marvellous place.'

'There's no place like Rome,' he said but she ignored it.

'The heat, the sounds, the smells – everything is different. Have you ever been?'

'No, but I have been to Croke Park in Dublin for the All-Ireland.'

She smiled and opened the Tupperware box and took another box from inside it. She gave the biggest one to Cal. She opened the next one and took a smaller box from that.

'How many have you in there?'

'That's the lot.' She gave the smallest box to Lucy and they began to pick from the untidy scribble of briars along the lane. The first berries dropped hollowly on to the bottom of Cal's container. They browsed like a family of animals along the bushes, staying close together.

'The Italians are very like the Irish in some ways. The friendliness, the religion thing, the family – the way they kill each other. Why is it that people who have a reputation for hospitality are also the most violent?'

'Search me.'

'Glasgow people are so warm – so are the Mafia. But the English are cold fish and yet you never feel threatened in London.'

'That's because they're all over here wearing uniforms and beating the shite out of us.'

'You're very anti-British.'

'Yes.'

5   'I thought I was detached from the whole thing. Being called D'Agostino kind of distances you from it. But when somebody kills your husband you're involved whether you like it or not. What about you?'

'I would like to see a united Ireland, but I haven't decided the
10 best way to go about it yet.'

'I feel sorry for it.'

'What?'

'Ireland. It's like a child. It's only concerned with the past and the present. The future has ceased to exist for it.'

15   'It will only have a future when the British leave.'

Tha backs of their hands became peppered with thorns and their fingertips coloured purple. Lucy had gathered three or four hard green knots of berries so Cal secretly poured the contents of his half-full container into the child's. The biggest berries when
20 touched inevitably seemed to fall down into the tangles of the bush. They gathered for half an hour, talking and joking. The happier Cal felt, the sadder he became. He wanted to confess to her, to weep and be forgiven. He saw the scene in his mind of her holding him, comforting him; he saw the scene as he knew it would be in
25 reality and it horrified him.

'Did you ever do anything – really bad?' he asked. She wrinkled up her face and said.

'Yes, I've just pricked my finger.' She sucked it and held it out for him to see the bright bead of blood.

30   'Maybe I shouldn't ask a woman that question.'

'No. It's all right.' She thought for a moment, still sucking her finger. 'Yes, lots of things.'

'They couldn't be all that bad then. For instance?'

She sat down on a part of the stone wall that was free of brambles.
35 Lucy was talking to herself farther up the lane.

'There was a boy once who made a date with me.' She spoke

slowly as if it was important to her. 'This was in Portstewart. I liked
him, I suppose, because he was very shy. I told some of my friends
and they absolutely ridiculed him. The girls who knew best fell
about laughing and because of that I stood him up. I think that
was bad – to go with the herd.' She leaned forward, picking berries 5
within her reach. Cal nodded. It was worse than he thought. The
slightness of her sin made his confession impossible.

'And I'm terrible with Lucy,' she said, looking again to check
her pricked finger. 'So selfish. What about you, have you done
anything really bad?' 10

'Yes.' He took a deep breath. She stopped picking and waited,
her eyes on him. 'The usual,' he said.

'What's that?'

'Sins of the flesh.'

'Naughty – not bad.' 15

'We beat a guy up once – in the school toilet. I felt bad about
that afterwards. Two to one.'

It was as if he was slipping down a wall of ice, trying to dig in
with his fingernails but, rather than hold, they bent. Lucy began to
whinge and came towards her mother. Marcella said. 20

'It's back to violence again. It frightens me. That people should
want physically to hurt one another. I suppose at school it's the
thing to do – young men of the species showing off to become the
leader of the herd – but you would think people would grow up.'

'Yes.' He was at the bottom of a gully, buried in an avalanche of 25
his own making. Lucy had set her container down and was clinging
on to Marcella's leg, trying to interrupt her by whining.

'She's bored, poor thing. I think we'd better go. We've enough
for about five pots of jelly.'

'Is that all?' said Cal. 'It's not worth it.' 30

'Wait until you taste it. Come along, Lucy.'

The child stood by the wall pouting. Marcella walked on slowly.
She put out her hand behind her and took Cal's hand in hers. It
was an unthinking gesture and the touch only lasted for a second
before she realized. She let go of him and seemed embarrassed. 35

'I'm sorry, Cal, I was thinking of the child.'

'It was nice,' said Cal and he was able to meet her eyes and hold them until Lucy came running. They put all the child's berries in the largest box in case they should spill.

Suddenly the air was ripped apart by an explosion. Cal felt the
5 shock-wave of it beat through him like the thump of a drum. Marcella screamed and ducked, protecting the child who set up an unmerciful crying.

'Jesus, what's that?'

Marcella lifted Lucy and hugged her. Cal looked all around.
10 Three or four fields away he saw a plume of white drifting smoke.

'I'd better go and see,' he said.

Marcella in a voice that shook said that she would go back to the house with Lucy.

'Be careful, Cal,' she called after him.

15 He climbed a gate and ran awkwardly across stubble. He was breathless by the time he reached the field where he had seen the smoke. He waited and watched. The cows had all run up to the far end of the field but had started grazing again. He saw something lying in the grass near the gate. At first he thought it was a cow. He
20 cautiously came out of the hedge and walked towards it. It was half a cow – udders, hindquarters with muscles red-raw and still jigging. He froze, frightened of stepping on another mine. He looked around him and saw something red, high on a tree in the hedge. He narrowed his eyes and recognized one of the Preacher's red tin
25 plaques.

'The Kingdom of God is within You.'

There was very little blood on the grass. He turned away, hoping not to find the rest of the beast, and started to walk back towards the Mortons' place. The cows were Friesians and as he passed
30 them he saw the white panels of their hides japped with blood. He heard them pull and tug and munch. He vomited twice in the muddy ditch before he had the strength to jump it.

Chapter Five

Two pots of bramble jelly, neatly dated, stood on Cal's shelf for six weeks before he could bear to open one. The other he took to Shamie. His father continued to be depressed and had stopped work. He sat for most of the day in Dermot's armchair shakily smoking and staring through the window at the grey back-yard wall. Cal found him difficult to talk to. If he showed the slightest irritation at the way his father was behaving Shamie broke down in tears. Coming away from Dermot's place one day, he had to duck into a garden to avoid meeting Crilly's mother. After that he decided not to risk a visit for a while.

Now that the weather had turned to wind and rain he had little opportunity or excuse to see Marcella. Once or twice he called at the kitchen door on the pretext of borrowing something but it was always Mrs Morton who dealt with him. After tea one night he was aware of flickering lights on the wall of his room. He had lost all track of the time of year and only when he looked out and saw cascades of crimson sparks did he remember that it was Hallowe'en. He went up to the farmhouse to join in with Mrs Morton, Marcella and her child. Rockets whirred and hissed into the dark and one expensive one burst at its zenith into a fountain of white which momentarily brightened the yard. The three faces were lit in awe but the only one Cal looked at was Marcella's. Behind her at a downstairs window he could not avoid seeing Mr Morton's pallid face, watching. The next day, crossing the yard, Cal stepped on the charred stick and burnt-out tube of a rocket embedded in the mud.

The only time he was sure of seeing Marcella was on Sunday mornings when she gave him a lift to mass. In the car she talked as if

she was trying to cram everything into the short time. Cal willed her to drive slowly, willed Lucy to curl up and go to sleep on the back seat. Sometimes she parked in the lane at the cottage and told Lucy to run home while she finished what she was saying. Cal loved
5 these moments, holding the car door half open pretending he wanted out, listening to her. One Sunday she talked for a full fifteen minutes with the engine running. She would touch his arm as she made a point and when he cracked a joke she would punch him playfully on the shoulder. Then one morning, as if it was a secret,
10 she told him that her mother-in-law was going away for a week.

'Where?'

'To Belfast. Grandad has to have another operation on his lungs and she's staying with friends to be near him.'

'And who'll mind Lucy when you're at work?'

15 She smiled at him asking the question.

'That's all arranged. Mrs Mc Glinchy in town. It's not everyone who would think of a thing like that.'

Cal was embarrassed at the praise and the warm stare she gave him.

20 It was lunchtime and Cal was having a smoke. He watched the ambulance arrive and old Mr Morton being wheeled out in a chair. Mrs Morton in her overcoat and carrying a suitcase fussed around the ambulance men, then climbed into the back beside her husband. They drove off, leaving the house empty.

25 At three Dunlop and Cal were having a cup of tea in the farmhouse kitchen when Dunlop said.

'I think we could knock off early today. What do you say, Cal?'

'There's not much to do, is there?'

'No.'

30 Dunlop left Cal in the kitchen pouring himself another cup of tea.

'Don't forget to pull the door after you. It's on the snib.'

Cal heard Cyril's engine start and fade into the distance. Here he was in Marcella's home. In the corner the fridge hummed. The
35 thermostat cut out and it shuddered to a stop. The silence of the

house was uncanny. He longed for Marcella to come back, ached to tell her of his love but knew that it could never become a reality. To speak of love he knew there had to be openness and truth. He was a lie to her constantly because of what he had done. What he got from her he had to steal. Her sincerity he was repaying with forgeries. He was obsessed with her – couldn't get close enough to her. He shut his eyes and remembered her lifting arm and tilted breast in the bathroom, the touch of her haunch in church, the way she had held his hand by mistake and how she had looked long and hard into his eyes afterwards. But she would probably laugh uproariously in her inimitable way if he gave the slightest hint that he loved her. Or even worse, say something sincere like she was flattered. He imagined her as the Sleeping Beauty in a drugged coma and how he would kiss her and touch her without her responding. How he would cup her cotton blouse against her breast and feel the warmth of her living. She would be displayed for him so that he could look at and touch any part of her. And she would not know it was he, Cal, who was the slayer of her husband. He opened his eyes. It was still light outside. Sometimes in her presence he felt like Quasimodo – as if the ugliness of what he had done showed in his face. The brand in the middle of his forehead would never disappear and seemed to throb when she was near. Alone, now, he relaxed into his ugliness. To hell, why not? If he could not take her like Sleeping Beauty then he could ravish the things which surrounded her. His impotence was something he could smell and touch.

He got up and went into the hallway and stood listening. A grandfather clock ticked slow and stately. He moved up the carpeted stairs and decided which was her room to the front of the house. The landing was dark but when he opened the door a rectangle of light brightened the wall behind him. The sun had come out from behind cloud and was lying just above the horizon, flooding the room with a wintry yellowness. It *was* her room. Several pairs of Scholls were set in a neat line by the window. There was a double bed made up with precision against one wall. He went over to it and touched the pillow nearest the window. He

didn't know why but he was sure it was the pillow she used. He put his face to it and smelt her perfume. Although he knew there was no one in the house he walked on tiptoe to her dressing table with its array of make-up bottles. He caught sight of himself in the
5 mirror and immediately turned away. Why did he do things like this? By trying to get closer to her he was putting another obstacle in his way. Could he ever admit that he had snooped in her bedroom? Her lemon dressing-gown had been flung over a basket-work chair and he felt its towelling stuff between his fingers. As he
10 lifted it he saw, curled beneath it, her brassière. He traced the delicate lace work of it, saw as he lifted it its cups form the exquisite empty shape of her breasts. Beneath, on the seat of the chair, her panties lay in a discarded double loop. He imagined her careless-ness as she undressed the previous night, the way she ignored them
15 as she rushed to dress for work that morning and he buried his face in them, on the verge of tears. He explored her wardrobe with its ranks of dresses and its floor covered untidily with shoes – spikes of high heels with the under-arch the colour of new leather, the soles blackened by use. There was a pair not much more than a
20 few golden straps. Then he glimpsed himself in the full length mirror on the inside of the door and, in disgust, closed it, swinging himself out of sight. By the window was a desk littered with books and papers. The sun touched the hill away over by Slieve Gallon but was still bright, making the room a butter yellow. He looked at
25 some of the titles on the spines of the books. He picked one up and spun the pages past with his thumb. There was writing on the first page. In dashed blue Biro it said, 'To Marcella with love instead of the dinner. Robert.' He set it down carefully in exactly the same position. There were two drawers in the desk and pulling open the
30 first one he found it full of felt-tipped pens, paper clips and drawing pins. In the second he found a fat navy blue book, its cover grained like wood. On the first page he read,

This book is the property of
Marcella D'Agostino, 4A,
35 Portstewart Convent

He turned the page over and saw in large red letters PRIVATE. The next page was full of closely written backhand. Convent writing. It was neatly dated August 4th, 1962. When she wrote it she was younger than he was now. He read some of it but could not make head or tail of it. 5

Bernadette and I were in Sister Assumpta's room. Everything is PR and we thought it rab-ding. She gave us orange juice and spoke in such an Ardviewetic voice – the whole thing was very Jonathan.

He flicked through, looking at the dates before each entry. The deeper into the book he got, the shorter the entries became. He 10 wondered if there was anything about him in it and in excitement looked for the last written page. But it was dated well over a year ago. He read some of the last entries.

Sunday March 16th

Today the weather was bright, crisp and springlike. We went up Slieve 15 Gallon. Huge landscape to be seen from the top. Most of Lough Neagh and the surrounding countryside bright but with areas of cloud shadow drifting across. Robert, as usual, sat in the car and read the papers. I play a game with Lucy – of listening. We stand completely quiet and identify the sounds that we hear. On the mountain total silence – not even a bird 20 – except for the slight blustering of the wind past our ears. In the woods yesterday we heard a variety of songbirds, a distant dog, crows, cars on the road. Lucy can name most of them. How different at night when Robert took me to the Foresters' Club. The Country and Western band is shat-teringly loud – no conversation takes place. People sit isolated in the din, 25 filling themselves with drink. They are all ugly with ugly emotions. Robert is no better. I had to drive home.

He continued to skip backwards through the pages.

Fri Nov. 22

Last night 19 people died and 200 were injured in Birmingham. A slaying 30 of total innocents – not even the callous excuse of a pub frequented by soldiers. I thought we would never reach the day of atrocities equivalent

to the Arab/Israeli unpleasantness. I am deeply ashamed of my country. From now on I think I will say I am an Italian. Violence is a bit like antibodies. Small doses build up until you can reject and be immune to the most horrific events. As yet the people of Birmingham have no anti-
5 bodies and it must be terrible for them to bear.

Saturday July 12th

Went to see the Orangemen's parade today. I am not a bigot but they disgust me with their hypocrisy. The parade led by Evangelists screaming about sin and death and damnation. The swaggering bands follow and
10 animality is very near the surface. Dervishes. It has been called 'the last folk festival in Europe'. This is true because they really believe in what they march for. It is so negative. They march against Rome and Popery. Their hatred is not hypocritical. Their banners are nice – colourful and crude. The huge drums are thumped so hard they vibrate in your body
15 like an external heart after sprinting. The air around the procession pulses like blood in fear. Saw Cyril Dunlop, strutting like a rooster. He's a big man but a wee coat fits him.

It became too dark to read and Cal did not want to risk turning on the light. Marcella's room could be seen from the road and she
20 was due back at any minute. He buried his face in her pillow, then patted it back to plumpness and left. In the kitchen he washed up the cups and tidied the mess that they'd left behind. Car headlights swung into the yard and flared at the kitchen window. He heard the child's voice and the banging of car doors. He opened the
25 kitchen door for them and Marcella came in with a box of groceries.

'Let me carry that,' said Cal.

'No, the heavy one is in the car. Will you get that for me?' He carried in the other box and set it on the draining board. Now Marcella had time to smile at him. Lucy had run off to the other
30 room.

'It'll be funny to have the house all to myself.' She gave a loud whoop and at the same time kept her face straight. Cal laughed.

'Who's all the food for then?'

'It's the beginning of my laying things in for Christmas.'

'I'll be off.'

'Oh Cal, do you like eating Italian?'

'I don't know. I don't think I ever have.'

'While the ancients are away I'm going to treat myself. They have nothing but Irish stew and mince. Why don't you come up here and eat?'

He stammered a little and then said he would.

'I hate eating on my own,' said Marcella. 'About eight o'clock, after I have shovelled the sausages and beans into this one.'

Lucy had come back in and put one arm round her mother's leg.

'OK, thanks,' said Cal.

He went home – he had learned to call the cottage that now – and sorted through the money on his mantelpiece. He walked the two miles to the Stray Inn and bought a bottle of wine and could only afford a half bottle of whiskey. When the barman asked him which particular wine he wanted Cal said red. The barman waved his hand vaguely at the shelf of wines and said,

'What's it for, sir? Drinking?'

Cal rolled about laughing and asked the barman to give him any one at his price. His step was quick and light on the way back and yet he was nervous that he might not be able to talk to her for such a long time.

He stripped to the waist and washed himself at the jaw-box, shivering and roaring when the cold water touched beneath his arms. He dressed in a clean shirt, clean socks and chose the best pair of shoes and trousers. He was ready too early and had to sit on the bed and smoke until eight.

When he went up to the house Marcella yelled 'Come in' as he knocked on the door. She was wearing an apron but beneath Cal saw that she was dressed up. A maroon skirt and maroon tights, and a white broderie anglaise blouse that fastened high at her throat. She was dashing about the kitchen juggling a casserole dish in her oven gloves.

'Be right with you,' she said. Cal set his bottles on the table. She turned to him, taking off her apron and smiling. 'Now, what would you like to drink?' Then she saw Cal's contribution wrapped in flame-coloured twists of tissue paper. 'Oh, Cal, you shouldn't have. I had already got some wine. That's very kind of you.'

Cal said that he would like to try a Martini. She looked lovely. It was as if she had prepared for him coming. Her hair was different and she seemed to have different, or more, make-up on. Cal sat down at the table and told her what the barman had said about the wine. 'What's it for, sir? Drinking?'

Marcella poured two Martinis and added ice and lemon. Cal clowned around, drinking his with his little finger sticking out, brushing his long hair back extravagantly.

'It tastes OK,' he said. 'Not at all like Guinness.'

She smiled and stood drinking hers with her back to the heat of the oven.

'It smells good,' said Cal. 'Can I set the table or anything?'

'My dear boy, it's already set. You don't think we're going to eat in here?' She was full of excitement and jokiness and when they finally did sit down in the candle-lit dining room she said.

'Isn't this great? Like lovers.'

He wished she hadn't said that. To say it out loud meant that it was the last thing in her mind. He was nervous about eating in front of her but she put him at his ease with her manner.

'*Minestrone*,' she announced, coming in with two plates of soup, 'Tinned. But Baxter's, I'll have you know, nothing common. We used to have a name for common things when we were at school. PR, we called them. Plasticky Rubbish.'

'Yes, I know.'

'How do you know? That was a secret between Bernadette and me.'

'I mean, I know what you mean.'

She served *spaghetti alla carbonara* and had to teach him not to be polite when eating it, told him to bite off mouthfuls and let them fall back on the plate. In Italy napkins were not just an extra. They drank Cal's bottle of wine with the *carbonara* and opened another for her *costolette di vitello alla modenese*.

'What in the name of God is that?'

'Veal and ham and cheese.'

'Veal?'

'I know, isn't it awful of us?'

'When a calf is too big to be born, do you know what the vet does?'

'No. Nor do I want to.'

'He gets a . . .'

'Please, Cal, not now. Don't tell me.' She lifted the bottle. 'More wine?'

Cal put his hand over his glass and told her to take it easy. He had drunk two glasses to her one. It occurred to him that if he got drunk his guard would drop and he might say something he would regret. Drink loosened his tongue and problems tended to become insignificant. I'm very sorry but I helped kill your husband last year. Pass the salt, please. He snorted into his glass.

'What are you laughing at?'

'Nothing.'

'Cal, I think you *are* drunk.'

The candles were becoming varicose with melted wax. Their light seemed to soften and shade her face so that she looked younger. They had crème caramel 'from the Spar'.

'No more like the real thing than I to Hercules,' she said.

Then they moved to the other room for coffee in front of the fire. She did not sit on the chair but on the rug, turning the side of her face to him. He sat in the armchair facing the television. There was a mushroom-shaped lamp on top of it throwing light down on to a photograph of her husband. It wasn't a portrait but an enlargement of a snapshot of him in his RUC Reserve uniform. He was leaning against a door frame with his face in a fixed smile. Cal continued to talk but the picture was an irritant to him and he kept losing the thread of what he was saying. Again and again his eyes strayed back to it. Marcella turned round to see what he was looking at.

'That's not my doing,' she said.

'What?' said Cal, looking away.

'The photograph. His mother wanted it and she paid for it. I don't know why but I don't approve of that sort of thing. I've never been to his grave since the day of the funeral.' She gave a shudder as if she were cold. 'But let's not talk about that.'

'OK,' said Cal, and he thought he nodded his head a little too pointedly.

'Did you ever read any of the books I gave you?'

'No, but I started one. I wasn't enjoying it so I stopped.' He felt he was hurting her by saying it.

'That's fair enough. Which one?' Cal tried to recall. He felt a flutter of examination nerves and said,

'It was something about a deaf-mute bloke in America.'

'Carson McCullers?'

'Aye, him. I think.'

'Her. And you didn't like it?'

'It was odd. Maybe I'll try again.'

'Yes do, Cal. It's really good when you get into it.'

He got up and moved to sit on the sofa. She said,

'It must really annoy you.'

'What?'

'That picture.'

'No. I just hate facing the TV when it's off. I keep wanting to watch it.'

She paused and gathered her knees into her arms. Cal lit a cigarette and was surprised when she asked him for one.

'I can smoke occasionally after a nice meal.'

'You're a very disciplined person, Marcella.'

'Robert taught me that.'

'Yes, that meal was magico,' said Cal. 'That's Italian for magic.' She leaned back and rested her elbow on his knee. He put his heel on the ground to stop her noticing the shake in his leg. She looked strange with a cigarette – like a film star in an old movie.

'Thanks for coming,' she said. 'It's good to have you here – without them. It makes me feel human again to entertain.'

'I'll help out any time.'

'Sometimes I feel very isolated out here. After Robert was killed I suddenly found I had no friends. Oh yes, they called and did everything they could for me for a couple of months. But they were all *his* friends. Then they just faded. I found I had little in common with them. That was one reason I went out to work again. Just to meet people.' She changed her position, moving closer to his knee, and sat cross-legged like a tailor, facing the fire and sipping her coffee. Cal imagined her thighs open to the heat of the fire. He glanced sideways and saw that the picture of Robert still had its fixed smile. She went on.

'I think that's a terrible thing about marriage. You have to move away from your own home to be with your husband and leave all your friends. Then bang – you're left without anything. Do you have many friends, Cal?'

'No, not many. At school it was different.'

'Yes, everything was so much more intense. There were people there you could die for. That was the test we used to apply to people. Would you *die* for him? Or her? That was all Sister Assumpta's doing. Did you ever hear of Maria Goretti?'

'Who?'

Marcella told him about Sister Assumpta's fixation with Saint Maria Goretti and how she died rather than lose her purity to an awful man.

'And we all believed that was marvellous at the time.' She laughed and went on with her story. Maria Goretti was only twelve and this man threatened to kill her if she didn't submit to rape. But she wouldn't give in and he stabbed her to death.

'But I always thought the best part of it was at her canonization the guy who killed her, after doing twenty-seven years in prison, received communion side by side with Maria Goretti's mother. Isn't that weird? That amount of goodness. We all thought it was the mother who should have been made the saint. We used to cry at that.' She laughed and slapped Cal's knee, turning her face up to him. He wanted to bend and kiss it. The wine gave him courage. Although the room was warm he was definitely trembling. He had to flex the knot of muscle at the corner of his jaw to keep it from shivering.

'It seems terrible at my age to be nostalgic for school.'

'You're not that old,' said Cal. His voice shook and sounded hoarse. In that posture her skirt was riding up and he could see the undersides of her thighs lit by firelight.

'No, but old enough to be nostalgic. How long have you been left school?'

5   Cal pretended to think. 'Oh, it must be six or seven years now.'

He put his hand out and touched the back of her neck at the hair-line softly with his knuckles. She moved her head back saying nothing. Cal leaned over her, with a slowness which gave her enough time to turn her head away if she wanted to, and kissed her
10 mouth. And again. The second time she made a small moan. After a long time it was she who withdrew from the kiss.

'I don't think we should, Cal.'

'Why not?'

'I haven't thought about you in that way.'

15   In his mind he went through the kiss again. The moist sweetness of her breath, the infinitesimal tremor in her lips, the way she opened her teeth to him, the involuntary noise she made in her throat. Their bodies had not touched and the noise could have been one of rejection.

20   'I'm a widow. With problems. You're a boy without . . . Somebody might get hurt and regret it. I still feel guilty about Robert.' The kiss had broken the spell and she rose, saying that she'd better make a start on the dishes. Also she wanted to have a bath and she had some ironing to do.

25   Cal helped her dry the dishes, dumb with disappointment, and listened to her.

'You're putting me out,' he said.

'No, I'm not. I'm doing the sensible thing for both of us.'

Cal thought of the extra make-up, the style, the candle-lit dinner,
30 her hand on his thigh. Was that just a woman or was she leading him on?

'I'll tell you now what they do to the calves. They cut them up with cheese wire. The vet puts cheese wire inside the cow and cuts them up before they're born. Then they get born in bits.'

35   Marcella rested her weight on her arms at the sink and spoke into the basin.

'You're trying to distress me.'

'I'm sorry,' said Cal, 'but I thought you should know.'

'No you didn't. You're being childish and trying to hurt me.' She turned to him, her face creased. 'Please, Cal, don't be like that.' He fiddled with the drying-up cloth and said genuinely he was sorry.

When he was going she took his face between her hands and kissed him affectionately on the mouth.

'Cal, you're my friend. Don't be so miserable. It is the sensible thing.'

Although he knew that she was going to have a bath he did not climb on to the roof but instead walked to the Stray Inn, demanded tick from the barman and quietly got drunk in the drinking time that was left.

That week Cal was working repairing fences at the far side of the farm. It was cold and wet but he didn't care. He thought of Shamie and wondered how he was. He would have to try and get into town and see him. Were misery and depression the same thing? Inside himself Cal knew that Shamie was sick, while he had something which would eventually go away if he ignored it long enough. Cal was just sick of himself. Rain dripped from his nose and his chin as his hands worked in front of him, red and glistening, driving in staples. He smiled when he realized that he was outside the boundary of the farm, fencing himself out.

At night he sat in the cottage trying to read the books she had lent him. He thought of hundreds of excuses to go up to the house and see her – but could not bring himself to do it. He spent hours lying on the bed staring at nothing, listening to the hiss of the Tilley lamp. Anything he did do to occupy himself he stretched out for as long as he could. He cemented two loose tiles back into the fireplace, keeping them the right distance apart with matchsticks, and it took him all evening. The next night he spent grouting between them.

On Wednesday the weather changed. In the morning there was a hard ringing frost as he walked across the yard. The fields were

whitened and he saw his trailing track behind him as he walked to where he had left off fencing. About midday it began to snow, finely at first, like smoke blowing, then heavy flakes falling from a sky as grey as slate. Cal worked on with his back to the angle of the
5 fall but the snow swirled around him, ascending and descending in front of him. He looked up and saw that everything except the nearest hedge had become invisible. The snow was beginning to lie thickly on the grass and whitely shadow one side of the fence posts. Eventually he gave up and trudged back, the snow over his
10 bootlaces at certain points where it had drifted, and told Dunlop that he thought he was going to die with the cold.

He lit a fire and changed his clothes and hung them steaming from the mantelpiece and the backs of chairs. There was a roll of carpet underfelt in the room with the stored furniture and he spent
15 the rest of the afternoon cutting it into strips and tacking it round the windows and doors to keep the draught out. And still it snowed an endless stream of flakes whirling to the ground. He saw the Anglia come home early. Everybody must be being sent home for fear of being snowed in. Dunlop left early too.

20 Cal heated a tin of beans and toasted himself slice after slice of bread at the fire. He fell asleep and when he awoke it was dark. He rubbed the window and looked out. Between the cottage and the lights of the farmhouse he could see the blizzard. It was after eight o'clock and the fire had died down. Shivering, he raked the embers
25 to redness and put on some kindling wood, then blocks on top of that. He pulled his chair nearer to the fire and put his feet up against the tiles of the mantelpiece. After such a long sleep he knew he would spend the night tortured with guilt and insomnia. There was a knock at the door and he leapt to answer it, knowing who it was.

30 'Is Cal coming out to play?' Marcella stood there wrapped up in a scarf, mittens, hat and sheepskin coat. Her jeans were tucked into long leather boots. There was a snowflake clinging to her eyebrow and melting.

'No he is not,' he said. 'But you come in.'

35 'Isn't it gorgeous?' Cal nodded, humouring her. 'Do you think we'll be snowed in?'

'If it goes on much longer, it's very possible.'

'Better still, do you think *they'll* be snowed out?'

'When do they come back?'

'Tomorrow. Gran phoned to say everything is fine and they're letting him out tomorrow.'

She tugged off her woollen knitted cap and shook out her hair, placing her mittens on the hearth to dry. Cal bundled up his damp clothes and threw them in the corner.

'Where's Lucy?'

'She's asleep – dead to the world. We played snowballs and made a snowman earlier. She was absolutely exhausted.'

Marcella sat down on his chair and rubbed her hands quickly together while Cal looked out at the snow, which was now rounding off the corners of the window-sill. The wood hissed and spat and flashed a flame.

'Cal, I'm sorry about the other night.' She spoke quietly after the exuberance of her entrance.

'It's OK It was my fault.'

'No, I hadn't thought enough about it. It should have been obvious. Do you forgive me?'

Cal nodded. 'So what can I do for you?'

'I just wanted to apologize, that's all. Before they came back.' She took up her excited tone again and she talked and talked about how cold it was, about her parents-in-law, about the library. She apologized for the melting snow from her boots ruining his hearth and then, realizing that Cal had said nothing, apologized for talking too much.

'Look what I've brought to warm us up,' she said and produced the unopened half bottle of whiskey. 'But the only way I can drink it is in punch. So I brought these as well.' She took a small twist of paper from her pocket and showed him some cloves.

'They always make me think of the spiky bits in a king's crown,' said Cal.

'So they do. Please let me make it.' She put on the kettle and put spoons in two mugs. When the water boiled she poured it into the mugs, added sugar and whiskey and floated the cloves in the spinning liquid. She opened the buttons her coat and sat on the floor, nursing her mug. Cal sat on the bed.

'I'm glad you put me out the other night,' he said.

'Why?'

5 'Because we have this to drink now.'

She put her nose down to inhale the drink but the fumes of the hot spirit caught her breath and she coughed even before she drank. The noise she made was mixed with laughter.

'Oooh, I've made it too strong.' There were tears in her eyes.
10 She sipped with her spoon, tightening her lips. 'This is one of the few good things that Ireland can offer the world.' There was silence between them as they tasted and savoured. Outside the snow seemed to have quilted every sound.

'I've been miserable this last few days,' Marcella said. 'I want
15 you to know that I am very fond of you and that I felt awful about hurting you.' She was choosing her words. She turned her face up to him and patted the rug beside her. Cal sat down on the floor with his back against the bed, balancing his mug of whiskey.

'You have not been married,' she said. 'You get used to things
20 and when they're taken away you miss them.'

'Such as?'

'Touching, the comfort of being held. Not necessarily sexual – but there's that too.'

'Anybody?'

25 'Good God no. You're the only person who's crossed my mind in that respect.'

She laid her head against him and it was awkward so he put his arm round her shoulders. He set his drink down on the hearth and stroked her face lightly, pushing back the hanging strands of her
30 hair.

'Like this.' His hands had become coarse with the job and he was embarrassed about the toughness she might feel. But she smiled and closed her eyes as Cal continued to touch her jaw line, her forehead, her cheekbones.

35 'Is this why you were so nervous when you came in?' His voice had that awful shake in it again. She nodded, smiling but still not

opening her eyes. His hand moved to her neck and he kissed her mouth, sure this time he would not be rejected. She said his name when he took his mouth away from hers. He put his hand inside the warmth of her sheepskin and, through several sweaters, cupped her breast in his hand. Again she made the same noise in her throat.   5

'I think I love you,' said Cal.

'Would you die for me?' She opened her eyes and smiled.

'Only if it was really necessary,' said Cal and they hugged each other close and laughed. Cal had never felt this way before. Previous sexual encounters in the backs of cars or dark doorways had been   10
sullen with lust.

'I've never kissed a man with a beard. It's nice,' she said. 'Let's get into your bed.' Marcella stood up to take off her coat and Cal put his arms about her thighs and buried his face in her. She began to take off her clothes layer by layer, at speed because of the cold.   15
He knelt, watching her, not believing. Two jumpers, bra, boots, woolly socks, her jeans, tights and pants in one, all landed beside him on the floor. Her breasts shook as she struggled with her sock and her arrowhead of black hair was small. Suddenly she was in bed beneath the blanket with a flash of back and buttocks which   20
showed a white triangle of bikini shadow. She faced him.

'Come in,' she said. He thought of the danger he had put himself in to glimpse the flesh of her neck and shoulder and one breast – on the roof with his knees trembling – and now here it was all displayed for him in an instant. Her body should have been like a   25
secret which was revealed pore by tiny pore – gradually, like opening the cards of a full house with his thumb. He stripped to his gooseflesh and climbed in beside her, terrified that he should make a fool of himself losing his virginity.

He kissed her and she opened her mouth to him and his tongue   30
probed. He felt with its tip, or imagined he felt, the ridges on the roof of her mouth. He saw himself again touching the back of the steering wheel lightly with his fingers, heard again the incessant barking of the dogs and Crilly trying to get sound out of the bell. Marcella touched his back with her fingernails descending his   35
spine, all the time staring unblinkingly at him. Unable to meet her

eyes, he closed his own and smothered his face in the curve of her neck. In his darkness he saw her husband genuflect and the sudden soiling of the wallpaper behind him. The unreal sound of the cap gun. Marcella touched between his thighs and he felt shame.

5   'Don't worry,' she said. 'We have all the time in the world.'

Cal tried to clear his head, shaking it as if he had a tic. He made a terrible effort to concentrate himself into the tips of his fingers as he traced her body.

'Relax,' she said. 'You're not on trial.'

10   'Oh God.'

If he could forget his impotence it might go away. He feared that, as far as Marcella was concerned, he had gelded himself that dark winter's night. Still she kept moving her head back to focus on him with her brown eyes. Her touches evoked no response in

15 him.

'Turn over,' he said.

She obediently lay on her stomach and he sat astride her back and began to knead her shoulders. He watched her brown skin crease and move under the pressure of his hands. He smoothed

20 the pale horizon of her strap mark outwards with his thumbs. With her face turned away from him at last he became excited and rolled down beside her. But he was on a hair trigger and shot wetly on to her stomach almost immediately she touched him.

'Never mind,' she said, holding his ashamed head to her breasts.

25   The shame of his weakness blotted out the sickening visions of her genuflecting husband. Gradually he began to take an interest in her again and explored her with boyish amazement and touches. Her erect nipples – 'It's the cold,' she said – the fragrance of her juices on his hands, above all the awareness that he was giving her

30 pleasure, were almost too much for him. She made her noises and he rose again and entered her, saying her name over and over again as with light fingers she taught him to time his thrusts.

Afterwards he smiled and, leaning on one elbow, hawed on his fingers and rubbed them on the imaginary lapel of his lean chest.

35   'Eventually,' she said, smiling.

They lay in each other's arms, eased and snug beneath the

blankets. Marcella said that she had to go back – just in case Gran should phone or Lucy wake. They dressed and she said that they should both go to the house. Cal kept kissing her and touching her even as she dressed.

Outside the snow had stopped falling and they walked, printing it with double tracks, she holding on to his elbow in case she should fall. Everything was still and crisp and bright as daylight. The snow squeaked dully as they pressed it with each step. Marcella looked back and said they were leaving clues. If there wasn't more snow they would be caught.

Cal said, 'What happens if you get pregnant?'

She smiled at him. 'I dusted off my diaphragm,' she said. He made a sound of amazement.

'Cal, I came to you hoping.'

In the house they drank more hot whiskeys and made love again on the rug in front of the fire, with the door held shut by an armchair against the possibility of Lucy coming down. When it was over they lay on their stomachs, their faces turned to each other. Cal's hand rested on her buttocks and she pushed his long hair behind his ear.

'You're such an attentive lover,' she said. 'You can see it in your eyes.'

'How do you mean?' His eyes flickered away from hers.

'Your attention to detail. You make me believe it's me.'

'I don't understand. It is you.'

'That's what I mean.'

'Isn't that how it always is?'

'Not always.'

'You're not making yourself very clear.'

She sat up and put her sheepskin coat round her shoulders and held her knees between her arms. Cal reached out beneath her ankles and delicately touched her. He lay with his head resting on his folded elbow, looking.

She ignored what he was doing to her and went on.

'I can't explain without talking about Robert – and that's not a very nice thing to do in the circumstances.'

Cal shrugged. 'I wish I'd met you before he did.'

She laughed. 'You'd probably have been in short trousers.' He looked hurt and she ruffled his hair. 'We had stopped making love for a long time before he was killed. We had occasional sex but he didn't make me realize I was me. He was having it off with some creature of his imagination. God forgive me, I shouldn't speak ill of the dead.'

'Were you in love with him?' Cal's voice still had echoes of a shake in it.

'Love is a very strange idea. I never know what it is. When you were young it seemed to be all intensity and no opportunity. Later when you did get the opportunity the fire had gone out of it.'

'I still have it,' said Cal.

'You're still young. Anyway that's too simple. It must be a mixture of friendship and desire. The friendship had gone out of our marriage long ago and Robert's lust was for someone inside his head – not me.'

'And you went on living together?'

She laughed. 'For God's sake, Cal, it's still going on. I'm living with his family.'

'Did you even like him?' Cal's voice was high with incredulity.

'Recently – not much.'

Cal laughed, a loud harsh guffaw with no amusement in it. It went on too long.

'What are you laughing at?'

He was unable to stop immediately he heard her tone. 'Nothing. It's a kind of joke. You really mean that? About not liking him?'

'Yes.' She looked perplexed, her face like a child's not under-standing but continuing to smile. 'Don't laugh like that again. It's not you.' She held out her arm and took him under her coat.

'Sorry,' he said. The fleece was warm against his back.

'He was so plausible – one of those people that everybody likes in company. He could charm the birds off the trees – everybody, men and women. He was witty and intelligent but you couldn't believe a single word he said. He told lies, Cal. All the time. About his affairs – I know he had two or three at least – about his drinking, about the money he spent. After a while I stopped asking and even then he *offered* me lies. It got so bad I think he actually believed them himself. And the worst of it was that his mother backed him up on everything. She took his word as gospel.'

Cal nodded, watching her staring into the fire. His hand moved on the bones of her back.

'He was one of those people whose company you love for an hour or so but you're glad you're not married to them. But I was.'

'Do you love me?'

'You're not listening, Cal. I need more time – to heal maybe.' She rested her chin on her knees and he thought she was on the verge of tears. He caressed the side of her face with the back of his hand and kissed her on the cheek. She acknowledged the gesture with a resigned tightening movement of her lips.

'I love you,' he said. As he said it he felt a new danger. The more he loved her, the more friendly he became with her, the more afraid he was that he would tell her what he had done. It was the one thing he wanted to talk to her about, to have her console him. He wanted to share his guilt with the person he had wronged. To commune with her and be forgiven. He opened his mouth to speak and she waited, listening with raised eyebrows. Cal paused.

'I would like – another drink,' he said.

She got up, leaving him in the cold, and went to the sideboard. She bent over, looking into one of the cupboards. With the inflexible nature of sheepskin the tail of her coat rose and Cal saw the sweet lines of her bare undercarriage.

'You're like a hot cross bum from here.'

'I'm a genius,' she said and flourished the substantial remains of a bottle of brandy. 'Gran always keeps it in case of illness.'

'A woman of foresight.'

They talked and drank on and on until Marcella was falling asleep.

'Cal, do you realize that this is the longest night of the year?'

'And the best,' he said. She told him that Lucy always tumbled into her mother's bed first thing in the morning and it would be unwise for him to stay; that she was happy for the first time in years; and that she would see him again the next day. Her mouth was slack from exhaustion or drink or both when he kissed her goodnight.

5 He walked back to the cottage, his feet splayed like Charlie Chaplin, scuffling the tracks they had made earlier. His excitement was such that he could not sleep. He lit a cigarette and sat on the bed smoking, going over again in his mind each nook and cranny of her, each look, each sound. Then he tried to look into the future 10 but what he saw there made him close his eyes. He held his head tightly in his hands, his elbows resting on his knees. He sat like that until he smelt the smell of his own hair singeing.

(3)

The next day was Thursday and despite the snow and the state of the roads he went into town early with Dunlop to do his Christmas 15 shopping. He wondered what he could buy for Marcella – something which wouldn't attract questions. Not that he could afford much. He bought her a tiny bottle of perfume which cost him the best part of three days' wages and in a bookshop he asked if they had any books by or about the artist who had so impressed her. 20 The assistant gave him a small paperback of Grünewald's paintings and he slipped it into his pocket. He bought Shamie a bottle of after-shave and a shaving stick, as he had done every year since he could remember. They seemed to last exactly from Christmas to Christmas. He also bought his father a one-thousand-piece jigsaw 25 to cheer him up. When Cal was a child Shamie had always interfered over his shoulder, wanting to put pieces into his jigsaws. In the toy shop he saw some 'Raggedy Anne' dolls flopped against the wall with their heads pitched forward like drunks. He bought one for Lucy.

30   Outside, the Preacher stood at the corner shouting at the top of his voice about God. He wore a black plastic apron with the words 'Repent ye; for the Kingdom of Heaven is at hand'. There was no one listening to him except a few of his cronies, also wearing black bibs, who were standing up against the wall. Everyone else bustled

past, some even stepping into the slush of the gutter to avoid him. He windmilled his arms and shouted as Cal passed him.

'Without the shedding of blood there can be no forgiveness.'

'Good evening,' said Cal.

He got no answer from Dermot Ryan's front door so he went round the back and found it open. He went in, kicking the snow off his shoes, and called for Shamie but there was no answer. He sat down to wait. Perhaps they had both gone out for a drink. If they had, it was a good sign. He took out the paperback of the paintings and began to look through it. He heard the front door open and shouted a warning that he was in. Dermot opened the door by himself.

'Where's Shamie?'

'He was worse than they thought, Cal. The doctor put him in for treatment.'

'Where?'

'Gransha.'

'Oh God, no.'

'They say this electrical shock treatment is bad. Very hard on you.'

'How the hell am I supposed to get to Derry to see him?'

Dermot shrugged and sat down, readjusting his cap on his head. Briefly Cal saw the track of the headband on the little hair that Dermot had.

'What about the van? Where is it?'

'A boy at the abattoir has it.'

'Crilly?'

'Aye, I think so.'

'Jesus.'

'Too generous for his own good. He's some man, your father. It broke my heart to see the way he was. Like iron to plasticine overnight.' He sat close to the fire, the top buttons of his trousers undone making a white V on his pot belly. One hand was on his knee, the other hooked in his braces.

'Cal, the world is full of gulpins who don't care who they hurt.'

'Will he be out for Christmas?'

'I doubt it – from what the doctor said.'

Cal went over to the table where he had left the presents.

'If you see him, will you give him this?' he said and handed the
large box to Dermot. 'And there's a present for yourself for putting
up with him.' He gave Dermot the wrapped after-shave and stick.
'It's the same brand as Shamie uses and I got to like the smell of
it.'

'Thanks, Cal. You're as like your father as two peas in a pod.'

(4) He went to the library to pass the time and was disappointed and
annoyed when he saw the bespectacled figure of the head librarian
behind the desk instead of Marcella. If he had thought about it for
a moment he would have realized that with nobody to mind her
child in the evening she would not be on duty. Now he would have
to walk home, or hitch-hike, which was dangerous.

He wandered down to the section which had the cartoon books
and opened one – a selection from the *New Yorker*. A voice behind
him said,

'Good to see you, Cal.'

He froze and without looking he knew it was Crilly.

'I didn't expect to see you in a place like this,' said Cal, turning
to face him. The big man stood smiling, his head hanging to make
him look less tall.

'Why not?'

'I read one book in school. That was one more than you.'

'The books is not for me. Here, c'mere.'

He led Cal over to the fiction section and cocked his head to the
side. He ran his finger along the titles and tapped a fat book.
Middlemarch by George Eliot. Cal said,

'So what?'

'There's plenty in that book.' said Crilly. He took it out very
gently and looked all around him and, seeing no one, flipped open
the cover. There was a square hole cut in the pages. Inside was a
small bag of powder wired to a watch. Crilly closed the book
carefully and slipped it back on to the shelf. He said,

'I don't borrow books. I bring them in.'

'Jesus, why do you want to burn down a library?'

'Government property, in't it? Orders is orders, Cal.'

'Fuckin' hell.'

Cal turned away from him but Crilly gripped his arm.

'Skeffington would like a word with you.' He added, 'Urgent.'   5

'I'm not interested any more.'

'We've been looking all over for you. I heard you were in England.'

'No, I'm still around.'

Crilly's hand remained on his arm.   10

'Where?'

'Here.'

The librarian looked over his glasses to see who was speaking so loudly. Crilly smiled and reduced his voice to a whisper close to Cal's ear.   15

'Now, Cal, don't fuck me about. Where are you living at?'

'Outside town.'

'Let's go to my house and Skeffington can drop in and see us, eh?' Cal shrugged. Crilly's voice had turned friendly but Cal knew that he shouldn't go. He allowed himself to be led out of the library   20 and on to the street. Crilly walked very close to him. He asked him what was in the parcel and Cal told him it was a doll. Cal thought of running but it seemed so stupid to run away from this guy he had been to school with.

'Too bad about Shamie. How is he?' asked Crilly.   25

'He's away in Gransha.'

'Yes, I know. He lent me the van.'

'You mean you took it.'

'Sort of.'

'I want it back. Like now.'   30

'It's being used, Cal.'

'Soon, then. I have to get out to Gransha to see him.'

'I've never seen a change in a man. Did you hear about Skeffington's father?'

'The wit? Don't tell me he spoke.'   35

'He got knocked down by a car.'

'Bad?'

'Bad enough. Just a minute.'

Crilly stopped at the phone box at the end of the street and opened the door for Cal. The two men stood with their knees
5 almost touching while Crilly dialled. Cal heard the receiver burr three times, then Crilly put it back. Cal was about to push open the door to leave when Crilly said, 'Wait.' They waited and the phone rang three times and stopped.

'Neat?' said Crilly. 'Saves money. Saves phone tapping.'
10 'It's a wonder the phone is in order.'

'It's in order because we want it to be in order. A bit of discipline around the district works wonders.'

In Crilly's front room they sat waiting for Skeffington. There was an electric clock on the narrow mantelpiece with a sweep
15 second hand which made slow progress round the face. Cal thought of the watch in the darkness of a closed book in Marcella's library. He did not dare ask Crilly what time it was set for but he guessed it would be well after closing time. Incendiaries could be put out if they went off when the staff were still there. Cal said,
20 'You were telling me about witty old Skeffington.'

'Oh, aye. He got knocked down by this drunken bastard of about sixteen. The wee shite had *stolen* the car. He fractured the old man's skull and broke both his legs. Christ, was Skeffington mad. He spent all night at the hospital and when I saw him the next day
25 he was biting the table. He said he wanted an example made of this lad. I've never done a knee-capping but, says I, "I'll have a go." Says he, "I'll drive for you. I want to see this one myself. And what's more," says he, "don't use a gun – get the captive bolt from work. I don't want this guy to walk again for a long time."
30 Wallop, wallop. Both knees he wanted, and your man on the ground squealing like a stuck pig with Skeffington sitting on his head.'

Cal said, 'That was stupid.'

'Why?'
35 'They'll be able to tell what made that wound.'

'Jesus, I hadn't thought of that.'

'An entry wound with no exit and no bullets? They'll trace it back.'

'Jesus, you're right.' Crilly scratched the top of his head. 'Cal, you should have stuck with us.'

Mrs Crilly looked into the room and, seeing Cal, bared her white 5 dentures in a smile:

'Hello, Cal,' she said. 'Tea or coffee?'

'He'll wait for Finbar, Ma. He should be along any second.'

When he came Skeffington didn't shake hands with Cal as he usually did but spoke to him across the room. He seemed serious 10 and anxious.

'I believe we share a problem, Cahal.'

'What's that?'

'Our fathers being ill.'

'Yes. How is yours?' 15

'They tell me he'll live. But broken bones at that age . . . He'll never be the same again.'

'I'm sorry.'

Skeffington sat down in the armchair. He turned to speak to Crilly. 20

'Well?'

'Easy. No bother,' said Crilly. 'That's where I met our friend here.' Cal tried to remember the name of the man who wrote the book. When Skeffington spoke to Cal his voice sounded deeply hurt. 25

'Cahal, why didn't you let us know where you were?'

'I told you before. I want out.'

'Sometimes there's a price to pay.'

'Yeah, I was just telling him,' said Crilly, 'about what we did to your friend last night.' 30

'Sometimes,' said Skeffington to Crilly, 'you are extremely stupid.'

'I was just trying to put him in the mood for listening to you. And it was *your* stupid idea to use the humane killer on him. Cal says they'll be able to trace it.' 35

'Highly unlikely. Have you not realized yet that Cahal is no

147

longer on our side? He should be told nothing. Cahal has had a change of heart, isn't that so?'

'I don't think I've changed all that much. I see things differently now.'

5 'That's what's called becoming a traitor to the cause. The next step is to become an informer.' Skeffington still had his overcoat and scarf on and held his left leather glove in his gloved right hand. He lay back in the chair, sighing. 'I really thought better of you, Cahal. In its fight for Irish freedom this kind of thing has dogged

10 the Republican Movement all through the centuries. Our own Lundys have thrown it away – nameless rats from Ireland's sad past.'

'I have not informed on anybody,' said Cal. 'I just felt bad about what I was doing. It was against my conscience. Was it you guys

15 who planted the mine out on the Toome road?'

'No. That must have been the lads from Ballyronan. Why?'

'They killed a cow.'

'That kind of sarcasm helps no one, Cahal. Mistakes are inevitable.'

20 'You mean it would have been all right if it had been a person?'

'Did you ever hear of Archbishop Romero? He talked about the "legitimate right of insurrectional violence". Oppressed peoples have the *right* to throw off the yoke in whatever way they see fit – and that's from an eminent doctor of the Church. If somebody is

25 standing on your neck you have the right to break his leg.'

'With a captive bolt?'

'Yes. If it will be a lesson to others. There are no rules, Cahal. Just eventual winners. I myself prefer the God of the Old Testament: "You who strike all my foes on the mouth, you who break

30 the teeth of the wicked".'

Mrs Crilly came smiling in again with her wobbling tin tray.

'It's bitter outside. Would you not turn on the other bar of that fire?' She set the tray on the table and asked Skeffington about his father, listening to what was said with concern.

35 'Och well, he'll be warm in the hospital tonight. The central heating in those places would boil you. I think it's why the half of

them die. That couldn't be good for you. When I was in for my
hysterectomy – I've had the whole works removed, y'know – the
sweat was breaking on me the whole time. The doctor said it might
just be the change of life but I thought it was the central heating.'

'Thanks, Ma,' said Crilly, holding the door open for her. When   5
she had gone Cal lifted his cup and blew on his tea. There was an
awkward silence. Cal looked at the clock. The library would be
closed by now. He remembered the noise of the fire in his own
house, the thunderous roaring of the flames. He thought of Marcella the next day tramping on the broken glass and the wet charred   10
floor, looking at the remains of her library, the stink of destruction
in her nose. The only books in Crilly's house were a set of four
bound *Reader's Digests* – green spines with gold lettering – held
upright by a plaster dog at each end. In the middle. Remember in
the middle of March – a month of the year.   15

'Well, Cahal?'

'What's this price you're talking of?'

'We want to know where you are staying – so's we can get in
touch with you if we need you.'

'So the price of getting out is staying in?'   20

'More or less.'

'And if I refuse?'

'Cahal, look. I have been extremely lenient with you up until
now. This is not a game we're playing. What you have done is
called desertion. You know the penalties for that in any other army   25
in wartime.'

Crilly stood up and walked behind Cal. Cal watched him out of
the corner of his eye. He held tightly on to his parcel.

'But look, I keep telling you I never joined. I helped out once or
twice . . .'   30

There was a long silence. Skeffington separated the fingers of his
limp glove. Crilly looked through the curtains and made a slurping
noise as he drank his tea. Cal heard the characteristic sound of a
Land Rover engine outside and was aware of Crilly stiffening. A
door slammed and Crilly hissed,   35

'It's the fuckin' cops.'

Skeffington jumped to his feet.

'Out the back.'

They moved quickly into the hall. The bell rang and almost
before it had ceased the door was hammered by a fist. They saw a
5 peaked cap at the bubbled oval of glass. In the back room Crilly's
mother and father were sitting watching television in blue darkness
and Skeffington told them not to answer the door for a while. The
three of them slipped out of the back door into the small snowy
garden. Cal was in the middle as they went crunching down the
10 path. Suddenly a voice shouted 'Halt!' and Cal glimpsed a peaked
RUC cap rise above the hedge at the bottom of the garden.
Skeffington stopped dead. Cal took one step to the side. Between
the tool shed and the coal house there was a gap of about a foot.
Crilly tried to follow him but a voice screamed again, 'Halt or I
15 fire.' Crilly stood still. Cal heard his own clothes scrape and brush
between the walls. His paper bag crackled so he quickly pulled the
doll out and dropped the paper on to the ground. He held his
breath and stepped up on a wire which separated him from the
next door garden. It twanged with his weight. He crept behind
20 some bushes, terrified he would be seen against the whiteness of
the snow, then through the hedge on hands and knees to the next
garden. He heard angry voices from Crilly's. The houses were in
terraces of four and there was a way on to the street from this
garden. Doubled over, Cal made it away from the backs and stood
25 at the front gate looking into the street. Others had come to their
doors and were standing watching the Land Rover. Somebody
shouted an obscenity at the policeman sitting at the wheel and a
snowball bounced hollowly off its roof. The snowball was followed
by stones. Cal walked away from the street as casually as he could
30 on to the main road, carrying the Raggedy Anne like a baby against
his shoulder.

On the corner next to the post office there was a telephone box
and Cal went into it and set the doll on the shelf. It slumped
forward, staring at its knees. The number of the Confidential
35 Phone was framed on the wall but somebody had rubbed either
mud or shit over it to obscure it. He made it out and dialled. He

told the voice at the other end that there was a fire bomb in the library and that it was in a book called *Middlemarch* by somebody called Eliot. No, he didn't know whether it was the only one. He put the phone down as if it was a black garden slug and left the box. Skeffington was right. He had turned informer.

It took him over an hour to walk home beneath a sky that was clear of cloud and thick with stars. Twice he saw shooting stars score the sky momentarily. It was freezing cold, and to keep himself warm he walked quickly and rhythmically in the black scar at the centre of the road which had been cleared of snow. There were few cars and at this time of night none stopped to give him a lift. He wondered if either Crilly or Skeffington would crack and give them Cal's name. How long did they question you? Did they kick the living daylights out of you, as he'd heard? Or did they just break you by keeping you awake and persistence? He'd heard of one trick they'd used, of blindfolding the guy and putting him in a helicopter, but only taking him up about two feet, then chucking him out. Or ball squeezing – hurting you in ways that didn't show afterwards. He felt sure that Skeffington would never break. Crilly on the other hand was not too bright and anybody could tie him in knots.

When he turned the bend in the road his first reaction was to look towards the farmhouse and, seeing a light on downstairs, he broke into a run. He rang the bell and heard Marcella ask, 'Who is it?'

'It's Cal.'

The door opened. She was in her nightdress and dressing-gown and when he passed her in the doorway she smelt clean and washed.

'Where were you? I went down to the cottage and you weren't there.'

'I was in town. I thought you'd be in the library,' he said. 'I had to walk it home.' The doll was beneath the crook of his arm and he offered it to her for Lucy, apologizing for the lack of wrapping. She thanked him extravagantly and they stood awkwardly facing one another. He unzipped his anorak and stood with his back to the fire. She smiled and after a moment's hesitation slid her arms around him inside his anorak and laid her head against his shirt front and thumping heart.

'I feel the cold off you,' she said.

He smelt the soft hair of the top of her head and kissed it, held
5   her as if to crush her. He wanted to tell her that he had saved her precious library but knew it would be too complicated. He wanted to be open and honest with her and tell her everything. To explain how the events of his life were never what he wanted, how he seemed unable to influence what was going on around him. He
10 had had a recurring dream of sitting at the wheel of a car driving and at a critical point turning the wheel and nothing happening. For miles the car would career along with the steering wheel slack and he would spin it round and round like a ship's wheel but nothing would happen. Eventually he would hit something – a
15 wall, another vehicle; once he woke roaring in his throat after seeing a child with bright amazed eyes disappearing beneath the front of the car and feeling the bounce of wheels on flesh and bone.

'Comfort me, Cal,' she said.

He stepped back and pulled the tie of her dressing-gown. He
20 put his hands beneath and round her shoulders. He felt the warm lines of her body through the thin material. He caressed her from neck to knee, feeling no interruption to the smooth passage of his hands. And they made love in an absolute and intense silence.

'Tomorrow they come back,' she said, 'and my life will just
25 become a fragment of theirs again.'

'Why don't you leave? Get a flat and I can come and visit you.'

'Yes, that sounds so easy. I've told her that many times. I wish I wasn't so weak. I wish I could fight with her and insult her. But when it comes to a crisis she always wins. The only way I could
30 do it is not be here when they get back. It's been a year now, and every time I tell her I'm moving something comes up and she persuades me to stay on. For Lucy's sake. For Grandad's sake. After Easter.'

Cal told her about his own father having to go in to hospital.

35 'And at Christmas,' she said. 'Cal, you must come here for Christmas dinner. It would be a relief for me to have someone to

talk to. And it could seem as if I'm acting out of charity. Will you do that for me?'

Cal nodded and yet he had the feeling he would never be there. So much so that he crawled naked to where he had flung his anorak on the chair and gave her her Christmas presents.

'Can I open them now?' she said. 'I can never wait.'

She touched between her breasts with the perfume and kissed him. Then in the book she sought and found Grünewald's picture of Christ crucified and held it up for Cal to see. The weight of the Christ figure bent the cross down like a bow; the hands were cupped to heaven like nailed starfish; the body with its taut ribcage was pulled to the shape of an egg-timer by the weight of the lower body; the flesh was diseased with sores from the knotted scourges, the mouth open and gasping for breath. She was sitting on the floor with her back to the couch, her legs open in a yoga position and the book facing him, just below her breasts. Cal looked at the flesh of Christ spotted and torn, bubonic almost, and then behind it at the smoothness of Marcella's body and it became a permanent picture in his mind.

They ate supper and went to her bed to make love again and she made Cal promise to leave before morning to avoid the attentions of Lucy when she woke. Marcella lay, her bottom snug in the cup of his thighs and belly and talked. The pauses grew longer until eventually she stopped altogether. Her breathing became deep and regular and her leg jerked in a dream. Cal lay awake beside her, touching her bare back with his cheek. The trust she showed in falling asleep beside him made him feel worse. Could he *ever* tell her the truth? Perhaps he could write it down. That way he could say what he meant and not get confused. He could write to her and if she replied he could begin to hope. But would she tell the police? A letter of confession would be evidence that would put him away for most of his life. She was what he wanted most and if he couldn't be near her he might as well be in prison. If he was ever caught – and there was an impending sense that it wouldn't be long now that Crilly and Skeffington were lifted – he would write to her and try to tell it as it was. He had her now like the Sleeping Beauty of his fantasy. He reached out his hand and touched her moistness but she grumbled in her sleep and jack-knifed, closing him out. He kissed the nape of her neck, got up and dressed in the darkness.

5 Walking back to the cottage he heard the sounds of a thaw. The black lane showed through the centres of footsteps when the moon raced from one cloud to the next. The air had warmed and melted snow was running down the sides of the lane. Everywhere was the sound of dripping and clinking and gurgling.

10 The next morning, Christmas Eve, almost as if he expected it, the police arrived to arrest him and he stood in a dead man's Y-fronts listening to the charge, grateful that at last someone was going to beat him to within an inch of his life.

Language Notes and Activities

CHAPTER 1

Focus

Why does the novel open in an abattoir?

In this chapter descriptions of the abattoir and the library are juxtaposed. Why?

Follow-up

'The wages of sin is death' is a quotation from the Bible which appears on the first page of the book. What might be the significance of this quotation within the novel and the quotation 'I am the Resurrection and the Life' which accompanies it?

'He could not bear to look up and see the flutter of the Union Jacks' (4.34). What does this line tell us about Cal and the community in which he lives?

Why will Shamie not be forced out of his home? What does Shamie's attitude tell us about him?

Why does Cal attempt to learn Gaelic? Why does he not succeed?

'He could not take his eyes off her, not because of what she was but because of what he might have done to her' (9.35). Explain the significance of Cal's initial feelings towards Marcella.

What do we learn in this chapter about the characters of Crilly and Skeffington?

Why is the name Marcella repeated four times within six lines on p. 9?

What is the significance of Cal's dream as recounted in the last paragraph of Chapter 1?

abattoir (3.1): a place where animals, such as sheep, cows and pigs, are killed for their meat.

baseball caps (3.3): close-fitting caps with long peaks, originally worn by baseball players, but now considered fashionable and worn by anyone.

carcases (3.4): the dead bodies of animals, especially those that have been killed for meat.

humane killer (3.8): a device for painlessly killing animals.

anaemic (3.12): pale and sickly looking; suffering from a blood condition where there is a shortage of red blood cells.

Adam's apple (3.13): the hard lump at the front of the throat, especially prominent in men.

tracts (3.17): leaflets or paper booklets, usually of a religious nature.

'The Wages of Sin is Death. Romans 8:5' (3.18): a quotation from the New Testament of the Christian Bible; the reference is to Chapter 8, Verse 5 of St Paul's Epistle to the Romans.

Magherafelt (3.49): a market town in Northern Ireland, in the south of County Derry and approximately thirty-five miles (fifty-six kilometres) from Belfast.

'I am the Resurrection and the Life. John 11:25' (3.20): a quotation from the New Testament of the Christian Bible; the reference is to the Gospel of St John, Chapter 11, Verse 25.

carborundum stone (3.23): a grinding stone made from a material formed by fusing together sand and coke. It is used for sharpening knives and other blades.

Da (3.24): a shortened version of *Dad*, a familiar form of *father*.

shanks (4.8): the lower parts of an animal's legs.

japped (4.18): splashed.

Embassy (4.19): a brand of cigarettes.

anorak (4.27): a waterproof, hip-length jacket, usually with a hood.

Giro (4.31): a cheque for the payment of a state benefit, such as unemployment benefit. These are usually cashed at a post office.

Union Jacks (4.35): The Union Jack is the flag of the United Kingdom. It is composed of the flags of England, Scotland and Northern Ireland.

Ulster (4.35): an alternative name for Northern Ireland.

estate (5.1): a large group of houses or flats, usually built to a similar design.

Loyalists (5.2): people who wish to continue Northern Ireland's political union with Britain.

Twelfth of July (5.3): the day on which Protestants in Northern Ireland annually celebrate William of Orange's victory over Catholic James II at the Battle of the Boyne (1690). (See below for definitions of 'Protestant' and 'Catholic'.)

kerbstones (5.6): large stones used to make a raised edge between the pavement and a road or street.

eviction (5.21): the forcible removal of people from their homes.

Protestant (5.22): a member or follower of any denomination of the Western Christian church that rejects the authority of the Pope and some basic Roman Catholic doctrines.

LP (5.35): a long-playing gramophone record.

tic (6.6): a sudden, nervous movement of the muscles which may become noticeable when someone is stressed; a twitch.

pidgin (6.13): a simplified language composed of two or more other languages.

cochon (6.15): the French word for *pig*.

merde (6.15): the French word for *shit*, a swear-word meaning 'excrement'.

crotte de chien (6.20): a French phrase meaning 'dog's droppings'.

Movement (6.27): a group of people who are interested in promoting and studying Irish music, language and culture. The Movement had its origins at the end of the nineteenth century.

Gaelic (6.28): a Celtic language used in different forms in parts of Ireland, Scotland and the Isle of Man.

Slieve (7.2): the Gaelic word for *mountain*.

plectrums (7.12): A plectrum is a small, flat, pointed piece of plastic or other hard material used for plucking the strings of a guitar or other similar instrument.

unsnibbed (7.18): unfastened, or unfixed, the catch of a door.

wire grille (7.25): bars of wire, sometimes criss-crossed, used as a partition, and usually as a form of protection.

warble-fly (7.29): a large hairy fly, which lays its eggs under the skin of horses and cattle, from which larvae hatch out and form painful swellings.

index file (8.20): a file or box which contains an ordered sequence of cards itemizing books in a library or collection.

sallowness (8.25): *sallow* refers to a pale-brown or yellowish skin colouring.

bland (9.28): lacking character, without definite features.

Biros (9.30): Biro is a brand of ballpoint pen; the word is now widely used for all types of ballpoint pens.

Perspex (10.15): a transparent, tough, acrylic plastic which is used in place of glass.

carbolic soap (10.20): soap made using phenol, a very strong disinfectant.

a fry (10.23): an informal name for a meal which comprises a variety of fried foods, such as bacon, eggs, sausages, etc.

black pudding (10.24): a dark type of sausage made from pigs' blood and pork fat.

yahoos (10.27): coarse, vicious, brutish people.

black lace edges (11.1): This refers to the outer edges of the white of an egg, which appear lace-like when fried and black when burnt.

Sellotape (11.6): a brand of adhesive tape.

deaf mute (11.8): someone who cannot hear or speak.

Catholic (11.10): a person who is a member of the Roman Catholic Church or a follower of the Roman Catholic religion.

entry (11.11): a passage in a terrace, either between or leading to the backs of houses.

Gerry Fitt (11.12): a former Northern Irish politician who led the Social Democratic and Labour Party (a Nationalist political party) from 1970–79.

tapes (11.31): strips of black-pudding skin.

eat again the ashes (12.3): an expression meaning, in this case, to think about and regret the terrible consequences of what he had done.

marbles (12.17): small, hard balls, usually made of coloured glass.

Control Zone (13.3): an area controlled and checked by the police or army.

spuds (13.16): potatoes.

bugger all (13.19): *bugger* is a swear-word and is used in a variety of ways; the phrase here means 'very little' or 'nothing at all'.

your arse (13.28): an offensive phrase expressing disbelief or disagreement.

compunction (14.26): regret.

blazers (14.28): a blazer is a type of jacket, often worn as part of a school uniform.

pornographic contact prints (15.2): sexually explicit photographs.

R.K. class (15.5): a class where religious education is taught. R.K. is an abbreviation for 'religious knowledge'.

lewd (15.6): indecent, obscene.

gulpin (15.7): someone who behaves badly, or acts in a rough and violent way.

fuckin' (16.1): *fucking*, a swear-word; a highly offensive term used to add emphasis to a word or statement.

delft horseshoe (16.7): delft is a type of earthenware (pottery), originally from Delft in Holland, which has an opaque, white glaze; *horseshoe* refers to the shape of the lavatory bowl.

crawler (16.31): a person who humiliates him- or herself in order to gain favour with somebody.

Nationwide (17.3): a former BBC television programme which featured a wide range of regional news reports and other items of general interest from around the UK.

aggro (17.7): threatening behaviour, particularly fighting or troublemaking.

Go mbeannuigh Dia duit (17.25): a greeting in Irish Gaelic; literally, 'God bless you'.

Dia is Muire duit (17.26): the usual reply to the above greeting, again a blessing.

Pioneer Total Abstinence (17.30): a group whose members have promised not to drink alcohol.

lifted (18.3): arrested.

internment (18.13): the imprisonment of a person who is regarded as a threat to security.

Dick Turpin (18.19): an eighteenth-century highwayman (a type of outlaw) who used to stop the carriages of the rich and rob them. He was celebrated rather than condemned for his exploits.

Robin Hood (18.19): a medieval outlaw, traditionally seen as a hero who robbed the rich in order to give to the poor.

wee (18.29): small.

a bookie's (18.30): *bookie* is a familiar form of *bookmaker*, someone who is in the business of taking bets.

New Lodge Road (18.31): a Catholic area in Belfast.

propaganda (19.6): information or publicity, often misleading and deceptive, published in order to spread and promote a policy, idea or cause.

off-licences (19.10): shops which sell alcoholic drinks for drinking away from the premises.

teaching your granny to suck eggs (19.12): a phrase meaning to try to show someone with more experience than yourself how to do something that he/she can already do.

'The Dark Side of the Moon' (19.18): a long-playing record by the British rock group Pink Floyd.

I have no stomach for it (20.8): a phrase meaning to have no desire, or lack the courage, to do something.

Reserve policeman (20.15): a member of the special reserve force attached to the Royal Ulster Constabulary (RUC), made up of 1,500 full-time and 3,200 part-time members.

ride on our coat-tails (20.22): an expression meaning that others can take it easy and have success while we do all the work.

Humes (20.23): a reference to John Hume, a Northern Irish politician who has been leader of the Social Democratic and Labour Party from 1979. He was joint winner of the 1998 Nobel Peace Prize for his attempts to bring about peace in Northern Ireland.

Brits (20.26): the British.

Attaboy (21.22): a slang word used to express encouragement, enthusiasm or approval.

Dr Scholl's sandals (22.8): a brand of particularly comfortable footwear, consisting of a shaped wooden sole and a single broad strap across the foot.

shrouded (23.17): covered, concealed.

Fenyan (23.20): usually spelt *Fenian*, an offensive term for a Roman Catholic, especially one who is suspected of having nationalist sympathies. The Fenians were an anti-British secret society founded in 1858 in the USA and Ireland, whose aim was to make Ireland a republic and end British domination.

UVF (23.22): Ulster Volunteer Force, a Protestant paramilitary organization. 'Paramilitary' means similar to an army, but not official and often illegal.

curlew (23.30): a type of bird with long legs and a downward-curving bill.

asbestos (24.1): a heat-resistant material.

pot-shots (24.3): shots taken quickly or on a chance opportunity, especially at something or somebody within easy reach.

skin crawl (24.7): experience a sudden, shuddering feeling of disgust or uneasiness.

.38 (24.24): a type of gun.

eiderdown (24.26): a warm bedcover which consists of a rectangular container filled with eider duck feathers or other soft fibres.

a bugger to get dried (24.29): In this context *bugger* means 'difficult', i.e. it was difficult to dry.

hot press (24.31): airing cupboard; a cupboard, usually warmed by the hot-water tank, where laundry can be aired or dried.

squatted (25.14): crouched or sat on the ground.

Continent (25.15): this refers to the continent of Europe.

static (25.22): a buzzing sound resembling electrical interference in a radio or television broadcast.

skillion (25.27): a made-up word meaning 'very, very many'.

Westerns (26.5): films set in the western part of the USA, usually during the second half of the nineteenth century.

disillusion (26.8): destroy or undermine a mistaken belief that is held by someone.

safe house (26.23): a house where people who are in danger can hide or meet secretly.

turds (27.9): pieces of excrement.

glove compartment (27.10): a small enclosed storage space in the dashboard of a vehicle.

gooseflesh (27.23): a rash of small, temporary bumps on the skin caused by sudden cold, fear or excitement.

crewneck (27.27): a close-fitting round neckline of a sweater.

innards (28.21): internal organs, especially intestines.

dole (29.35): a regular amount of money paid by the state to people who are unemployed.

digs (28.36): lodgings; a room or rooms that someone rents in another person's house.

insomnia (29.12): inability to go to sleep.

janitor (29.14): caretaker; someone who looks after the cleaning of buildings such as schools and offices.

brain haemorrhage (29.19): bleeding from broken blood vessel in the brain.

combs (29.30): pieces of plastic or wood with long, thin teeth to keep the hair in place.

mass (29.34): a religious service, usually in Roman Catholic churches.

communion (29.34): the religious ceremony in which the priest consecrates bread and wine and distributes it to the people in church in commemoration of the Last Supper of Jesus Christ.

rosary (29.35): a series of Roman Catholic prayers.

missal (30.1): a book that contains all the prayers, hymns and responses used in the Roman Catholic mass.

memoriam cards (30.1): cards intended to remind people of someone who has died.

novenas (30.1): in the Roman Catholic Church, prayers which are said over nine days in order to achieve a particular purpose.

love-bites (30.14): small patches of bruised skin caused by sucking the skin very hard.

engrossed (30.23): totally involved in, taking up the whole of someone's attention.
bay window (31.1): a rounded or three-sided window built to stick
   out from an outside wall in order to extend the room inside.
skewered (31.9): pierced by.

CHAPTER 2

Focus

Write a brief character study of Cal, based on what has been
revealed about him in the first chapter. In particular, note his
attitude towards (a) his father, (b) his mother, (c) Marcella,
(d) Crilly. To what extent does his character change in the course
of this second chapter?

Follow-up

What is the significance of Cal seeing Marcella at mass in Magherafelt and realizing that she is a Catholic?

'Cal drove the sixty miles to Clones. Once over the Border he
experienced the feeling of freedom he always got. This was Ireland
– the real Ireland' (36.11). Can you explain Cal's feelings?

'The hard men and the bandits are the real revolutionaries, if you
see what I mean. They get things done, they punch the hole for
us to get through later' (37.28). In the terms defined here by
Skeffington, is Cal a 'hard man'?

In the middle of this chapter, Cal is beaten up on his way home by
three other young men who are neighbours of his. What is the
reaction of both Cal and his father, Shamie, to the beating?

Why does Mrs Morton offer Cal work?

What is the significance in the novel as a whole of Mrs Morton
being a Protestant and her daughter-in-law, Marcella, being a
Catholic?

usher (32.22): a person who shows people to their seats in such places as churches and cinemas.

aisle (32.22): a passage usually down the middle or down the sides of the interior of a church.

altar (32.24): a raised structure, usually a table made of wood or stone, where religious ceremonies are performed.

leaded windows (33.6): windows containing small panes of glass held together with strips of lead.

mantilla (33.11): a lace scarf which covers the head and shoulders.

lectern (33.13): a reading stand, usually a tall table with a slanted top.

gospel (33.14): an extract read from one of the four Gospels in the New Testament as part of a religious service.

sermon (33.16): a talk on a religious or moral topic given by a priest as part of a religious service.

limbo (33.20): In the Roman Catholic religion, it is believed to be the home of the souls of unbaptized children and of the righteous who died before Jesus Christ.

atonement (33.24): making amends for a sin.

lapped (33.27): wrapped.

mortified (33.30): decayed, rotten.

Matt Talbot (33.31): (1856–1925) a popular Catholic martyr.

congregation (35.13): a group of people who have gathered in a church for a religious service.

haunch (35.24): upper part of the leg.

holy water font (35.31): a container, sometimes made of stone, usually found at the entrance to a Roman Catholic church. Holy water is water that has been blessed by a priest.

Anglia (36.08): a type of car that used to be made by the Ford Motor Company.

cork tips (36.9): the ends of filter-tipped cigarettes.

Clones (36.11): a small town in County Monaghan, in the Republic of Ireland (Eire).

Border (36.11): This refers to the border between Northern Ireland and the Republic of Ireland (Eire).

umpires (36.23): people who supervise play and make sure that the rules of a game are obeyed.

fishmongers (36.27): A fishmonger is someone who sells fish for eating.

mortal and venial sins (36.28): In the Roman Catholic Church, a mortal sin is considered so wicked that a person committing it could be sent to Hell unless the sin is forgiven, whereas venial sins are less severe and ones that are easily forgiven.

confession box (36.31): a small enclosed room, divided by a partition behind which the priest listens to people who admit to their sins.

mildewed (37.5): covered with a white or grey powdery fungus.

cinders (37.15): small pieces of burnt coal.

hard men (37.28): men who are considered vicious and are probably criminals.

slabbered (38.8): splashed.

reprieve (38.33): the halting or delay of something harmful or dangerous.

fit (39.9): ready.

copse (39.14): an area of small trees.

lop (39.16): cut.

girned (39.18): to girn is to moan or complain; the saw made a loud noise as if moaning or complaining.

thrush (39.23): a wild songbird.

pub (39.26): a shortened form of *public house*, a place where you can buy and drink alcoholic drinks.

Guinness (39.27): a famous brand of Irish stout – a dark beer with a creamy top.

sledge-hammer (39.30): a large, heavy hammer.

wedges (39.30): solid blocks that are thin on one end and thick at the other and are used to separate two objects.

blisters (40.6): painful swellings on the skin that contain a watery fluid and are caused by repeated rubbing of the skin against something hard.

negro (40.14): a term, now considered highly offensive, for a black person.

clutch (40.28): a pedal in a car that activates a device that enables power to be transmitted from the engine to the gear box.

unmetalled (40.31): unpaved; referring to a road that does not have a proper, firm surface.

bucked (40.32): moved in a jerking, erratic way.

Rayburn (41.15): a brand of large iron stove used for both cooking and heating.

gable-end (42.10): a triangular structure; a canopy over a door or window.

baby-sitting (42.15): looking after a child, or children, in the child's own home while the parents are out.

livid (42.21): a bluish colour like that of a bruise.

denim (43.02): a hard-wearing cotton material, typically used to make jeans.

veered (43.05): suddenly changed direction.

snot (43.22): mucus; slimy liquid produced from the nose.

anaesthetic (43.25): a substance that reduces sensitivity to pain and can cause a person to become unconscious.

stubble (43.35): short stalks which are left in the ground after a crop has been harvested.

pickhandles (44.4): fairly long, thick wooden poles.

saliva (44.21): clear liquid produced in the mouth.

Jesus, Mary and Joseph (44.31): an exclamation of surprise. Christians believe that Jesus is the son of God; Mary and Joseph were his earthly parents.

tremor (44.36): a slight shaking or trembling.

sherry (45.2): a wine that is high in alcohol because brandy has been added to it.

cloying (45.3): sickening.

head-butt (45.16): to hit someone with a deliberately hard blow using either the forehead or the top of the head.

national anthem (45.20): This refers to the official song of the United Kingdom, which is 'God Save the Queen'.

bloody (45.23): a swear-word, used to add emphasis to what is being said.

dressing table (46.1): a piece of bedroom furniture that consists of a low table with drawers and a mirror on the top.

welts (46.7): raised ridges on the skin, caused by a lash or a similar blow.

landing (46.21): a passage at the top of the stairs.

tripe (46.25): the lining of a cow's stomach.

Royal Baking Powder (46.29): a brand of powder used in baking in order to make cakes rise.

vertigo (46.32): a dizzy, whirling sensation.

Our Lady (47.1): another name for the Virgin Mary, the mother of Jesus Christ.

Adeste fideles (47.13): the Latin version of a religious song, 'O Come All Ye Faithful', which is usually sung at Christmas.

Orange march (47.34): in Northern Ireland, a march along the streets in which people who belong to, or support, the Orange Order (see below) take part.

Orange Order (47.35): a Loyalist organization in Northern Ireland which was formed in 1795 and which seeks to celebrate and defend Protestantism. 'Orange' comes from William of Orange (William III of England), who defeated the Catholic James II in 1690.

flouncing (48.11): deliberately making the water splash.

toddler (48.17): a small child.

wellingtons (48.22): waterproof rubber boots which reach to just below the knee and are worn in wet or muddy conditions.

nuzzling (48.31): rubbing or pushing gently with the nose in such a way as to show affection.

Girl Guides (49.22): a world-wide organization, the female counter-part of the Boy Scouts. Groups meet weekly, and the basic aim is to train girls to be good citizens with high ideals of duty, service to others and self-reliance.

Land Rover (50.1): a four-wheel-drive vehicle that is capable of being driven over all types of surface.

RUC (50.8): Royal Ulster Constabulary, the police force of North-ern Ireland. The RUC is responsible for dealing with politically motivated crime as well as ordinary law enforcement. The membership of the force is mainly Protestant.

sickle (50.12): a curved shape, crescent-shaped.

muslin (50.36): a thin cotton fabric.

ring-pull (51.2): a ring of metal attached to the top of a tin can which is pulled in order to open the can.

tea-caddy (51.13): a tin or box with a lid, used for storing tea.

lifting (51.18): digging up.

death throes (51.36): the agony suffered by someone who is dying, or the effects of sudden pain, such as felt by people when they are dying.

felt his gorge rise (52.2): was filled with a feeling of loathing or revulsion.

crooning (52.8): singing or murmuring in a soft, comforting voice.

larynx (52.12): the upper part of the windpipe where the voice is produced.

hee-haw (52.27): mimicking the sound made by a police siren.

drizzle (52.33): light rain.

buff (53.7): a pale, dull, yellowish-brown colour.

repetitiveness (53.24): referring to something that is done over and over again.

switched off (53.27): not paying attention; not thinking about anything.

jaundiced (53.33): a shade of yellow that is similar to the skin colouring of those suffering from liver disease.

kettle (54.9): a large metal pot with a lid; *kettle* more typically refers to a vessel with a spout for boiling water.

foreman (54.18): a man who is in charge of a group of workers.

CHAPTER 3

Focus

'He felt that he had a brand stamped in blood in the middle of his forehead which would take him the rest of his life to purge' (88.18).

Explain this statement about Cal, with reference to the events described in this chapter.

Follow-up

Why do Cal and Crilly rob the off-licence in Magherafelt? How does Cal feel about it?

'Not to act – you know – *is* to act' (64.4). What does Skeffington mean by this statement?

Describe the relationship between Cal and Dunlop.

What is Shamie's reaction to their home being set on fire?

Why is Cal made uneasy by Marcella in the library when they discuss his reading habits?

The murder of Marcella's husband – Robert – took place a year previously. Why is it described at this point in the novel, rather than earlier?

pliable (55.7): able to be easily bent, flexible.

pedal-bin (55.23): a metal or plastic container used for waste, opened by pressing a pedal at its base.

Belfast (55.26): capital of Northern Ireland.

Strabane (55.26): town in County Tyrone, Northern Ireland.

Derry (55.26): also called Londonderry, a city and county in Northern Ireland.

Newry (55.26): a town and port in County Down, Northern Ireland.

Long Kesh (56.14): a prison in Lisburn, County Antrim, where political and paramilitary prisoners were held.

Cortinas (57.7): A Cortina was a type of car that was produced by the Ford Motor Company.

takings (57.10): money received through making sales in a business.

pebble-dash (57.22): small stones set in plaster and used as a surfacing for walls.

a chara (57.25): in Irish Gaelic, *friend*; used as a form of address.

Language Notes and Activities

forestry plantation (57.33): an area of land planted with trees which are being grown for commercial purposes.

saplings (57.35): young trees.

stilts (58.11): long poles with foot rests set high off the ground on which someone balances and walks.

frosted-glass (58.27): glass with a roughened or dull surface so that it cannot be seen through clearly.

double parking (58.31): parking a vehicle alongside one that is already parked and so causing an obstruction.

peed (59.11): *pee* is an informal word meaning 'to pass urine'.

jukebox (59.21): a coin-operated machine that automatically plays chosen gramophone records.

revved (59.21): increased a vehicle's engine speed.

Harp polythene bag (59.27): a plastic carrier bag advertising a brand of lager (a light beer).

like lightning (59.32): with the speed of lightning, very quickly.

squealing the tyres (59.36): pulling away very quickly so that the car tyres make a squealing noise.

cinch (60.2): something that is done easily.

sink the boot (60.8): an expression similar to 'put your foot down', meaning to make the car go faster by pressing down on the accelerator pedal.

dilapidated (60.19): in a condition of disrepair, in a poor condition.

in aid of the Black Babies (60.30): referring to charities which collect money for impoverished children living in places such as Africa.

the Cause (61.3): the Republican cause, the movement that believes that Northern Ireland should be joined with the Republic of Ireland and that political ties with the United Kingdom are cut.

Alsatian (61.16): a large breed of dog, also known as the German Shepherd Dog.

flock wallpaper (61.18): wallpaper with a raised pattern.

Arse-licker (61.26): an offensive term for someone who flatters, or slavishly follows the orders of a superior in order to gain favour.

barriers (62.6): structures that are designed to prevent access or separate one place from another.

transistor (62.6): a small, portable radio.

frisked (62.11): quickly search for hidden weapons by running hands over clothing.

Waterford crystal (62.15): heavy, cut glassware made in Waterford in the Republic of Ireland.

at the runt-end of the school (62.20): at the bottom of the class at school.

psychopaths (62.21): people who suffer from a personality disorder which leads them to act in anti-social and often violent ways.

spin a great yarn (62.23): tell a good story.

pit (63.8): a slang word for *bed*.

slip a few quid (63.28): give a few pounds.

primary classes (64.10): classes for younger children.

presumptuous (64.18): disrespectful, inconsiderate.

Pearse (64.20): Padric/Patrick Pearse was an Irish poet who was a leader of the Easter Rising in 1916 (see below), after which he was executed.

1916 (64.30): This refers to the Easter Rising in 1916, an armed rebellion that took place in Dublin, against English involvement in Ireland.

Paras (65.13): an informal, abbreviated name for soldiers who serve in the Parachute Regiment of the British Army.

cowering (65.22): crouching in fear.

Last Rites (65.27): a Roman Catholic ceremony for someone who is close to death.

trespassers (65.32): people who enter another's land and property without permission.

Brown stomach, lungworm, black scour, bankrupt worm (66.10): diseases of cattle.

showing off (66.11): behaving in a way that attracts attention and invites admiration.

reek (66.13): strong smell.

muck out (66.17): clean manure out of a cowshed, stable or barn.

byre (66.17): a shed where cows are kept.

the hewers of wood and the drawers of water (66.20): a quotation from the Bible (Joshua 9:21); literally people who cut wood and haul up water – in other words, people who work manually.

Civil Rights (66.22): a movement formed to campaign for fair treatment from the law and government for all the people of Northern Ireland.

spasmodically (66.27): at uneven intervals.

surplice (66.28): a loose-fitting outer garment worn by priests.

slacking (66.34): avoiding work.

derelict (66.36): no longer lived in; in a poor condition.

cuffed (67.3): hit lightly.

putty (67.4): a dough-like paste used for fixing glass into wooden window frames.

lino (67.6): a shortened form of *linoleum*, a hard-wearing, washable floor covering.

prattling (67.21): talking in a silly, childish way.

out-and-out (68.1): thorough, extreme.

the troubles (68.3): the name given to the periods of political and civil unrest in Northern Ireland from 1919–23 and, more particularly in this context, after 1969.

layabout (68.5): a lazy person who does no work.

give him his cards (68.6): dismiss him from his job.

hanky (68.9): a shortened form of *handkerchief*.

rosaries (68.10): Roman Catholic prayer beads used for counting prayers.

of the first water (68.12): of an extreme kind.

for the rest of her natural (68.15): for the rest of her life.

flak-jacket (68.18): a reinforced vest or jacket worn as protection against gunfire or fragments from exploding bombs.

sten (68.19): a light submachine gun.

imperceptibly (68.20): gradually.

her eyes riveted (68.33): with her attention completely fixed/totally concentrated on.

white line (68.33): this refers to the white line which is painted down the centre of the road.

Sunday Independent (69.2): a weekly newspaper.

parka (69.13): a warm, knee- or thigh-length jacket with a hood that is often lined with fur.

Punch (69.15): a humorous magazine.

browsing (69.15): looking through something in a casual, leisurely way.

fart-like noise (69.18): a rude, offensive noise, as of breaking wind.

alcove (69.26): a hollowed-out space in a wall.

polo-neck (70.14): a sweater with a high collar that fits closely to the neck.

Under the Greenwood Tree (71.6): a novel by the British novelist Thomas Hardy (1840–1928).

transaction (71.23): a procedure that has been settled or completed.

Sir Edward Carson (71.32): (1854–1935) a controversial Irish-born British politician, strongly reviled by Catholics, who was against Irish Home Rule.

Sir James Craig (71.33): (1871–1940) an Ulster Unionist politician and first prime minister of Northern Ireland. He discriminated against Roman Catholics and was very effective in organizing resistance to Irish Home Rule.

Reverend Ian Paisley (71.33): a Protestant clergyman and Northern Irish politician, leader of the Democratic Unionist Party since 1972. He is a Loyalist and extremely opposed to the idea of a united Ireland.

God-awful (72.2): a slang expression meaning 'very bad'.

squint (72.2): a condition where the eyes are not aligned in parallel, sometimes giving a person a cross-eyed appearance.

Women in Love (72.12): a novel by the British novelist D. H. Lawrence (1885–1930).

intellectual (72.15): intended for, or appealing to, intelligent people.

daft (73.23): silly.

pensioner's (74.9): a pensioner is someone who is over the age of sixty-five, has retired from work and receives a state benefit.

bungalow (74.9): a single-storey house.

petrol bomb (74.15): a bomb that is made by filling a bottle with petrol, or other flammable liquid, with a rag for a wick which is lighted just before it is thrown.

inferno (74.22): literally, 'hell'; a place which is burning very fiercely.

eye-shadow (74.34): a coloured powder that is put on the eyelids.

débris (75.1): fragments of something that has been broken or destroyed.

stalactite (75.15): an icicle-like pendant which hangs from the ceilings of limestone caves, and is formed gradually by water dripping through the roof of the cave.

compensation (76.17): money given to pay for loss or damage.

hearth (76.24): the raised floor of a fire-place that extends out into the room.

range (77.4): an old-fashioned type of cooking stove with one or more ovens and with hotplates on top, heated with solid fuel and often kept constantly burning.

fire door (77.4): the door of the compartment in the range where the solid fuel is burned.

castrated (78.32): removed the male organs of reproduction (testicles).

vice (78.34): a tool with two metal plates (jaws) that close by a lever or screw. It is used to grip something tightly (e.g. a block of wood or metal) and prevent it from moving.

blokes (79.4): a slang word for *men*.

staunch (79.26): loyal.

Orangeman (79.26): a term used to describe members of the Orange Order (see Chapter 2, above); a Loyalist who supports and defends Protestantism in Northern Ireland and wishes Northern Ireland to continue its political union with Britain.

Republican (79.27): a person who supports the idea that Northern Ireland should be united politically with the Republic of Ireland (Eire) and should stop being part of the United Kingdom. In a Northern Irish context, the term Republican is taken to imply that the person gives tacit or actual support to the use of physical force by paramilitary groups with Republican aims.

fervent (79.30): passionate enthusiasm.

salvaged (80.6): saved.

a goner (80.7): something that is beyond saving.

tape deck (80.7): a device that plays and records tapes, especially audiocassettes.

porch (80.12): a covered entrance to a building.

meths (80.20): a shortened version of *methylated spirit*, a substance used as a fuel and as a solvent.

Not to be taken (80.20): a phrase meaning 'not to be drunk'.

hardboard (80.23): thin, stiff sheets made of compressed wood chips and sawdust.

disgruntled (80.32): dissatisfied, irritated.

pint (81.4): a measurement of liquid. Beer is served in pints in the United Kingdom.

antennae (81.8): thin, movable, sensory organs found on the heads of insects.

hunkered down (81.9): crouched down close to the ground.

squatting (81.10): a play on words as *squatting* can mean both 'crouching down' and illegally living in a house that belongs to someone else.

nicked (81.14): stolen.

chugged (81.17): tugged.

minute (81.28): very small.

menial (81.33): a servant.

gate-lodge (81.33): a small house at the gates of a large country house.

serenaded (81.35): performed a love song.

cell (82.2): a very small, simple room.

vegetables (82.9): an offensive term for people who are brain-damaged.

cop (82.31): a slang word for *policeman*.

we do him (82.33): we kill him.

UDR (83.8): Ulster Defence Regiment, a regiment of the British Army which was recruited in 1972 from within Northern Ireland. The regiment was almost entirely Protestant.

condensation (83.10): a film of water droplets.

hardware (83.27): guns or other weapons.

wheels (83.29): an informal term for *vehicle*.

belched (84.16): let out gas from the stomach through the mouth.

wind (84.16): gas that builds up in the stomach.

Spar (84.18): a chain of small supermarkets.

juice (84.20): a slang word for *petrol*.

navigated (84.22): kept the car on the right route.

automatic (84.25): a gun that fires continuously as long as the trigger is pressed.

liable to jam (84.26): likely to stick or stop working.

jumpy (85.3): very nervous.

piss (85.12): a slang word for *urinate*.

idling (85.17): running gently.

stall (85.19): when a car engine suddenly stops working.

carpet slippers (85.31): soft, comfortable footwear worn inside the house.

genuflected (85.33): To genuflect is to make a gesture of religious respect. This involves bending the knee to the floor and rising again.

slewed (86.9): swerved, twisted violently.

nosey (86.20): too curious about other people and what they are doing.

corrugated-iron (86.31): sheets of iron that are alternately ridged and grooved.

whumph (86.35): expressive of a dull thump.

maple floor (87.17): a wooden floor, especially suitable for dancing.

tempo (87.28): the speed at which music is played.

ballroom dancing (87.29): formal dancing with a partner, in which the dancers follow a set pattern of steps.

mole (88.5): a small, dark, often raised patch on the skin.

brand (88.18): a sign or mark of disgrace.

purge (88.20): to make pure and free from guilt and sin.

CHAPTER 4

Focus

'He was in love with the one woman in the world who was forbidden him' (91.21). To what extent does this feeling condition Cal's attitudes towards Marcella?

Follow-up

What do Marcella's recollections about her childhood and her visit to Rome tell us about her?

What is the significance of Cal's dream about being in Rome?

Describe how Dunlop's attitudes to events in Northern Ireland are further revealed during the course of this chapter.

'Cal was unsure of God but it came to him that the gift of suffering might work without Him' (105.13). How would you explain this statement?

At the end of the chapter, while out walking with Marcella and Lucy, Cal comes across a cow which has been blown apart by a land-mine. Why do you think this episode is the final event narrated in this chapter?

jaw-box (89.16): sink; the word possibly derives from a Scottish term describing the hinged flap attached to a sink and covering a coal container next to it.

pub grub (89.18): an informal name for hot and cold food produced and sold at a public house.

clientele (89.19): customers.

sheepskin-coat brigade (89.20): a derogatory phrase describing wealthy town-dwellers who only visit the countryside infrequently and for leisure purposes.

vigil (89.26): a time spent keeping watch, usually through the night.

light years away (89.27): as distant as the stars, very far away.

extension (90.11): an extra area or room added on to an existing building.

bubbled glass (90.14): glass which has a rippled surface so that you cannot see through it.

plummeting (90.27): the sound of water falling steeply.

shit (91.9): an offensive word meaning, in this instance, a horrible, unpleasant person.

slaying (91.29): killing.

deserters (91.36): A deserter is someone who leaves his or her post (usually in a military organization) without permission and does not intend to return.

tramp (92.9): a person who has no home and usually travels around begging for a living.

chafing (92.13): rubbing so as to make sore.

vulnerability (92.14): lacking protection, in an exposed state.

hair shirts (92.17): shirts made from very rough, scratchy material that were once worn next to the skin by religious people as a form of self-inflicted punishment.

hermits (92.17): people, often religious, who choose to live alone and have no contact with society.

Y-fronts (92.18): men's underpants; originally a brand name, but now widely used for all underpants of this style.

Cow and Gate (92.27): a brand of dried baby milk.

Freeze (92.34): Stay still.

spread-eagled (93.2): forced to stand with arms and legs wide apart.

cock (93.4): a familiar way of addressing a man, similar to 'chum' or 'mate', usually associated with the speech of Londoners.

posh (93.29): upper-class.

towelling dressing-gown (94.10): a dressing-gown is a coat-like garment that is worn over night clothes. Towelling is a soft fabric of looped cotton, from which towels are made.

fucked (94.19): a swear-word, meaning 'ruined' in this context.

hairnet (94.27): a fine cap, made of netting with elastic edges, used to keep the hair in place, especially in bed.

fluorescent strip (94.33): an electric strip light.

Pyrex (95.11): a brand of heat-resistant, glass kitchenware.

Dettol (95.12): a brand of antiseptic disinfectant.

scare the living daylights out of (95.20): frighten greatly.

talc (95.25): a shortened form of *talcum powder*, a pleasant-smelling, fine powder that is often applied to the body after bathing.

Elastoplast (95.36): a brand of adhesive plaster which is put over cuts and wounds in order to protect them.

simpering (96.16): coy and irritating.

compromise (96.21): reach an agreement by making concessions.

tenant (96.23): someone who rents a building or rooms.

tousled (97.3): untidy, messy.

sludge (97.22): a solid wet mass.

stall (97.23): employ a delaying tactic.

wellies (97.31): a familiar term for *wellington boots* (see Chapter 2, above).

mesh (98.8): a net-like structure of wires forming the base of a bed on which a mattress is placed.

pillow slips (98.10): fabric covers for pillows.

ferrying (98.12): carrying from one place to another.

Tilley lamp (98.13): a portable lamp fuelled by paraffin.

card table (98.13): a small, light table used when playing cards.

reserved (98.17): behaved in a cool manner; restrained.

kindling (98.24): material, such as dried twigs, used for lighting a fire.

pump (99.1): a device for raising water from underground.

Portstewart (99.10): a seaside town on the north coast of County Antrim.

quadrants (99.12): patterns in the shape of a quarter of a circle.

gouged (99.12): scooped out.

nuns (99.13): members of a women's religious community.

Convent (99.13): a religious community run by nuns, sometimes incorporating a school for girls.

Elsinore (99.14): a castle in Denmark, the setting for Shakespeare's *Hamlet*; it suggests a large, forbidding place.

callous (99.22): showing no concern for others.

widow's weeds (99.26): black clothes once worn by women whose husbands have died.

yogi (99.34): someone who practises yoga.

trance (99.35): a dazed or stunned state.

second-hand (100.25): used, not new.

jumble sale (100.29): a sale of used or old clothes and other items.

hallway (100.35): an entrance passage with doors leading to other roms.

nondescript (101.10): without interesting or marked characteristics.

middle-age spread (101.13): weight gained during middle age.

primary reader (101.20): a reading book for young children.

drawers (101.33): trousers.

steep (102.1): soak.

brambles (102.6): prickly shrubs that grow in the wild and produce edible berries such as blackberries (see below).

whin bushes (102.6): gorse bushes – prickly shrubs covered in bright yellow flowers.

blackberry (102.8): a dark-coloured, juicy berry which can be eaten.

canopy (102.14): a overhanging structure.

rake (102.16): a long-handled garden tool with a long-toothed cross-bar at one end used for clearing leaves, grass cuttings, etc.

meat cleaver (102.17): a heavy knife with a broad blade.

nodes (102.26): the bony parts of the spine which stick out.

Good on you (103.9): a phrase expressing approval.

hawed (103.10): blew.

brambling (103.14): blackberry picking.

briar (103.18): a prickly, wild plant (usually a rose).

curtness (104.22): abruptness, making no effort to be friendly.

Lent (104.35): the period of forty days before Easter, a time which some Christians spend in prayer, penance and self-denial.

wooden mushroom (105.2): a mushroom-shaped wooden object that is placed under fabric to keep it rigid while it is being repaired by sewing.

darning (105.3): a criss-crossed sewing stitch used for repairing holes in fabric.

decadent (105.21): self-indulgent, pursuing one's own pleasure.

Julius Caesar (105.32): a play by William Shakespeare.

boiler suit (106.33): a long-sleeved, one-piece garment worn over other clothes in order to protect them while doing manual labour.

crucifix (106.4): a cross; usually the cross on which Jesus Christ died.

flange (106.10): a rim which sticks out.

hawser (106.10): a heavy cable.

gristle (106.11): tough, elastic tissue.

togas (106.15): outer garments worn by people in ancient Rome.

Crime and Punishment (106.34): a novel by the Russian novelist Fyodor Dostoevsky (1821–81).

unclenched (107.17): ungripped; untightened.

threshed (107.17): to thresh is to beat out grain from wheat, etc.; the wind is 'beating' the trees.

glassy (107.22): expressionless.

Parkinson's disease (107.33): an incurable nervous disorder whose symptoms are an uncontrollable shaking and trembling of the limbs.

mural (108.34): a large picture painted directly on to a wall.

deodorized (109.4): all unpleasantness removed.

Grünewald (109.10): a German painter (1475–1528). His paintings of religious subjects show an intense emotional involvement with them.

insinuate (109.24): introduce oneself gradually and stealthily into a place.

de-mister (109.26): a device that blows warm air on to the wind-screen of a vehicle in order to clear it.

even a rat . . . will suck eggs in the presence of a chain dog (109.32): even someone small and insignificant will be brave if the enemy is not able to, or is prevented from, attacking.

Beat the shite out of (109.33): an offensive expression meaning to hit or kick someone repeatedly, or, more generally, to completely defeat and destroy.

IRA (110.2): Irish Republican Army, the main Republican parami-litary group involved in the Northern Irish conflict. The central aim of the IRA has been to end British control of Northern Ireland and to achieve the reunification of the island of Ireland.

blow their brains out (110.11): kill.

lunatic fringe (110.20): people whose views are not in agreement with those of most people and are considered dangerous because of this.

When you're fed up shadow-boxing, you sometimes turn and hit the referee (110.22): when you are unable to hit your enemies, you sometimes turn on someone who is neutral.

voodoo (110.27): unpleasant magic.

mumbo-jumbo (110.27): religious beliefs that appear to be pointless or meaningless.

Ach (111.8): a word used to express annoyance, frustration or acceptance.

kitchenette (111.12): a very small kitchen.

snap out of it (111.24): pull yourself together, stop being depressed.

Valium (112.29): a brand of drug taken to make you calm and less nervous.

Martini (113.32): a brand of alcoholic drink made from wine flavoured with herbs.

Cheers (113.34): used to express good wishes just before an alcoholic drink is taken.

Slainte (113.34): 'Cheers' in Irish Gaelic.

bigoted (114.12): holding very forceful opinions in such matters as politics, religion and race, and unwilling or unable to accept differing views.

mitch (114.17): leave school during the day without permission.

macs (115.11): short for *macintoshes*, waterproof coats.

Tupperware (116.31): a trade name for lidded, plastic containers for holding food.

Donegal (117.9): a county in the north-west of the Irish Republic.

Croke Park (117.20): a sports ground in Dublin.

All-Ireland (117.20): this refers to the All-Ireland Senior (Gaelic) football final.

Mafia (117.35): a secret criminal organization in Italy and the USA.

Friesians (120.29): a breed of cows.

CHAPTER 5

Focus
Why does Cal become an informer?

Follow-up
What does Cal learn from reading Marcella's diary?

What does Marcella reveal during the course of this chapter of her feelings for her dead husband?

What is the significance of Marcella's story of Maria Goretti?

'Her sincerity he was repaying with forgeries' (123.05). Is this true?

Cal imagines telling Marcella that he had a part in the murder of her husband. How do you think she might have responded if he had really told her?

What do the references to Grünewald's painting of Christ and to the fairy tale of Sleeping Beauty contribute to our reading and interpretation of the novel?

What does Cal recollect as he is making love to Marcella?

Is there any irony in a bomb being placed in the library, hidden inside a novel?

What is the significance of Cal and Marcella talking about being prepared to die for love?

Hallowe'en (121.17): 31 October, the eve of All Saints Day.
rockets (121.19): fireworks.
zenith (121.20): the highest point.
knock off (122.27): finish work.
snib (122.32): door latch.
inimitable (123.11): unique; impossible to imitate because it is someone's own particular style or characteristic.
Sleeping Beauty (123.13): a princess in a fairy tale who is bewitched, falls asleep for a hundred years and is awoken by a prince's kiss.

coma (123.14): a state of deep unconsciousness.

Quasimodo (123.20): the hump-backed bell-ringer in Victor Hugo's novel *Notre Dame de Paris* (1831).

impotence (123.25): lack of power or strength; a man's inability to perform sexually.

grandfather clock (123.28): a tall clock that stands on the floor.

snooped (124.7): searched through someone's possessions or affairs in a sneaky way.

Lough Neagh (125.16): a large lake in Northern Ireland.

Country and Western (125.24): a type of American popular music, based on the music of the rural south and the cowboy music of the west of the United States.

Birmingham (125.30): a city in England which was bombed by the IRA in the 1970s.

antibodies (126.3): the body's immune response to disease.

Evangelists (126.8): a Protestant Christian group that attempts to convert others to become Christians.

Dervishes (126.10): people who act in a frenzied, uncontrolled way.

Popery (126.12): an offensive term for the Roman Catholic Church, its practices and teachings.

draining board (126.28): a metal or wooden grooved surface next to the sink, where dishes can be left to drain.

laying things in for Christmas (126.34): buying things in/ storing things up for Christmas.

ancients (127.4): old people.

mince (127.5): finely shredded meat.

broderie anglaise (127.31): a fabric decorated with a pattern of small holes with stitched edges.

casserole dish (127.32): a deep, heavy, lidded dish which can be used for cooking food (e.g. a stew or 'casserole') in the oven.

minestrone (128.22): a soup made from vegetables, herbs and pasta.

Baxters (128.23): a brand of tinned soup.

spaghetti alla carbonara (128.30): pasta with a bacon and egg sauce.

varicose (129.18): covered with lumps of wax, resembling 'varicose' or protruding veins on a person's legs.

than I to Hercules (129.21): an expression meaning nothing like the real thing.

deaf-mute bloke (130.10): a man who cannot hear or speak.

Carson McCullers (130.11): an American novelist (1917–67) whose books were mostly set in the south of the USA, where she was born.

fixation (131.18): a preoccupation or obsession.

canonization (131.25): the formal procedure or decree by which a dead person is proclaimed a saint by the Roman Catholic Church.

nostalgic (131.35): relating to a mixed feeling of happiness, sadness and longing for the past.

infinitesimal (132.16): very, very small.

cheese wire (132.33): very fine wire used for cutting cheese.

tick (133.13): credit; obtaining goods which will be paid for later.

grouting (133.32): filling in the gaps between tiles with a cement-like substance.

blizzard (134.23): a very heavy snowstorm.

mittens (134.31): gloves that have only one covering for all four fingers and a separate covering for the thumb.

exuberance (135.17): enthusiasm, high spirits and vitality.

savoured (136.12): enjoyed with unhurried appreciation.

sullen (137.11): silent in a hostile way, unsociable.

full house (137.27): a winning hand at cards.

cap gun (138.3): a toy gun that fires small explosive devices that are noisy but not dangerous.

gelded (138.12): removed the male sexual organs.

hair trigger (138.22): something that needs very little pressure to activate it.

diaphragm (139.12): a contraceptive device that prevents women from becoming pregnant.

having it off (140.5): an informal term for *sexual intercourse*.

speak ill (140.6): talk badly of.

guffaw (140.23): a loud laugh.

plausible (140.32): believable.

gospel (141.4): the absolute truth.

commune (141.21): talk, communicate.

inflexible (141.25): stiff and unbending.

foresight (141.31): the ability to see possible future problems.

nook and cranny (142.8): every small part of a place.

singeing (142.12): burning lightly.

shaving stick (142.22): a stick of soapy substance applied to the face before shaving.

Raggedy Anne (142.27): a type of rag doll.

cronies (142.33): close friends.

electrical shock treatment (143.19): an electrical treatment for people suffering from mental illness.

plasticine (143.31): a brand of soft modelling material.

New Yorker (144.16): an American magazine.

don't fuck me about (145.16): an offensive phrase meaning 'don't mess me around'.

phone tapping (146.9): placing a listening device on a phone in order to listen secretly to conversations.

incendiaries (146.18): bombs designed to cause fires.

biting the table (146.25): an expression meaning 'very angry'.

knee-capping (146.26): shooting someone in the knees deliberately as a punishment.

captive bolt (146.28): another term for *humane killer*, a device for painlessly killing animals.

Lundys (148.11): traitors. This refers to Robert Lundy who is considered a traitor by Loyalists, whom he betrayed during the siege of Derry in 1689, and whose effigy is burnt annually in Derry.

insurrectional (148.22): rebellious, especially rebellion against the rulers of a country and often involving conflict.

hysterectomy (149.2): an operation to remove a woman's womb.

change of life (149.4): the menopause, the time in a woman's life when menstruation lessens and then stops.

Reader's Digests (149.13): collections of abridged novels.

lenient (149.23): tolerant; showing mercy.

obscenity (150.27): a word, statement or phrase that is offensive; a swear-word.

Confidential Phone (150.34): a telephone number that you can call and give confidential information about illegal activities.

shooting stars (151.7): brief streaks of light that meteors create in the night sky.

persistence (151.15): continuing steadily and in a determined fashion.

scourges (153.13): whips.

bubonic (153.17): as if suffering from bubonic plague and covered with swellings.

jack-knifed (154.2): doubled up.

Further Activities and Study Questions

Imagine that Cal keeps a diary. What would be the main entries in the diary to cover the events of the first chapter?

Write a letter from Shamie to a relative in which he expresses his concerns about Cal. (60 words)

Make a list of the sayings and statements about the political conflict in Northern Ireland which are made during the course of the novel by (a) Skeffington, (b) Crilly, (c) Dunlop, (d) Cal. Select two statements which you consider to represent best the situation as you have read about it.

Read again the final paragraph of Chapter 4. Make brief notes on the connections between this paragraph and the first three paragraphs of Chapter 1.

Explain the final paragraph of the novel. How would its impact be different if there was no reference to 'Christmas Eve', or to 'the dead man's Y-fronts'?

'*Cal* is a story in which tenderness and innocence can only flicker briefly.' Discuss.

'In *Cal* the future is always inhabited by the actions of the past.' Discuss.

'A divided society produces divided individuals.' How many individuals in *Cal* would you describe as 'divided'?

'There are no rules, Cahal, just eventual winners' (148.27). Does Cal follow any rules? Could Cal be described as a winner or a loser?

The film of *Cal* starts with the shooting of Marcella's husband by Cal and Crilly. How would the novel be different if it had opened in such a way?

Is *Cal* too short as a novel? If *Cal* were twice the length, what parts of the action would you want to devote more space to developing and why? In what ways would it become a different novel?

Cal is a novel that has a very economical, pared-down and terse style which relies on a range of linked images. Find three examples of such stylistic features. Is this style appropriate for the narrative? If so, why? If not, why not?

In what ways would *Cal* be different if it were not narrated from Cal's point of view? Could the novel be narrated by Marcella or Skeffington, for example?

Character Notes

Cal

Cal is the central figure in the book, and although it is narrated in the third person, all the events and characters are seen very much from his point of view and thus he is the most complex and fully rounded character. Cal is a Catholic living in Northern Ireland in the 1970s at the height of the troubles. He is vulnerable, introverted and rather lonely. Cal is not particularly well-educated; he is unemployed and because of the political situation has few prospects. Although involved in illegal activities, he is basically a decent, ordinary young man who is caught up in a desperate situation. He appears to be involved in the violence against his better nature, drifting into it because of his association with Crilly and Skeffington. Yet, he is politically aware to some extent, but has become disenchanted with the 'Cause' and the violent means used by its members. His distaste for violence is evident in his inability to continue working in the carnage of the slaughter-house.

Essentially a tragic and flawed figure, he is totally consumed by guilt. It would seem that throughout his life, he has been drawn to vicious acts, but has immediately regretted his involvement in them. Initially, this is demonstrated by the incident at school when Crilly bullied a younger boy. Cal was marginally involved and later tried to make amends. This incident is repeated to a greater extent with the murder of Morton. At the outset, Cal's obsession with Marcella can be seen as a result of his guilt, but this soon grows into attraction and then love. He seems to punish himself for his brutal acts at every point. His visits to the library, his job at the farm and even his relationship with Marcella are to some extent attempts to confront his guilty conscience. Yet he is never able to confess his sins or find absolution. In his relationship with Marcella, he is only momentarily able to transcend both the violence and the guilt, but ultimately he perceives there to be no hope for the future, and as such this mirrors the seemingly hopeless situation that existed in Northern Ireland at that time.

Marcella

Marcella is older than Cal, a widow with a small child. Although a Catholic, her duty and responsibility lie with the Protestant family of her dead husband. At first, she appears a serious, reserved woman, a figure of pity and a focus for Cal's obsessional guilt. However, as her relationship with Cal grows, she develops into a more interesting character. Again this may be because we see her through Cal's eyes and we learn of the conflicts of her personal situation only when he does. She seems a less complex character than Cal, but nevertheless appears to bear some similarity to him. She too is lonely and filled with guilt, about her desire to escape her duties and responsibilities to her parents-in-law. As the book progresses, she becomes more carefree and seems younger and less serious. Like Cal, but for different reasons, she realizes that their hope of happiness is futile and that escape for her is impossible.

Shamie

Shamie, Cal's father, is an ordinary, decent, hard-working man and as such represents many of the people in Northern Ireland. He is popular with both Catholics and Protestants and is bemused by the troubles and the hostility that surrounds him. His relationship with Cal is close, but not so close that Cal is able to share his secrets and guilt with him. He is a character who is almost always able to make the best of a bad situation, which is evident in the way that he has kept a home for Cal after the death of Cal's mother. It is obvious that this home is very important to him, as its devastation proves to be the ruin of Shamie. The loss of the house and the splitting up of the family lead to the destruction of Shamie's personality. Increasingly suffering from depression and then mental illness, Shamie's disintegration personifies the disintegration of a society torn by violence, loss and hatred.

Skeffington

Skeffington and Crilly represent both ends of the Republican spectrum. Skeffington is cold, hard, fanatically dedicated to the Cause and totally immersed in the history of the troubles. He is the ringleader, the planner and obviously the person in charge, and as such is possibly more dangerous than the violent Crilly. Although fastidious and not directly involved in violence, Skeffington has no qualms about ordering violence to be committed, as is witnessed by his ordering Crilly to punish brutally the young boy who knocked down his father.

Crilly

Crilly is less politically committed than either Skeffington or Cal. He is a sadist and is caught up in the violence because he enjoys it. This is evident in the way he relishes telling Cal about punishing the young boy in the stolen car and in the means chosen as punishment. He is not well-educated and has always had a brutal nature, as evidenced by the bullying incident at school. His involvement in the Republican cause merely allows him to give free rein to his vicious tendencies. Cal's friendship with him appears to some extent to be based on fear rather than comradeship.

Dunlop

Dunlop is representative of the hardline, extremist Protestant loyalism. The foreman at the farm, he is a member of the Orange Order and takes part in marches, although he is not involved in any paramilitary group. He is a bigot and unable to see any other person's point of view if it differs from his own. He is blindly prejudiced against Catholics, stereotyping them as lazy and workshy. His remarks to Cal are casually cruel, though apparently Dunlop does not recognize them to be so. His presence in the book enables us to put the Cause into perspective. Despite being on the opposing side, his character is similar to that of Crilly's; both are bullies, although Dunlop's violence is verbal rather than physical.

Text Summary

CHAPTER 1

Cal, an unemployed, young man living in Northern Ireland, visits
his father, Shamie, at work in a slaughterhouse in order to borrow
some cigarettes. Cal has recently left a job there because he hates
the violence of the work. He has been replaced by his friend Crilly.

Cal returns home and listens to some records. Later he goes to
collect his unemployment benefit and then visits the library where
he notices a new, female library assistant. He seems shocked when
he hears someone call her Marcella. He quickly goes home, but is
restless and returns to the library. Eventually he borrows some
tapes and leaves.

His father returns home from work and Cal talks about Marcella.
He appears disturbed and preoccupied. The next day, he visits the
library again and seems almost obsessed by Marcella. Later Shamie
and Cal talk about Crilly, Cal's friend, and Cal remembers being
revolted by an incident at school when Crilly violently bullied
another boy.

Cal then visits Crilly, and another man, Skeffington, is also
there. It is implied, though never directly stated, that Cal, Crilly
and Skeffington are all members of a Republican organization.
Skeffington seems to be in charge and tells Cal that he wants him
to drive during a robbery as they need funds for the 'Cause'. Cal
is very quiet and appears concerned about the possible violence.

Marcella is mentioned and also the murder of a Reserve policeman. Eventually, Cal agrees to drive and the meeting ends.

Some days later, Cal encounters Marcella in the street. He has been waiting for her to leave work. She drops her shopping and he helps her to carry it to her car. Returning home, he finds a threatening letter from a Protestant group telling him and his father to leave or the house will be burnt down. Cal and Shamie are Catholics, but live in a mainly Protestant area, and some of the other residents are hostile to them because of their religion. His father shows him a gun which he has obtained for protection. During the night, Cal thinks of Marcella and remembers an incident involving Crilly and a gun. He has very little sleep, but the house is not attacked. The next morning, he thinks about his mother who has died some time ago, then falls asleep and has a disturbing dream.

CHAPTER 2

One Sunday morning, Cal oversleeps and misses the service at his local church and so has to go to mass in Magherafelt. During the service, he again thinks of his mother and his relationship with her and then he notices Marcella and her daughter in the congregation. He is surprised that she is a Catholic as he knows that she was married to Robert Morton, a Protestant farmer, who is now dead. He follows her out of the church without speaking to her. Cal then goes to a Gaelic football match where he meets Skeffington who continues to persuade him to work for the Cause.

The following week, Cal is nervous as he is waiting for Crilly to contact him. This does not happen. At the end of the week, Shamie and Cal go and cut up a fallen tree. Cal then attempts to sell the logs at a nearby farm which belongs to the Mortons and which is Marcella's home. The elderly woman at the farm, Mrs Morton, agrees to buy them. On his return home, he is beaten up by some Protestant youths. The next day he returns to the farm to cut up the larger logs and receive his payment. This time Marcella and the child are there. Old Mrs Morton offers Cal a job picking potatoes and tells him about her husband who was seriously injured in the same attack in which her son was shot and killed.

The next day, Cal works on the farm. The work is hard, but he enjoys it and is a good worker. After the potato picking is finished, Mrs Morton offers him a permanent job on the farm, which he accepts.

CHAPTER 3

Returning home from the farm, Cal tells Shamie about the job. Cal and Shamie listen to news reports of bombings and murders and then Cal goes to visit Crilly, who wants him to drive the get-away car in a robbery that evening. They drive to a wood where Crilly picks up a gun. Cal waits in the car while Crilly robs an off-licence, terrorizing the customers who are in the shop at the time. After the robbery, they drive off at speed and take the stolen money to Skeffington, who introduces them to his father. Cal still does not want to be a part of the violence, but Crilly and Skeffington tell him that by not taking an active part in the struggle, he is assisting in British domination of the Northern Irish people. Skeffington tries to persuade him of this by talking about past atrocities.

The following Monday morning, Cal begins work at the farm, under the supervision of Cyril Dunlop, the foreman. Dunlop is a Protestant and is rather antagonistic towards, and scathing about, Catholics, although he pretends that he is not prejudiced. Despite working at the farm, Cal sees very little of Marcella, so he visits the library one evening. Marcella discusses books with him. Cal reads very little, preferring to borrow tapes, but on this occasion he chooses a book in order to impress her.

He gets home to find that the house has been bombed and is on fire. Shamie is safe but the house is in ruins. They both go to stay with an elderly relative, Dermot Ryan. During the night, Cal goes home again in order to get Shamie's gun before it is found by the police or the fire brigade. Shamie remembers that Crilly wants to see Cal, but Cal tells his father to inform Crilly that he has disappeared.

The next morning, Cal returns to the farm and he explores a derelict cottage which is on the Mortons' land. He decides that he will stay there rather than at Dermot's as it will be easier to avoid Crilly. On his first night at the cottage, he thinks about the time when he and Crilly went to the farm and Crilly shot Marcella's husband, Robert, and wounded old Mr Morton. Cal is overcome with guilt.

CHAPTER 4

Cal continues to live in the cottage without anyone knowing. One night, he creeps to the farm and spies on Marcella when she is taking a bath.

Then, alerted by a light, the army raid the cottage. They treat Cal very roughly and take him to the farmhouse. Mrs Morton decides that he can stay at the cottage legally as long as he fixes it up. Next morning, Marcella and her daughter, Lucy, help Cal to carry things to the cottage. Marcella is more light-hearted and less reserved when she is away from her mother-in-law. They tidy the house, clear the water pump and Marcella tells Cal something of her life. She offers him some of her dead husband's clothes to wear while she washes his dirty ones. Cal is uneasy about this but accepts. That night, Cal again thinks of his guilt and shame but determines to have a new start. He falls asleep and has a terrible nightmare. The next night, Marcella returns the clothes that she has washed. She stays to talk to Cal who comforts her when she begins to cry about her father-in-law's suffering. She tells Cal that she does not really like living with the Mortons, but feels that it is her duty.

One Thursday night, Cal has a lift with Dunlop into town. During the journey, Dunlop expresses hostile opinions about Catholics. Cal thinks that he is angry because of the cottage. Cal visits his father, who has become very depressed. Cal is worried and makes him promise to see a doctor. Shamie tells Cal that Crilly keeps asking about him. Cal leaves and then waits for Marcella to finish work at the library. They call at a public house on the way back to the farm.

The following Saturday, Cal, Marcella and Lucy go blackberry picking. Cal and Marcella talk a little about the political situation. Cal is happy when he is with Marcella, but cannot help remembering the evil thing that he has done to her and her family. They hear an explosion, Cal investigates and finds that a cow has stepped on a landmine and been killed.

CHAPTER 5

Some weeks have passed and Cal has had little opportunity to see Marcella. Shamie has become more depressed and has stopped working. Mr and Mrs Morton go away, so that Mr Morton can have an operation. When they leave, Cal and Dunlop are left alone on the farm. Dunlop goes home. Cal looks round the house and thinks of Marcella and the part that he played in the murder of her husband. He goes to her room, looks through her things and reads her diary.

Marcella returns home from work and invites Cal to the farmhouse for a meal. They spend the evening together, but Cal is uneasy and cannot take his eyes off the photograph of her husband. Marcella talks of her marriage and tells Cal that she was not very happy just before her husband died. Eventually, they kiss, but then Marcella becomes withdrawn, as if she is frightened of her emotions. She sends Cal away, saying that they are friends, but they must be sensible. Cal is upset and goes to the public house and gets drunk.

Cal is miserable, but cannot think of any excuse to go and visit Marcella. The weather changes and snow begins to fall. Marcella visits the cottage and apologizes to him. They share hot whiskey, talk together, and Cal confesses that he is in love with her. They embrace and Cal tries to make love to her but cannot as he cannot get the image of her husband's death out of his mind. Eventually, he is able to blot out the sickening vision and they make love. Then they both go to the farmhouse where they make love again. Marcella talks of her husband and confesses that her marriage had become unhappy because of her husband's lies and his affairs with other women.

The next day, Cal goes shopping for Christmas presents. He visits Dermot and learns that his father is in hospital. He then goes to the library where he meets Crilly, who shows him a library book in which has been placed an incendiary bomb. Cal is horrified. Crilly urges Cal to return home with him. He tells him that Skeffington's father has been knocked down by a stolen car driven by a young boy. As punishment Skeffington had ordered that the boy should be shot in the knees. Skeffington then arrives and accuses Cal of being a deserter. There is a police raid, the others are arrested, but Cal escapes. Cal wonders if Skeffington and Crilly will betray him to the police. He is so disenchanted with Skeffington, Crilly and their Cause, that he calls a confidential phone number and warns of the bomb in the library. He returns to the farm and goes to Marcella. She is upset because Mr and Mrs Morton are coming back and soon her life will become dull and monotonous again. Cal comforts her and gives her the Christmas presents which he has bought. They make love for one last time and then Cal returns to the cottage. The next morning, he is arrested by the police.

Audio Extracts 🎧

Total = 70 minutes

READ MORE IN PENGUIN

In every corner of the world, on every subject under the sun, Penguin represents quality and variety – the very best in publishing today.

For complete information about books available from Penguin – including Puffins, Penguin Classics and Arkana – and how to order them, write to us at the appropriate address below. Please note that for copyright reasons the selection of books varies from country to country.

In the United Kingdom: Please write to *Dept. EP, Penguin Books Ltd, Bath Road, Harmondsworth, West Drayton, Middlesex UB7 ODA*

In the United States: Please write to *Consumer Sales, Penguin Putnam Inc., P.O. Box 12289 Dept. B, Newark, New Jersey 07101-5289.* VISA and MasterCard holders call 1-800-788-6262 to order Penguin titles

In Canada: Please write to *Penguin Books Canada Ltd, 10 Alcorn Avenue, Suite 300, Toronto, Ontario M4V 3B2*

In Australia: Please write to *Penguin Books Australia Ltd, P.O. Box 257, Ringwood, Victoria 3134*

In New Zealand: Please write to *Penguin Books (NZ) Ltd, Private Bag 102902, North Shore Mail Centre, Auckland 10*

In India: Please write to *Penguin Books India Pvt Ltd, 11 Community Centre, Panchsheel Park, New Delhi 110017*

In the Netherlands: Please write to *Penguin Books Netherlands bv, Postbus 3507, NL-1001 AH Amsterdam*

In Germany: Please write to *Penguin Books Deutschland GmbH, Metzlerstrasse 26, 60594 Frankfurt am Main*

In Spain: Please write to *Penguin Books S. A., Bravo Murillo 19, 1° B, 28015 Madrid*

In Italy: Please write to *Penguin Italia s.r.l., Via Benedetto Croce 2, 20094 Corsico, Milano*

In France: Please write to *Penguin France, Le Carré Wilson, 62 rue Benjamin Baillaud, 31500 Toulouse*

In Japan: Please write to *Penguin Books Japan Ltd, Kaneko Building, 2-3-25 Koraku, Bunkyo-Ku, Tokyo 112*

In South Africa: Please write to *Penguin Books South Africa (Pty) Ltd, Private Bag X14, Parkview, 2122 Johannesburg*

READ MORE IN PENGUIN

LITERARY CRITICISM

The Penguin History of Literature

Published in ten volumes, *The Penguin History of Literature* is a superb critical survey of the English and American literature covering fourteen centuries, from the Anglo-Saxons to the present, and written by some of the most distinguished academics in their fields.

New Bearings in English Poetry F. R. Leavis

'*New Bearings in English Poetry* was the first intelligent account of the work of Eliot, Pound and Gerard Manley Hopkins to appear in English and it significantly altered critical awareness . . . Leavis gave to literary criticism a thoroughness and respectability that has never since been equalled' Peter Ackroyd, *Spectator*. 'The most influential literary critic of modern times' *Financial Times*

The Uses of Literacy Richard Hoggart

Mass literacy has opened new worlds to new readers. How far has it also been exploited to debase standards and behaviour? 'A vivid inside view of working-class culture and one of the most influential books of the post-war era' *Observer*

Epistemology of the Closet Eve Kosofsky Sedgwick

Through her brilliant interpretation of the readings of Henry James, Melville, Nietzsche, Proust and Oscar Wilde, Eve Kosofsky Sedgwick shows how questions of sexual definition are at the heart of every form of representation in this century. 'A signal event in the history of late-twentieth-century gay studies' Wayne Koestenbaum

Dangerous Pilgrimages Malcolm Bradbury

'This capacious book tracks Henry James from New England to Rye; Evelyn Waugh to a Hollywood as grotesque as he expected; Gertrude Stein to Spain to be mistaken for a bishop; Oscar Wilde to a rickety stage in Leadsville, Colorado . . . The textbook on the the transatlantic theme' *Guardian*

READ MORE IN PENGUIN

LITERARY CRITICISM

The Practice of Writing   David Lodge

This lively collection examines the work of authors ranging from the two Amises to Nabokov and Pinter; the links between private lives and published works; and the different techniques required in novels, stage plays and screenplays. 'These essays, so easy in manner, so well-built and informative, offer a fine blend of creative writing and criticism' *Sunday Times*

A Lover's Discourse   Roland Barthes

'May be the most detailed, painstaking anatomy of desire we are ever likely to see or need again ... The book is an ecstatic celebration of love and language ... readers interested in either or both ... will enjoy savouring its rich and dark delights' *Washington Post*

The New Pelican Guide to English Literature   Edited by Boris Ford

The indispensable critical guide to English and American literature in nine volumes, erudite yet accessible. From the ages of Chaucer and Shakespeare, via Georgian satirists and Victorian social critics, to the leading writers of the twentieth century, all literary life is here.

The Structure of Complex Words   William Empson

'Twentieth-century England's greatest critic after T. S. Eliot, but whereas Eliot was the high priest, Empson was the *enfant terrible* ... *The Structure of Complex Words* is one of the linguistic masterpieces of the epoch, finding in the feel and tone of our speech whole sedimented social histories' *Guardian*

Vamps and Tramps   Camille Paglia

'Paglia is a genuinely unconventional thinker ... Taken as a whole, the book gives an exceptionally interesting perspective on the last thirty years of intellectual life in America, and is, in its wacky way, a celebration of passion and the pursuit of truth' *Sunday Telegraph*

PENGUIN STUDENT EDITIONS

Series Editors: Ronald Carter and John McRae

Penguin Student Editions have been specifically designed for readers who are studying a text in detail. They include a helpful introduction and explanatory notes, character sketches, a text summary, a chronology, language notes, a selection of questions and topics for discussion and analysis, as well as suggestions for further reading.

Published or forthcoming:

Also available:

American Short Stories of Today
British Short Stories of Today